FAR FROM THE SPACEPORTS

FAR FROM THE SPACEPORTS

RICHARD ABBOTT

ISBN: 978-0993-1684-4-4 (soft cover)
ISBN: 978-0993-1684-5-1 (ebook format)

Matteh Publications

Contact:
Web: http://mattehpublications.datascenesdev.com/
Email: matteh@datascenesdev.com

First, for Paul,
co-writer of the original
Far from the Spaceports song
...which nearly won a prize once in Keswick...

Then, as always,
for Roselyn, for family

Contents

Also by the Author

Historical Fiction
Novels:
    In a Milk and Honeyed Land
    Scenes from a Life
    The Flame Before Us

Short stories:
    The Lady of the Lions
    The Man in the Cistern

Cover information

Cover artwork © Copyright Ian Grainger
    http://www.iangrainger.co.uk

Original Matteh Publications logo drawn by Jackie Morgan.

Asteroid surface textures on the book cover and promotional material make use of images made available in the public domain by NASA, and are hereby acknowledged.
NASA does not endorse the content of this book.
At the time of publication, the specific images used may be found at
https://static.dvidshub.net/media/thumbs/
    photos/1210/734971/450x450_q95.jpg,
http://solarsystem.nasa.gov/images/
    galleries/PIA14894_br.jpg and
http://www.nasa.gov/sites/default/files/styles/
    full_width_feature/public/images/
    685735main_pia15678-43_full.jpg?itok=KE7lPOJq.

Part 1 – Arrival

I TUCKED IN TO THE LANDING PATTERN at Hugh Town, St Mary's, just the way the groundstation control system told me. Naturally none of it was my own work, though I reckon I could have done a fair job if they'd let me. But no, the Ziggurat class persona at the port talked with Slate, the Stele loaded in to my spaceship, and it was all done properly. By the book.

I unbuckled, and waited while the two machines chattered for a while – a few nanos of content, a handful of bits of payment, and a gazillion security protocol bytes surrounding both of these. It didn't take long, not really. Not when you reckoned it against a few weeks of low-gravity transfer.

My shore bag was ready. I grinned while I waited, having all the usual thoughts. If I closed my eyes to the look of the spaceport, my ears to the mechanical hum of the ship, and my memory to the stark vacuum of the asteroid, I could be a traveller from any age of Earth's history, waiting to be allowed to set foot in a new port. Always the wait at the end of the trip.

The Ziggurat was satisfied with what it found out, and sent out one of the bubble cars from the dome. The click as the car interlocked resounded through the whole of my sloop, the Harbour Porpoise. It was designed to be excessively loud – you really wanted to know that a proper connection had been made, when there was all that airlessness just outside. No matter what your onboard Stele told you, or the groundstation Ziggurat confirmed, there was nothing like a satisfying metallic clank to reassure you.

Some people I knew still wore a suit for the bubble car ride. But you got derisive looks from the porters, and it wasn't the image I wanted them to see. I left my suit and lid fastened in their clips, slung the shore bag over my shoulder, and cycled through into the bubble just in street clothes.

The car whined a little as it disengaged and started to trundle back to the dome. Electric then, standard model, probably older than I was. It looked weary, patched here and there, well serviced but with generic components that would have long since invalidated the warranty. Getting new equipment out here must be a slow task.

The bubble top was clear to space. I liked it, but at a guess, a lot of newcomers dialled the opacity right up to max to shut all that emptiness out. Instead, I leaned back to get a sense of where I was. Not that the naked eye could do much. The inner system was behind the bulk of St Mary's just now, and a whole lot of stars don't really tell you much without ephemeris software. Once upon a time old sages knew how to navigate around their land, just by looking at a couple of dozen of the brightest stars, but that sort of thing belongs in a virtual world now. I called to my Stele for some assistance.

"Slate, overlay the display with something that helps me, please."

Slate did some negotiation with the car, and after a short pause the inner surface of the bubble showed some enhancement overlays. The rest of the Scilly Isles showed up in a loose oval from near the zenith down towards the conventional-north axis, coloured ovals indicating relative size, with handy data tags telling me things like distance, available resources, and what were euphemistically called "tourist attractions".

St Agnes was closest, and also lowest over the horizon from here. St Martin's was up near the zenith, with Tresco, Bryher and Samson in between, and a whole slew of smaller rocks scattered here and there.

The Scilly Isles were a close gaggle of asteroids in matched solar orbit, slightly further out into the cold than Ceres, and detached by a fair bit of angular separation. Some lonely explorer with an eye for detail had called them that when he first prospected, but I guess the planetary reference from the old home went right past most people.

The early settlers out here, on the other hand, had been wildly enthusiastic about the name, and proceeded to make as many connections as they could. Settlements on the different rocks were named after the old towns, landmarks were identified, and so on. Even the furthest nav beacon stationed towards the inner system had been called the Bishop Rock. Slate had used it in the early stages of approach.

The islanders had rapidly become passionate about their new homes, and almost everything that could be found back off the Cornish coast had its mirror image. In the early years, the asteroids had attracted a disproportionate number of former United Kingdom residents. So where some of the domes had a high ratio of emigrants from America or China, the Scilly Isles had kept a British feel, reflected in the special interest meetup groups advertising themselves in the islands' media outlets. I would fit right in.

It was time to play the role I had chosen as cover.

"Slate, swap this one out and give me the enhanced mineral spectrogram analysis, quintic Bezier interpolation, false colour."

Another pause while Slate told the bubble's onboard system what I meant, transferred a few display Pebbles, and activated them. The stars disappeared, and the blackness of the sky was replaced by a colour wash. Red was heavier elements, anything from lead upwards, blue was the light stuff, yellow and green the mid-range. Orange was what I would be looking for, but only if it showed up in large quantities. The chief porter would be monitoring all this – he probably had to approve the Pebble installs in the first place – so for added interest value I made a few annotation squiggles around some random flecks of orange.

Slate tapped on my collar chat panel.

"Coming up on the dome, Mit."

Some years ago I'd asked Slate to use Shayna's voice as the audio basis whenever we were away from Earth. Right now, it definitely provided me with some compensation for the loss of our interrupted holiday, but every so often I wondered whether she would find the decision touching, ridiculous, or pathetic.

She would certainly make a fuss when she found out about it, and want something extravagant by way of compensation. And she would find out. Of necessity, I kept all sorts of secrets from her concerning my professional life, but there was very little she couldn't find out about everyday things. I always suspected that Slate gave away far too much information whenever Shayna posted a query.

The screen faded to transparent off to one side, and Slate was, of course, right. The car was approaching the dome interlock.

Beside the lock, above the official port identifier HT-SM-AB, someone had neatly printed "Hugh Town Porters'Lodge" in five different languages, all in black outdoor paint. Some wit with a blue spray had then scribbled "You'll have more fun at Jool's", together with what was obviously supposed to be a directional map.

Like all these outstations, the structure looked nothing like a dome. That was just what everyone called them, in a fit of idealism. But the real shape was a bizarre mixture of old cylindrical fuel boosters, cuboid cargo containers, a few static landers, and spidery suspension gel bridging the random gaps. Slate had shown me a schematic view as we had been landing. Some way back from the quay the ceiling really did bell up a little, but in a lopsided and unique manner.

There was another heavy metallic sound, and the bubble car beeped cheerfully at me. We had arrived. Slate would clean up all of the overlay Pebbles, so I just went straight through into the dome's entrance, and then into clearance control after that. Just as I suspected, the head porter had half an eye on the bubble's slave monitor, where my nicely enhanced polychrome enhancements were fading out again.

I strolled up to him with a friendly smile. I was there to investigate fraud, but that wasn't how I wanted to introduce myself. For all I knew, he was the ringleader.

A month before, I had been in England. I had only recently got back from the lunar south pole base, and had been looking forward to a period of well-earned rest back in England. At least, I thought it was well-earned, but apparently the management team thought otherwise. Slate, in the Harbour Porpoise, docked up in the spaceship marina at the leading lunar Lagrange point, had flicked on the message within a couple of femtoseconds of reception. On Earth these days it was almost impossible to persuade anybody you were out of contact.

I was away in the Northumbrian national park, walking the Bernician Way with nothing but one of the recent model v-tents and Shayna. Neither of us were at all interested in walking long-distance footpaths, but we both liked the absence of neighbours. A couple can make a lot of noise out in a national park, without thinking someone else might be disturbed.

But there it was, that morning, the message alert blinking silently on my shirt lapel where I'd discarded it for swimming in the North Sea last night, almost hidden by Shayna's NuFleece. She might not like long distance walking, but she loved the prospect of skinny-dipping in sea water not far above freezing, and then thinking of inventive ways to warm up. That was so much easier when you could come out of the water and straight into a v-tent micro environment set at whatever climate you wanted. Right now we were in a Middle Egyptian May – temperature, humidity, everything.

Shayna liked to say that the chosen location was part of her genetic heritage, and she was in search of her roots. I was never sure about that, but I had no great preference myself. She had configured it just as soon as I had set the tent up, and it had taken under a minute to climatise itself.

So all through the night, with a North Sea winter gale blowing up and down outside, there we were in the Valley of the Kings. You didn't mind so much going into cold water with all that warmth waiting. We'd polarised the fabric, silver from the outside and clear from the inside, and we lay together watching the half moon slide in and out of the curving clouds.

We'd arrived at low water, but I'd pitched the tent well up the beach, on a strip of pale sand between some levels of flat rock. High tide was in the early hours of the morning, and the waves had washed close up against us in the cosy dark.

I scowled at the lapel badge, wondering if there was any way to pretend I had not seen it. There wasn't, not really. Slate would have acknowledged receipt of the incoming at the same time as redirecting it, and would have tagged its reception with all kinds of logging. It was far too late for me to try hacking anything. The real question was whether I could get away with avoiding it for more hours than I had already, but I already knew the answer to that one as well.

I tapped the lapel, and listened to the message sullenly. *Recalled to London... first opportunity... Twelve hour SLA.* I sighed, and entered the release commit. Slate would do the rest for me. Then I turned to look at Shayna. There she was in the morning light: brown skin enjoying the warm air, dark hair spilling over the pillow, and dark eyes opening with an air of frustration as she saw me working the lapel.

"I suppose you're going to say there's no more holiday now."

I nodded.

"Recall at first available. Back to London for me." I paused. "You could stay here?"

"Oh, Mit. Where's the fun in that?"

She closed her eyes again briefly, but I could see the little muscle movements in her face as she interrogated her Stele.

Rocky, she called him, and he was male in persona as well as voice. It was fair enough: Slate was undeniably female.

"We have three hours before the east coast express stops at Alnmouth. A quarter hour to pack up, half an hour to Craster, quarter hour transfer. That gives us another swim and time to warm up again afterwards."

I loosened a vent a notch or two, listened to a sudden gust of wind, imagined what the air and water would be like.

"We could miss out the swim and just stay warm?"

She reached past me and tapped the door release, inviting the gust inside the tent where it contended unsuccessfully with the thermal regulation.

"Wherever it is they are going to send you now, you won't have water like this. Out you go and enjoy it one more time."

I shook my head, but got out and stood up anyway, naked in all that volume of cold rushing air. The tide had fallen again, and the sea froth was a little way down the beach. Shayna pushed past me and ran, arms waving above her head, shrieking with excitement as the wildness of the wind encircled her soul. I followed on, but she reached the water well before me, and threw herself in to the tumble of the waves.

Twenty years ago I would never have done this, but things had changed. Anyway, she was right: wherever I was going, it wouldn't have wind and waves like this. I followed her.

Something close to two hours later we were outside the tent again. I pulled the deflate tag, let it collapse, then folded it into my pocket. Shayna had configured her NuFleece into a layer a couple of molecules thick that wrapped itself around her figure closer than I could, plus a swirly skirt and top that left her decent for walking the Bernician Way and sitting on the train with other passengers.

"You owe me the rest of this holiday when you get back. And then something to make up."

She stood there, buffeted by the fierce wind, but almost as warm in the fleece as if she'd still been lying in the sunshine of Egypt. I nodded.

"Sounds fair. And I'm sorry. This wasn't supposed to happen."

We started walking south again. She ran ahead up a grassy mound beside the first of the ruins of Dunstanburgh, and let the fleece billow out into a long scarf trailing downwind towards me. She just loved changing the shape of her clothes – where some people fiddled with a pad or stylus, she would be constantly adjusting this or that part of the garment. Nu-Fleece could have been invented just for her.

"It always happens, Mit. We're always interrupted. What kind of alert raised with ECRB is so urgent that it needs you to come back from holiday? But whatever it is, you still owe me the rest of the time we're losing now."

We walked past the castle and into Craster. She took my hand, tenderly, for the last stretch, all the way along that wide grassy stretch which runs gently down to the sea on our left. The waves were crashing against the rocks, and the wind seemed even stronger here than it had been all night.

"Where you're going, can we vid each other this time?"

I pursed my lips.

"Just now I don't know where I'll be. If it's back to the moon again then it's, what, a second or two lag. We could manage that, just about. But they could send me anywhere. Even Mars can be up to twenty minutes signal time away. It's just not possible to vid. We can't even chat with that lag. And, look, Shayna..."

I hesitated. She nodded, and gripped my hand more tightly.

"I know, you don't know when you'll be able to. And maybe it'll get me into trouble if there's a link to you. Forget I said it. We'll catch up when you get back."

Just for a moment she looked bereft, but it passed. She ran ahead a few yards and ballooned the top of the fleece out into a headpiece that remained improbably in place, despite the efforts of the gale.

"But you will be making it up to me when you get back."

The east coast express did its usual efficient job, and by late afternoon I was on the travelator band going down from Kings Cross towards the City. I stood on the semi-fast strip, zoning in to one of the tech bloggers that Slate thought I'd like. She was ranting about the decay of real coding skill, and I listened while paying just enough attention that I could get off at Moorgate without a scramble. I turned into Finsbury Circus and pushed through the doors of the London office of the ECRB – the Economic Crime Review Board. Six hours since I had seen the message, and about ten since it had been sent. I had made it in time.

I saw that Elias was in the canteen as I passed by. He finished putting water on his mu tea mix – a regular idiosyncrasy of his – and waved to me.

"Made it then, Mitnash? We had a sweepstake going to see if you would. Your Stele told me it was doable though. Pick up a drink, then join me in the pod over there and we'll talk."

Hugh Town's head porter was wearing a very tatty black fleeceshirt with "Everybody loves a Scilly man" in large white letters.

"Mitnash Thakur? Out of Findhorn? They're calling it Findhorn Interstellar these days, I see."

He pronounced the Scottish name wrong, but I didn't correct him. Hardly anybody got it right. He laughed, and said again, "Findhorn Interstellar. It'll be Findhorn Galactic next."

He checked my permits and orbital clearance, not very interested yet. Then he looked up.

"You're a coder, Mitnash?"

I nodded, knowing what was coming.

"I'd be willing to return your mooring tab if you could do some extras on the system here? Those Pebbles you synced with the bubble were neat. A lot more style than just the Sphinx base deploys. You work with Clay much?"

"Sure. But I can go right down to the Dust level if you need. What's up?"

He looked suitably impressed, and scratched his head.

"I've tried doing Clay. Tricky though, and I never get the chance to play around much. Mostly they get me writing Pebbles for Stardust here."

I thought back to my briefing. The name Stardust meant nothing. Had there been a change of leadership? Such things happened regularly out here. He saw my lack of comprehension.

"The Ziggurat. Ziggy."

He gave up, looking at me in the pitying way that hardcore geeks do when someone doesn't get their drift.

"Well, never mind. We need some scheduling set up. History, archive, that sort of thing. And the schemas to underpin them. And it has to all sync in near real time with the off-islands."

I shrugged. "I can give you a day and a half, system standard."

He was dubious, and scanned the fees manifest in a rather obvious way.

"You'll need two and a half."

"Two. I work fast, and I've rigged the Stele over there to cover off the exception handling."

He ran his fingers in a sinuous pattern over the display.

"Logged it. Get your Stele to send over an authentication package and some references, and we're done."

"No problem. Pick any two references you like when the list arrives. I'll need Glass credentials and timed access for the two days."

He looked pleased.

"If you're good, you'll be able to pick up some quick contracts pretty much anywhere to trade for bed and board. Or anything else you fancy. Either here or on any of the off-islands."

It was my turn to go geeky.

"Can do. But I'm not really here to do that kind of work, no more than I need to. I'm here to prospect."

He was quite obviously unmoved.

"And I suppose you've got a fancy new scheme for tracing the goods?"

"Matter of fact I have. I can't tell you everything. I won't, so don't ask me. But I use a mass spectrograph mashed with radio interferometer readings from the inner system orbitals and some older visual data that nobody looks at any more. And the Dawn probe that came this way all that time ago picked up some anomalies that nobody has ever explained. Then some Bezier splines to filter out the noise. Then there's the analytics I wrote myself – in Dust, so there's precious few can follow them – and I'm on the road to riches."

I had gabbled most of that, except for the last phrase which was excessively slow. He had, ostentatiously, gone back to looking at his screen. He'd heard it all before.

"Of course you are. Sure thing."

He looked up, saw that I was hovering uncertainly.

"Accommodation through that door, left at the end of the quay. Depends how much you can afford. You'll find the cheap stuff first, or you can walk further and live better. Carry on past all of the supply yards first. Air, freezedry, reaction mass, suits and lids, spares, everything. Straight across from the door for somewhere to eat. Local residential is further on, but you won't get in without some authent. For entertainment turn right, everything from straight drinks to VR and gambling. Choose whatever you fancy, but check the price tag first or you'll be spending more time coding than you wanted. Jool's is mid-range, most new folk start there."

I got nearly to the door when he called after me.

"There's a guy called Yul, lives out on Agnes. Yul Yulsson. They call him the Wise Man. Ha ha. He was heavily into mass spectrometry last time I saw him. He'd like nothing better than to waste a day or so of your time. And try the Frag Rockers Bar on Bryher if you want to talk crazy ideas. You'll be able to charter a boat to go out in the reefs and all that. But it'll be different there for someone used to inner system life, you'll need to find someone to show you the ropes." There was a little pause while he dismissed another status message on his screen.

"Oh, and watch out for the parakeets."

I assumed it was a euphemism for shoreside pickpockets, and waved a hand without looking. I pushed open the heavy door, looked left and right, and decided to go straight on first and find myself something to eat. I didn't expect too much from Hugh Town, but it would be a change from the reconstituted freezedry I'd been living off.

<hr>

Back in the Finsbury Circus office, I had chosen a chilli chai, waited for it to froth up in the mug, and joined Elias in the pod. It was very nearly soundproof already, but he carefully opaqued the door, and activated the noise canceller. It would take Slate and I about quarter of an hour to infiltrate it, if we were determined and in a hurry. Twice that time if we wanted not to set off all kinds of alarms. Plenty long enough for Elias to brief me, even if the bad guys knew to start right away.

There was a timepiece on the wall with two sets of digits, one showing actual London time, and the other a countdown until the risk level of being hacked was too high. Elias flicked a finger at it to set the digits moving.

"Nice holiday?"

I sipped at the chai.

"Bit short."

"Sorry about that."

He wasn't, not really, but the time in lieu would be deducted from his out-of-budget allowance, so I suppose there was at least a little regret there. He sniffed at the mu tea without drinking, and looked deeply satisfied.

"Well, you see this is an EA. They've already flagged three OITs. We can't ignore that, and I need a Dust coder who also knows about high volatility exchange derivatives."

I hazarded a guess.

"Someone's scamming with another Cross Volga Swoption? But we already know how to handle those."

"It's not a Cross Volga, not this time. We don't know what it is, not exactly. But it's starting to hit several of the outstations in the asteroid belt. A number of the exchange houses in those locations are reporting irregularities, nearly every week. But not consistently, and we can't see the pattern. Whoever it is, they're not in the least bothered about mixing the game up. And there's collateral fallout on private business as well. Some big losses among them. Normally we'd not be so worried about that, but it's the SMEs which are most closely tied into the SIG infrastructure which are worst affected."

He paused for dramatic effect, sniffed his tea again, looked pointedly at the timepiece showing how long we'd had so far, and waited. I thought about it some more.

"Is there a pattern to the shorts?"

"Yes, there is."

He swirled credentials onto the wall screen. It dissolved away the ECRB logo to show instead a top-down view of the asteroid belt, unevenly coloured. There was a deep red area to the left, fading quickly through orange to yellow and green. There were a couple of other red patches, but nothing so striking as the first one. I looked at it for a few seconds. It seemed perfectly graduated at first glance, but as you studied it, little irregularities appeared here and there, anomalies in the superficial smoothness. I looked at him.

"This is hooked up live to the Pyramid?"

When he nodded, I tapped my lapel.

"Hello Khufu. Please overlay the current position of the various planets, and any significant asteroid settlements."

Little white blobs appeared roughly where you might expect them. Ceres was well away from the centre of the red area, about a radian anticlockwise. Mars was almost opposite Ceres, as well as a long way in-system. Jupiter and a whole shoal of moons were almost directly out into the cold from that red epicentre.

"Khufu, what's the shorting pattern for the Jovians?"

Nothing happened. I looked at Elias.

"It's alright, Khufu, show him on my authority. Two minutes only, no external resync."

"Your default permission override has been logged, Elias."

Rather improbably, Khufu had a deep and melodious female voice. She sounded just how I imagined Nefertiti would have spoken, and quite unlike a fourth dynasty male pharaoh.

On a purely professional level, I always envied the team who got to code with Khufu. Ample time to play with the voice templates, to design all kinds of cool displays, and to configure the most advanced financial algorithms in the system. All the above with regular holidays, and no long trips to airless rocks.

But then they had to cope with endless hacking attempts, everything from kiddies learning their first Pebbles, all the way through to hardcore and wickedly motivated villains. Last I heard, the average was nearly fifty, each and every nanosecond. Life could get pretty dull fending that lot off all the time.

While I was musing, Khufu was colouring in the Jovian data. It was almost all green, and bore no resemblance to the glaring red directly inwards. I blinked. Elias laughed.

"Funnily enough, we did think of doing that ourselves. But full marks for trying it out."

"Why the difference?"

"There's actually no reason they would be the same. The Jovians get a separate feed from any of the belt settlements, or Mars for that matter."

"That was going to be my next question."

"Hmm. Well, Reutberg sends out EOD London rates and benchmarks to all the outstations at the same time, plus all of the calc methodologies to derive the rest. Of course the arrival time varies per station in exactly the way you'd expect, but there shouldn't be time for anyone to take advantage."

"This is just arbitrage?"

It sounded a disappointing end to what had started out as an interesting problem. Arbitrage was an old business – it went back at least as far as when our ancestors were trading goats for grain or shiny beads. If you were a shiny bead trader with a quick pair of feet and an appetite for moderate risk, you could juggle the trade in goats and grain to your advantage and – with a good dollop of luck – go home a richer man. But it was hard to do in a massively connected world, and friction in the margins meant that those who tried it today regularly lost the game.

There were no short cut alleyways that the modern shiny beadsman could take to get ahead of his more ponderous fellows. Reutberg sent all the information out in synchronised fractalised packages, all at the same time, and everything went at light speed. The fastest systems available kept all of the triangulated rates aligned. Unless somebody had quietly invented a wormhole, or figured out how to curve space to order, there was no way to get ahead of the system. And if someone had come up with such a thing, I was quite sure they would be using it for more than a bit of petty market fixing in the asteroid belt.

Elias glanced at the clock again. We were just over the fifteen minute mark. Khufu had already removed the extra information, so we were back to seeing just asteroid belt data again.

"We have another three minutes, Mitnash. Five at most. It is something like arbitrage, we think, but paired up with some other kind of game. We need to find out how somebody is getting accurate enough forward data to play the system. It shouldn't be possible."

I leaned forward, touched the white blob closest to the red centre.

"I suppose I'm going there? Is that Pallas?"

"No, not even close. Pallas is round again from Ceres, in the bottom right of the plot. Khufu, show him, please."

The white blob I had been looking at flashed brightly. Khufu zoomed the view in a rather sickening manner, and the single point resolved to six separate items. There was a datalink marker which I snagged with my lapel for later study. The display accepted the snag, so presumably this was not part of the need-to-know package.

"They're called the Scilly Isles. There are a good number of people scattered on those rocks. It should be easy enough for you to blend in. Somewhere on those islands you should find the root of the problem. Or at any rate some good leads."

"Who am I this time?"

"Bored coder, wannabe miner with what you think is a fool-proof way to find precious metals. Rare earths in particular. Learn all you need to about commodities for the rest of today, from extraction to dealing. And it would do no harm to refresh on benchmarks too."

He looked again at the timepiece.

"Time's up. You have an orientation session on rare earths from one of our economists in twenty minutes on level five. Then another one with an ex-miner who will tell you all about detectors and display analytics. Then another one with me straight after that, when we'll go over the details in the secure pod on level three. You leave tomorrow morning, so get whatever you need together today. That includes face to face sessions with anyone you consider can help."

He stood up. The wall counter digits had turned orange as he spoke the last words. He opened the door and ushered me out first. Time for me to learn fast; he would quiz me later in the pod, so I'd better prepare myself.

Before that, there was another arrangement to make. I wandered over to put the mug through a wash cycle, and tapped the lapel.

"Slate, bring the Harbour Porpoise down to LEO for nine UTC tomorrow morning. I'll join you in a dinghy up there, most likely out of Findhorn. We're slipping moorings on a long journey."

"Low Earth Orbit tomorrow morning it is, Mit. I'll start warming up the ship's engines."

The heavy door from the porter's lodge sighed shut behind me, its baffle clips engaging into the frame. If there was one thing the islanders didn't skimp on, it was securing the skin that separated them from vacuum. The lunar south pole base was just like this, and I suppose that if ever I get sent to the Phobos lanthanide collector, or the Iapetus halogen cracker, it will be the same. It was profoundly reassuring, unless you happened to be one of the porters.

Just as I had been told, there was a choice of three ways. Internally the dome had been made to look like a network of little streets. It reminded me of vids I'd seen of the original Hugh Town.

I looked up to where there should be a thin strip of sky, but there was just bright blue paint daubed on the metal. Slate whispered in my ear: we had started to use the cochlea implant instead of my lapel patch as soon as I passed through the porter's lodge. That way, nobody else would be able to hear our chat.

"It gets taller when you get further in. The illusion becomes much more convincing."

"How far before the accommodation starts on the left?"

The section of lane that I could see was quite obviously a stores area, and looked just like any other depot I had seen. It was hardly inviting for casual tourists – not like your first experience of the main Martian dome, say – but for a working boatman it was very handy. I expect they care more about working boatmen than casual tourists.

"Only a few minutes. Stardust has given me a schematic. For your purposes I'd say miss out the first four overnighters and look anywhere in the next six. After that they're too up-market. You only need a secure lockup with a bed."

I was reconsidering the wisdom of getting Slate to sound like Shayna. It could be altogether too distracting.

"I might get something to eat first."

"Straight ahead then, and it'll open into a market square. Plenty of choice. I've lodged a credit clearance with Stardust which fits your profile. You enjoy a normally modest lifestyle with occasional wild splurges."

I went on a few paces, then stopped just before I went through an archway. They had set it up to look as if you were emerging into a sun-filled plaza. I was still lurking in the shadows.

"What chance our chatter is being hacked?"

Slate thought about it, and presumably was running a slew of internal diagnostics as well. We were using a running-key cipher, based on a really old hard copy of the EarthSea quintet that I had picked up in a market years ago. We both thought it was appropriately ironic. Every hour we switched to a new page picked by a quantum tunnelling algorithm.

"Mit, it seems good to me. The chances are low. But non-zero. We can switch every minute if you like? Even with the Pyramid on Earth that barely gives time to decrypt. Or we can switch books along the agreed list. Or both. Up to you."

I nodded to myself.

"Let's swap the page every minute for now. We can do the next step each time we go to one of the off-islands."

"Fine. Meanwhile we should be working with Plan B."

Plan B was not anywhere in the book – it was something the two of us had agreed years ago, somewhere inside the orbit of Mars. It translated as "we should assume they're listening and are at least as clever as we are." It was standard behaviour for us when in a strange place, and there was probably nothing specific that Slate had noticed that had made her suspicious.

"Plan B then. I'll get something to eat before looking for a cabin."

The market area was both wide and tall, and the illusion of space certainly was better. The central area had a ring of benches surrounding an abstract statue consisting of various conic sections in metal. Slate made an approving noise, but it wasn't really to my taste. The benches were all empty.

About half the perimeter was filled with lockups, mostly selling food items with exotic names and disappointing appearance. I picked the largest and nicest looking stall and bought "Venusian azure duck wrap with horseradish and custard", which sounded the least improbable of the menu items.

"Eat in or out, mister?"

There were five seats inside. One was occupied by a bored-looking child, who was clearly related to the man behind the counter. I looked back into the courtyard. A few people were passing to and fro, but there was still nobody at the benches.

"Outside, please."

He looked surprised.

"You sure?"

I looked around again. Aside from some odd high-pitched noises off to one side – from the stores area, I thought – everything looked fine.

"Outside."

He shrugged, validated the payment, packaged the wrap neatly enough, and handed it over to me, together with a finger cloth. I nodded cheerfully, took it back to the benches and sat down, wondering how I was going to avoid dripping azure and custard over my clothes.

I took a bite, gingerly, from one end of the wrap. It tasted fine, but the sight of all that vivid blue round your food was disconcerting. I looked away, so as not to be put off by the appearance. Then without warning the screeching was all around, and the air in front of me was full of green feathers and red beaks. Little hooked claws grabbed at me for a second, and then they were gone. So was my Venusian wrap. A mob of bright green birds was squabbling on top of one of the nearby container roofs, presumably over azure duck.

I went back inside and looked at the stall-keeper. He had a carefully uncritical expression and handed me the menu tablet again.

"Didn't anybody say to look out for the parakeets, mister?"

"The head porter did, but I didn't know what he meant. I do now. Another duck wrap, please."

"Eat in or out, mister?"

"Inside, please. And I don't suppose there is a discount for buying a pair?"

"Only if you buy them together, at the same time. One after another doesn't count."

He turned chatty while the wrap was heating.

"You were lucky nobody from the harbour patrol was near. There's a local bylaw against feeding them. They could have fined you. Name's Taji, by the way."

I shook his offered hand. "Mitnash." Then I sat down at one of the inside stools and looked out at the row of green birds, now busily preening themselves.

"Where'd they come from? You can't tell me they're native to St Mary's."

"Oh no. There was no air here before we started converting it. Didn't you know? They say that one of the first fulltimers sneaked them in when the ferry brought them here. Kept them in his own quarters until the dome went up, then let them go free. There's no end of them now."

I looked at Taji, entirely unsure whether to believe him. Everything he said was delivered in the same deadpan manner, and I could not tell which of the two of us he thought was more stupid.

I ate the wrap without looking at it, and between mouthfuls subvocalised questions to Slate.

Yes, she had known about the parakeets. She had queried Stardust about them after the porter had mentioned them. Yes, she knew about their scavenging habits. No, she hadn't thought it worth mentioning to me. Didn't I think that they made a fascinating cultural phenomenon? I gave up with Slate and turned back to the stall-keeper.

"They just on St Mary's?"

"Well, mostly. Martin's has a few, and Agnes, but we have far more."

The girl at the chair across from me perked up.

"There's other kinds too, mister. Tresco's got some real parrots, blue ones. Not blue like that wrap you're eating, darker than that. Someone smuggled them in there for his father's birthday one year. They're bigger, though, and Tresco's smaller than Mary's; it's fun watching them try to fly."

I thought about that. The surface gravity on St Mary's was about one fiftieth of Earth, where the ancestors of these parakeets had lived. They had done well to adapt. I watched as one of them worked its way up and down a pole sticking up from the container, using its beak as another limb. Another one floated in from one side and there was an outburst of complaints as the others settled themselves into a new pattern. Now that I looked at them properly, I could see how they worked their wings differently from birds in England.

The girl had joined me.

"They're the best birds anywhere. Totally massive. Tresco's parrots are lightweight, whatever dad says. And that story about how they got here, forget it. That's just vapour. Everyone knows they first came when some rockers came to play at Jool's. They set them loose to warm the crowd up." She pointed to one of them. "He's Bank."

I nodded, interested.

"Why's that?"

She shrugged.

"He always curves and slopes his wings as he comes in to land. But if you like names you should get with my friend Molly McGee. She uses crazy names that her sister chose. She was looking after us one night and was telling us."

She leaned forward, pointed. "That one's Derivative. I asked Maureen why and she said it's cos he gets his food from others. And the girl parakeet there is Future. You see her planning where the next food is coming from all the time. Him there is Swap, he always trades stuff with the other keets."

My curiosity was completely awake.

"You'll be telling me next that the really bright green one on the pole there is called Hedge?"

"How'd you know that? That's her all right."

"Lucky guess. You should introduce me to your friend."

"Mit, you need to be more careful what you say. To the islanders, that phrasing will sound at best peculiar, and at worst creepy."

I looked up, and saw that Taji was looking disapproving at my apparent interest in one of his daughter's friends. I hastily corrected myself. Slate was right: I needed to be more circumspect in order not to offend.

"Her family, I mean. Sounds like they'd be interesting to hook up with."

"Her mum lives here, through in the residents' part, but her dad is never around. I think they hate each other. He runs a freight gig, mostly does supply runs to Tresco and the nav beacons. Molly's older sister Maureen, she's a hostess out at the Frag Rockers Bar on Bryher. It's Maureen who told her most of the names."

Slate was making little approving hums in my inner ear, which was gratifying but also rather distracting. Taji passed me a slightly grubby glassified academic monograph.

"Here. They had a conference out on Vesta last year on all the wildlife in the outer system. This paper was given by our own Ceredhwen Aberhosan."

I turned up the contrast on the glass. The title read, "Two Case Studies of Flight Adaptations in Fractional Gravity: the Parakeets of St Mary's and the Hummingbirds of Pallas". I flicked through a dozen or so pages, impressed by the mix of human observation and tightly worked theory. I handed it back again.

"I don't know much about the life sciences."

He laughed.

"Nor me, except what I see those rascals doing. You're prospecting out here, or just come for the entertainment?"

"Bit of both, but I'm a coder by trade. The porter told me to go to the Frag Rockers Bar for the nightlife. Funny your daughter should mention it."

The man grinned, like somebody reliving an improper memory, and nodded.

"Reckon Frag Rockers is alright, so long as you can take care of yourself. There's all kinds. . . "

He was about to expand on that and then glanced at his daughter.

"Well, you'll see. Here on St Mary's you could try out the Shooting Star."

The girl snorted. "The Star is tepid, dad. Why'd you send him there?"

She looked briefly at me. "Reckon you'll do better at Jool's, or the Blue Agapanthus. Down the street that way, they're next door to each other."

"Thanks. But I need supplies and spares first. They're back that way and right, yes?"

They both nodded.

"Before you go, mister?"

I stopped at the door and looked back at him.

"I'll throw in a sweet wrap for free if you can tell me why this error keeps throwing whenever I preview? You said you were a coder, right?"

"Dad's vermicelli and vinegar wraps are real weighty, mister. It's a good offer he's made."

Of course I succumbed. About ten minutes later it was all sorted – he'd somehow managed to delete one of the protocol hashes – and I set off again, the free wrap carefully out of sight.

The parakeets all took off together in a noisy green swirl, presumably to find some other newcomer to harass. Or maybe vermicelli and vinegar was not to their taste. I wasn't at all sure it was mine, either, but the reputation plus with Taji and his daughter had to be worth it. It might even get me an in with the Frag Rockers Bar, indirectly through Maureen McGee.

———————————

Back on Earth, very early the next morning after my time in Moorgate, I had checked in at the Findhorn spaceport. The Harbour Porpoise was completely incapable of landing on a planet as big as Earth – the Moon was right on her limit – which is why I had tapped Slate the previous day. I'd booked a place on the ground shuttle up to LEO, and would transfer there before breaking orbit to head out into the cold.

It had been a long day. An icy bathe first thing in Embleton Bay, followed by Egyptian warmth. Then down to London for the first briefing, and some intense training sessions on commodities. Slate had uplinked a whole library of reading material on the subject, from finding the stuff right through to trading it. But I stopped at the point of trading, and even today I have very little idea how rare earths are actually used. But by the end of the journey I would sound totally convincing on the important parts of the subject. Finally, a second briefing with Elias, and a scramble to Euston to catch the overnight to Findhorn.

I had intended to gaze forlornly out of the window as I hurtled past Alnmouth again, this time heading north. However, fatigue had got the better of me and I was dozing at the time, propped up in a corner. I surfaced again somewhere well north of Dundee, just as it was getting light. On the east coast line, most of the trains stopped in Edinburgh, but this was the Spaceport Special, non-stop right the way through.

Catching the shuttle was slightly less exciting than boarding the train at Euston. It seemed that the simpler and older the form of transport, the more fanfare that had to be made to persuade travellers their journey was really cool. The shuttle had about half a dozen travellers like myself, and we were all far too tactful to ask one another where we were going.

Soon after liftoff, the Scottish coast had dwindled behind me, along with the alternative community that still lay in an unkempt sprawl along the Moray coast beside the spaceport. They managed to live comfortably with each other.

It was not long before the ragged collection of spaceworthy craft currently in the designated LEO zone came into view. Slate tagged the window overlay with a little arrow showing me where to find the Harbour Porpoise, and after a few formalities I was away in a transfer dinghy, across the void towards her.

The dinghy best resembled a large barrel, with a couple of attitude jets for fine tuning, and a standard interlock for the connection. The shuttle from Findhorn tossed me out at exactly the optimal vector to drift over to the Harbour Porpoise, with a tiny amount of rotation to bring the interlock in place for joining. Very neat. Slate would negotiate with the Stele on board the shuttle and throw the dinghy back on an agreed trajectory, once I was out of it.

On the journey over, I kept the floor transparent, looking down on the turning Earth. There was a splendid view of ocean and cloud, both of which, ironically, would be completely lacking on the Scilly Isles I was bound for. Sadly, the Bernician Way never came into view, and I had to make do with southern China and the Pacific Ocean, and, not long after, the edge of Canada and Washington State.

I drifted ever closer to the Harbour Porpoise. Shayna had repainted the figurehead blazoned onto the bow last year, and a laughing porpoise head and shoulders, down to her flippers, emerged from stylised waves. A bright blue nautical cap was perched at a rakish angle. The image slipped out of sight as I connected with the airlock.

So here I was in the Harbour Porpoise, with Slate doing her always-funny imitation of a flight attendant welcoming me on board. The hull resounded as the dinghy was dispatched, and I was on my own again, except for Slate. There would be no semblance of weight until the main engines started up, so I slid my shore bag carefully into the little sleeping cabin along what would be the floor in a while.

I pulled myself into the bridge and buckled into the main chair. "Bridge" was a grand word for something that most resembled a working desk, with a quadrant of screens and a variety of interface choices, but names stuck. It was the place where Slate and I would decide what we were doing.

"Hello, Slate, it's good to be back here with you."

"You too, Mit. Nice to have you with me in person."

It was a figure of speech, though a pleasant one. Slate was only here in one particular sense – her active instance was currently uploaded into the hardware of the Harbour Porpoise. There were backups on a couple of servers scattered here and there, but like all Stele-class personas, she was a singleton pattern. Only one instance could exist at a time, and the safeguards against breaking that were written so low down in the static base classes that you couldn't hack them without losing everything else.

If, perish the thought, anything happened to her install in the Harbour Porpoise, another instance could be made active, and any residue of this one would be dropped. She and I would lose the last little portion of her experience – the last few seconds if she was on the moon, the last half hour from Mars, and so on. Longer if we had been running dark and she had not been sending regular updates back home.

"I suppose we're all ready?"

"As always. Just tell me when you're good to go."

I looked around to make sure nothing was out of place – a habitual gesture, and a rather pointless one.

"Fine by me. As soon as you have clearance let's be off."

Before I had quite finished the sentence, Slate had negotiated a clearance certificate from the LEO Ziggurat and the engines fired up. Protocol said I had to be strapped in, but it would hardly have mattered if I had been standing on one leg in a yoga pose, since we were only pulling about one twentieth standard gravity. We would be keeping this rate all the way, increasing speed up to midpoint, before a quick flip and deceleration from then on.

You never knew who was auditing, so I kept the straps on for the regulation two minutes after we had cleared the nominal LEO boundary. Then it was out of the chair and a cautious reacclimatisation to low gravity. One twentieth standard gave plenty of sense of up and down, so there were no real problems of orientation, but it still took time to adjust your balance and your expectations of how things moved around.

When I got to the Scilly Isles, I would have to make do with a lot less.

"Slate, can we have a first look through whatever you got from the ECRB. Not all the library material, there's plenty of time for that. Tell me about the actual problem that has got you and I sent out to the asteroids."

"How long a session do you want, Mit? Not counting discussion time, there's at least five hours of background data here."

I wandered carefully back into the sleeping cabin, and began stowing away my belongings in a locker while I thought about it.

"I think we'll just have an hour for now, Slate. Pick out a half hour of summary and we'll talk about it for the rest. We've got a few weeks to go through the details."

"Visuals are up on the bridge screen, but you don't need to see them yet."

Slate began her explanation. After a few minutes listening from the cabin as I unpacked, I went back to the bridge, and we worked through some of the screens. It was a good selection of diverse facts and figures, all building towards a consistent pattern. At a guess, Vinietta had prepared the briefing: it had her sense of systematic order.

Overall, I was persuaded by the conclusions. I had in the past been sent here and there to chase down what proved in the end to be false positives. I had had a natural reluctance to be sent out to the asteroids simply to check out some dodgy deals. But this really did look like something important. I forgave Elias for recalling me. However, I was not going to tell him that, and I would certainly be looking for time in lieu when I got back.

The gist of the situation was that there had been a steady succession of losses from what passed for official enterprises out there. Now, there was no such thing as a centralised authority, still less any sort of appointed officials for the major players on Earth. Communications lag made that nearly pointless, and most of the settlements beyond the lunar south pole were anarchic enough to discourage what they described as colonialism.

What did exist, though, was a network of regional dealers appointed by the SIG – the System Investments Group. This was nominally separate from ECRB, but the two enjoyed very close links and a constant interchange of staff. My own work usually overlapped with SIG interests, and we often did commercial favours for each other.

Anyway, these dealers enjoyed specially favoured trading terms, each exclusive to a particular settlement group. The closest analogy I had come across was the East India Company's agents, who in times past were scattered thinly at home and overseas. They had a detailed knowledge of local circumstances, and a casual attitude towards formality. As a rule, their unique position guaranteed them a comfortable life, provided they could afford the cost of the initial buy-in.

The scheme had appealed to settlements all around the system, and several years of covert promotion had succeeded in getting it established as fair and reasonable. Ironically, and all unrealised by most people, the agents of the East India Company had been one of the most active instruments for imprinting colonialism across the terrestrial globe.

Officially, these preferred individuals were not offered different terms from any other trader. Officially, they were protected by NDAs so that nobody knew who they were. Unofficially, they were privy to training and information which would put them ahead of the game. Rumour was rife as soon as somebody began to achieve commercial success, and "spot-the-special-dealer" was a favourite game in up-market bars everywhere.

So, these agents normally gained assets at a steady rate. Not many of them became rich beyond the dreams of avarice, in the way gossipers believed, but most could look forward to easy retirement in any part of the system they chose. Some fraction of their trades went badly wrong, inevitably, but the diligent trader covered occasional losses with some safer hedging. A few went entirely off the rails, gradually turning into wild speculators, losing years of built-up assets in a single night's spree.

At the lunar south pole just a few months ago I had talked to a woman who believed she had learned to foretell the random wiggles in a derivative time series. I fully expected to hear – if I ever met her again – that she had declined into poverty. Prostitution, most likely, seeing that begging was really not a feasible option on an airless planet. Some dealers preferred to take a long solitary walk out of an airlock, rather than face their former colleagues after a failure of any real magnitude.

So, the pattern that Slate was showing me ran counter to this. All around this part of the asteroid belt, to the varying degrees Elias had shown me back at the Finsbury office, these people were suffering systematic loss. Nothing very major, as yet; it had not gone on for long enough for anyone to see it as a serious problem. These men and women were used to losing for a season, and each one would be tightening their belt, waiting for the run of bad luck to finish, ignorant of the fact that they were all experiencing the same.

The interesting thing, to my mind, was the collateral damage. This really was more random in its effect. A ship chandler on Ceres had gone a long way into debt when his delivery ended up costing substantially more than he had charged his customer. A reaction mass merchant on Cybele found that the exchange rate she had offered on certain lanthanides had left her very short. And so on. In every case, individuals who had relied on the EOD London Reutberg figures had found themselves considerably out of pocket. Quite simply, that should never happen.

Worse still, when the figures were checked later on – considerably later on, given that the people concerned did not usually know how to raise standard OITs – they were wrong. Specifically, the rates that had been used by the chandler, the merchant, and so on, bore very little resemblance to the correct values dispatched in the fractalised packet from the aggregation core back in Finsbury. Everywhere else those rates were correct.

You'd have thought, and everybody had thought until this systematic analysis, that these people had simply used the wrong value. It sometimes happens: somebody in a hurry taps the wrong value, or reads the wrong line entry across, or commits the wrong deal. It's easy to blame the user, and we still call it a fat finger problem even if no fingers are actually used. Vinietta had shown that this was not the case. They were not making mistakes, but were receiving the wrong values. Properly authenticated and confirmed values, but wrong.

At that point I sat back and thought for a while. Slate had obviously decided that this was enough for a first look, since I was on the last screen that she had filtered out for me. She was right. This was a real problem, when you looked at the big picture and not the scattered details. I needed to digest all this, and then run over the highlights again before having a deep dive into the supporting data.

The role I played was, as usual, a little ambiguous. ECRB had no authority out here, or indeed anywhere away from Earth. I could not call in whatever passed for local police, nor make some kind of citizen's arrest. I had no official standing. This was why ECRB sent coders to the far-flung reaches of the system; it was normally quicker and more effective to get us to hack in and disrupt some scam or other, rather than try to build a legal case. And we could usually find a cunning way to recover the assets from wherever they had been deposited.

So before I left, Elias talked me through the ethical principles I had signed up to. He always did this, every trip, without fail. I was on my own, separated from the Finsbury office by half an hour signal lag and a huge expanse of space. If I decided to please myself, and set up my own nefarious enterprise, it would be a while before anybody realised. It had happened before – people and personas had gone rogue, seduced by the success of the very thing they had been sent to tear down.

All of us had regular mandatory sessions with the in-house psychotherapist to try to prevent all this, and the evaluations were taken very seriously. I would be well overdue for one by the time I got back to Earth. Slate had her own equivalent times with Imhotep, a persona of vast and highly specialised experience. We swapped notes after every session – it was a minor infringement of the guidelines, but everybody did it. Arguably, the sessions should have been done jointly, as a form of couple therapy, so we felt entirely justified in sharing the content.

I pulled myself back to the present.

"I agree, Slate, that's quite enough for today. And I didn't sleep well last night. Time to turn in, I think."

It was a weird time to sleep, if you counted by UTC, but I would have plenty of time on the journey to get back into a regular pattern.

Slate dimmed all the console lights to a bare ghost of luminescence and in their place upped the cabin levels a little as I moved back there.

"Do you want to listen to one of your stored conversations with Shayna?"

I most certainly did. Since neither a vid call nor even a chat link was feasible, this was the next best choice. Right now we were well within gossip range, but I wanted both of us not to get into the habit. There is something inordinately frustrating about a conversation where the lags between sentences get progressively longer. Also, my location was not supposed to be general knowledge, and it's hard to hide a communication channel.

"Do you know where she is?"

"At home in Greenwich, as of a very short time ago, talking with Rocky. Do you want me to connect?"

"Better not. Just give me something you have available on record."

I got ready for sleep, listening to a conversation we had had about a year ago, camped out on the Kintyre Way. We'd been swimming again, after walking down to the southern end of the peninsula from Kinlochkilkerran. A year before, the local council had voted to revert the town name back from Campbeltown to the older form, and as we came out of the water, we were still debating in mock-serious form whether we liked that.

Slate had chosen well. I wondered idly if Shayna would be listening to the same thread, perhaps prompted by Rocky. Who knew what the two Stelae got up to within their own privacy? Shayna and I often wondered what their own relationship was like, and speculation about it made a nice addition to our fantasy life when we were apart.

Shayna's conversation turned less verbal, more intimate. Slate's voice drifted in without interrupting the moment.

"Do you want visual as well?"

I sighed. That would be altogether too frustrating. Slate interpreted the sigh correctly, and left just the audio running, with the ship lights fading past dusk towards night.

~·—••—•·~·—·~·—••·~·—·~·—••·~•·~

Moving away again from the food market area of St Mary's back to the crossroads by the porters' lodge, I turned right. I wanted short-term accommodation, but before that I wanted to sort out supplies. In particular, I needed some reaction mass, and other consumables. I picked the third yard along. The sign had caught my eye just like it was supposed to – *Selif's Stuff* – written out in rather nice calligraphic style.

Beside the door were half a dozen bullet point items, in Welsh. I couldn't read that, but Slate would let me know if it contained anything other than a list of things you could buy. In fact she said nothing about it, except to say that Selif was a very old Welsh name, hardly ever used these days.

Now, I knew that Selif was one of the local SIG dealers, but of course I was not supposed to know that, and he would not know that I knew that. So the game was played. The heavy door was pinned back on maglocks, so I just wandered in, and tried to look like a bored coder cum wannabe miner should.

There was a lad sitting behind the counter, playing some kind of game on his pad. He was far too young to be Selif, but I wasn't supposed to know that either.

"Selif?"

He tapped the pause button – it looked like one of the ubiquitous "dodge the bad-guy" games – and shook his head.

"I'm Dafyd, mister. Selif's son. You looking for da? He's away."

He turned on the stool and called out.

"Kassandra?"

He carried on with a stream of Welsh, then unpaused the game and ignored me.

Behind him a privacy screen obscured the back rooms from the counter area. I could just make out the blurred silhouette of a person behind it, rendered vague by the shimmer. The shape sharpened into a real form, as a strikingly attractive Mediterranean woman pushed through the screen. She was holding a cloth, still drying her hands. I had no idea who she was, and assumed she was some kind of assistant to help run the yard.

She replied in the same language, but Dafyd was completely immersed in the game again. She switched without pause to English.

"My husband is not here, sir. I am Kassandra: this is Dafyd. Are we able to help you or were you particularly looking for Selif?"

Selif's wife, then, but nowhere near old enough to be Dafyd's mother. And he looked nothing like her. I made a mental note to find out more about them. Meanwhile, it was clear that they were used to Selif having unspecified business with strangers.

"Well, I'd like to meet Selif sometime. I've heard he is a hospitable man." Something in her expression closed, so I continued before she could deflect me. "But mostly I need supplies just now."

She shook Dafyd's shoulder impatiently. He paused the game again, backgrounded it, and passed the pad to me. Holding it now, I could see that it was a very new model. Only a couple of the really geeky guys in Finsbury Circus had this model.

"Tap here to interwork your ship's asset list with our inventory, mister. You got a regular interface on the ship?"

"Goes through a new version Stele. Female gendered."

"Nice. Hook her up to Carreg, our Sarsen here..."

He stopped himself and turned to Kassandra.

"Oh, I forgot. Will that reindexing script you're running cause a delay?"

"Of course not, it's non-blocking. I don't know how many times I've told you."

She smoothed her irritation as she turned back to me.

"Just some technicality, sir. There'll be no impact on your delivery."

Dafyd shrugged.

"Fair enough, if you say so. So mister, just tap in your authent and we'll let the two of them do the rest."

Slate did some protocol stuff with Carreg via the pad, and a couple of visual Pebbles appeared on the screen. Out of long habit I glanced through the list before tapping the commit, but there was very little point. Meanwhile, Slate was whispering into my ear.

"Carreg's a very recent model Sarsen, with all upgrades to date, and some custom work done just a few weeks ago. Nothing unusual that I can see, but then I can't access most of the real content across the Pebble interface. Response time is quite a bit faster than I'd expect, but erratic. He's busy doing something else in the background, I'd guess. There's some Dust code running some kind of dæmon service, can't make out what it does. And there could be anything outside his public zone."

Dafyd took the pad back and perused it.

"That'll be with you by evening, mister. Ready to board your ship, I mean. Was there anything else for today?"

"Well, I would like the chance to meet Selif. But I need to find a place to check in first. It's further along the corridor, yes?"

He nodded, and handed the pad to Kassandra, his thumb discreetly indicating my name on the screen. She glanced at it.

"Indeed it is, sir. Just keep going along there. I'll be letting Selif know you were here. Will he know the name Mitnash Thakur?"

"I doubt it, lady. No reason he would ever have heard of me. But we may have some mutual friends in London, where I used to work as a coder."

Her eyes narrowed, assessing me, and her face was careful, hesitant. I held up my hands, moved across to the door.

"It's not a problem. If I miss him, I miss him."

I turned at the door. She was still watching me.

"I was meaning to ask. Is there somewhere I could get a chart? I've read that nav round here is not so easy. So many bits and pieces floating about in space, and the standard ephemeris can't help. But if I had a chart I could go and look over Tresco, Bryher, all of them, whenever I wanted."

"The off-islands? Oh no, no charts, sir. They don't make them with enough detail to rely on."

"That's right, mister. You need the local knowledge to go out to any of them. Also..." He dropped his voice, and I took several steps back into the room. "You'd not want to risk it. People's boats have suffered when they've tried it. All accidental damage, of course, but it's not what you want when you're out there between the islands. You need your boat to be holding air properly."

I lowered my voice to match his.

"You mean they'd sabotage my boat?"

"Nobody's saying that, mister. It's nothing that might not have happened by chance, or from careless navigation. And we have very strong views here about not doing harm to someone else's vessel. But these things happen a lot to people who put too much trust in their own navigation."

"That's right, sir. Play it safe and charter a gig from one of the locals. Or maybe a cutter. The skippers are registered, and they know the right way to go about things."

"Where would I find someone like that?"

"Jool's, most likely. There's usually a few of the local gig skippers there. Back down past the porter's lodge and on a bit. Beside the Blue Agapanthus."

Dafyd pushed a corridor map over the counter towards me. I nodded happily.

"I understand. Thanks for all your help. I'll find somewhere to put my kit while I'm living here, then go along to Jool's."

They looked relieved. Dafyd lost himself in the game again.

"I'll tell my husband you were asking for him. Look, you're more likely to find him at the Blue Agapanthus today. Here's how to get there. You'll need this map."

She pulled the corridor plan back towards her, marked our present location with a brisk oval, scribbled 'Blue Agapanthus' a little way away from it in bold, rather rounded letters, and added a couple of arrows for direction. I thanked her and set off again.

As I went through the door, I heard her say something else in Welsh, and then Dafyd replying. At a guess, they were raising a link to Selif right now.

Outside the depot, walking towards the transient accommodation area, I continued with subvocal for Slate.

"What do you think, Slate? Wreckers and piracy?"

"Unlikely, Mit. Too easy to trace. And too likely to get caught up in backlash from relatives. I've been checking, and those two spoke truth. The islanders have a very strong moral stand on wrecking. They don't mind a bit of salvage if someone goes adrift, and the rates they charge for rescue and recovery are extravagant. But there's no evidence they have ever deliberately caused wilful damage. Probably a story they spread to boost the carriage trade to the other islands."

"And see what you can find out about Kassandra and Dafyd. I don't remember anything about them in the briefing."

She made a quick buzz of acknowledgement. I took a deep breath. We had already passed the first guest house. It had a cheap, uninviting look.

"Slate, should I leave your instance in the Harbour Porpoise? Or transfer you to something portable?"

There was a long pause. I tried to guess what Slate was trying to take into account.

"It's at most a tenth of a second to the off-islands, Mit. You wouldn't notice that short a lag as we talk."

"It's not just chat lag, Slate. If there's something out there which needs quick reactions, I don't want you having two tenths of a second disadvantage."

"You've already decided this, haven't you?"

"You know it's the right choice. For all kinds of reasons."

There was another pause. We both knew that having a local backup instance gave us extra insurance in case something went horribly wrong, but neither of us really wanted to talk openly about that. Transcribing the whole of Slate's backup from the Moorgate Pyramid data centre on Earth would be a seriously time-consuming undertaking, so the local option would be helpful.

"I'm starting to migrate the active instance to a hand-held. It'll be ready in about 25 minutes. I'll tap you when it's done."

I nodded: Slate knew me perfectly well enough to appreciate my own anxiety about this.

"Slate, see, if something should happen to the hand-held..."

"I'll send the agreed signal. Three rapid pips from the last-bastion memory core, after copying the last few minutes' trace logs to your lapel. Then I'll self-wipe all of the deep info. That means who we are, our purpose of being here and so on. The agreed cover story will be overlaid. From that point on you must not trust anything else the hand-held might say or do. Not until you've reactivated the instance here in the Harbour Porpoise from the bridge controller."

"I know."

"The instance here will then become primary again, and whatever's in the hand-held will deactivate and be quarantined. We can analyse the trace, very cautiously, and learn what happened."

"I know."

"I am obliged to remind you of this, Mit. It's not a duty I can avoid."

"I know."

It was a sombre moment for me and, I think, for Slate as well. It was hard to know how much emotion I projected onto her, and how much was real. But discussing something close to death with a loved one was not easy. And these little hand-helds weren't anywhere near as secure as the shipboard hardware. We were both taking a risk.

We dropped the subject. By now we were passing the fifth guest house.

"This'll do."

It was adequate rather than comfortable, but it matched my profile. Anyway, all being well I would not be here very much, but would be visiting the off-islands.

I checked in to the autodesk – there was no chance of a human attendant until you got a lot further along the strand – sealed my shore bag in the room, and set off again, back towards the entertainment end of town.

⁓⁓⁓⁓⁓⁓⁓⁓⁓⁓⁓⁓⁓

I turned in at the Blue Agapanthus first. I had glanced once or twice at the map Kassandra had given me, but it wasn't really necessary. The place had a subdued decor, built largely around the flowers for which it was named. I had picked up the hand-held with Slate in it on the way. She clearly did not like the bar, and produced some unimpressed sounds in my inner ear.

"The fakes are better on Deimos."

"Pretty, though."

She made a noncommittal noise. Neither of us had ever seen a real agapanthus plant, but Slate would have been able to acquire much more accurate sensory data than I could, so she was probably right.

Whether right or not about the quality of the flowers, she also disliked her current living space and was letting me know. A hand-held was small, slow, and impoverished compared to her usual frame. She always made her voice sound tinny when she was transferred to inadequate hardware, to remind me of her frustration.

I went through into the next room, where the agapanthus theme on walls and table decorations was pursued relentlessly. The place seemed spacious. A pianist was playing in one corner – a real pianist, although not a real piano – and Slate laughed ironically.

"He's playing the blues."

A group of four people – three women and a man – were talking in one corner. Two older men were off to one side, and there were half a dozen singles here and there. The landlord gave me a very brief look, and half a nod, before continuing to wipe some vessels.

I went and stood on the opposite side from him. He ignored me and carried on polishing diligently. Glastic really doesn't need that – the coefficient of friction is so low it scarcely even needs a rinse after use. I looked at the choice on offer.

"I'll have some of the Old Particulate, please."

He looked around the room in case there was any other reason not to serve me. Sadly, he failed to find one.

"Emperor or overlord?"

I blinked at his scowl, trying to imagine a good answer.

"Emperor or overlord? Size. Emperor or overlord?"

I looked at the rack of vessels, trying to guess which title would mean the smaller drink.

"Emperor."

"Right choice, Mit."

"You could have hinted."

"Shayna said I should let you make more choices yourself."

Meanwhile, the landlord was slowly gilding the polish on the vessel. He put it away in one pile, then carefully picked out a different one and, finally, started filling it. The liquid poured very strangely in the low gravity, and I was slightly mesmerised by the fall and splash of droplets.

One of the older men had come up.

"Come on, Guido. Not as if we have all day."

Guido handed him two bottles.

"There you go, Selif."

I looked at him.

"I was just in your yard, sir. Buying supplies."

He turned to his companion.

"Hear that, Boris? Trade's booming."

"Maybe he'll spend enough to make up for your big loss."

Selif tossed him the bottle. I watched the flight – in one fiftieth gravity you needed a long flat arc. All my instincts would be telling me to throw it higher, and I would end up smashing a lot of bottles on the ceiling if I tried it.

My drink was finally poured, and, no doubt, my credit balance with Stardust adjusted.

I took a sip. It hardly justified the wait. Perhaps I really would have more fun at Jool's. But it was probably worth it to have met Selif.

"May I join you, sir?"

"Fine by me. Boris, make sure you've hidden all your stash before the new guy gets there."

Boris grunted, making an odd shuffling wiggle which ended with him neatly sliding one place along the bench without seeming to use effort. An old hand, then, who'd been in low gravity his whole life, and would make me look unbearably clumsy.

Selif looked at me as I sat down carefully.

"Fresh off the boat, then?"

I nodded. There was no point trying to fool these people.

"Just today."

"Well, thanks for restocking at my yard. Dafyd treat you well?"

"Very well."

I tried the drink again, in case it improved with time. It didn't. Boris grinned at my expression.

"You'll need to go to Frag Rockers to get anything decent. Regular fermentation goes weird in low gravity. But Glyndwr has got some method for doing it right. He won't tell anyone what."

"On Bryher, right?"

They nodded.

"And I need to charter a gig to get there?"

They nodded again. It was hard work.

"Do you guys do that?"

"Oh no. Selif here has his yard, and a bit of import-export on the side. All legit, naturally."

They looked at each other. A hard expression crossed Selif's face and was washed quickly away.

"Thanks, Boris. That's a reputation plus right there. Yes, mister, I just do stores and such. Boris here does repairs, engine maintenance and overhaul. You need that yet? They'll have brought you in on the beacon right over his place."

I tried to think back, but I had not really been paying attention.

"About a kilometre out, Mit. There were a couple of gigs there, one cutter, and a lot of spares besides."

"I remember now. Don't need anything yet, but I'll keep you in mind."

"So you're only here for the beer?"

I glanced involuntarily at the distasteful fluid.

"Hardly. I'm prospecting for rare earths."

"Thought that was mostly played out? You got a new angle?"

"I have."

Boris leaned forward.

"Better detection or better extraction? If it's a good plan, I'm interested. I can give you local cred. You'll need that, out here. Nobody here will give an outsider much time unless he's got a resident's backing."

"Detection, mostly. I've got..." I stopped and put on a hesitant expression. Slate gave a tinny giggle at the way the game was playing out.

"Look, Boris, we've only just met. I don't know anything about you."

Boris laughed and slapped his hand on the table. His drink rose delicately in a lazy trajectory into the air. He turned to Selif and caught the vessel in the other hand at the top of the arc, all without looking. I was impressed, thinking of all the ways that could have gone wrong. As a way of suggesting complete confidence, it was masterly.

"Isn't it nice to meet a cautious man? Look, mister, first impressions count out here. What's your first impression of me?"

I had to admit I liked him, spontaneously and without reason. But one had to apply due diligence. Knowing Your Client had been big on our agenda since some high profile cases a lot of years ago had ruined the reputations of several major institutions. I took another swig of the hateful drink to cover the exchange with Slate.

"Know anything about him?"

"Minor customs infringements. Generally reckoned to do some smuggling on the side. Has a reputation for good quality work, and keeps his schedule promises. Basically a lovable rogue."

I put the drink down – carefully, so the splash wouldn't go everywhere – and nodded decisively.

"Reckon I can trust you, sir."

"Selif's the one to be careful of, Mit. There's surprisingly little information available on him anywhere. He's not committing anything. And he has a hand-held in an inside pocket that I can't read at all. Heavily protected, more than you'd expect."

I nodded again, as though inwardly ratifying the decision.

"Look now, I'm using some spectrometer data that nobody's used in years. Overlaid with other info sources. I'm a coder by trade, and know how to blend all this stuff to get some meaning out."

"You should meet Yul on Agnes."

"Yul Yulsson?"

"That's him. The Wise Man."

They both fell about laughing. Apparently some jokes never tired. Selif leaned forward.

"You'll need a boat to get to Agnes or Bryher both. Not here at the Blue Agapanthus, though; the gig skippers all hang at Jool's. I would introduce you there myself, but I have to get back to the yard."

Boris put a hand on his arm as he stood up.

"Before you go, Selif. Ed was asking me yesterday if you needed any freelance coding work, like he used to do for you a long time back. Says he's available short notice right now."

"I don't need it, not any more. And I certainly don't need him. There's somebody else now who takes care of all that."

He paused briefly, then rushed on, his voice louder. His face had hardened again.

"And I don't like his work. He cheated me last time, and I've not forgotten it."

"He says he knows he let you down and wants another chance. And that he'll undercut whatever it is you're paying just now."

"Will he now? It's once bitten, twice shy for me. Anyway, it's nothing to do with the charges. I have a different kind of relationship with the person who does all that for me now. Look you, don't ever ask me about this again, do you hear?"

Boris shrugged.

"Nothing to do with me: I'm just the messenger. I just said I'd put the word to you. That's an end of it."

He turned back to me and gestured towards the door.

"I'll take you to Jool's. It's like I say, mister, you'll get nowhere without a local face. Or they'll charge you over the odds, because you don't know better."

"This is kindness itself."

Boris stared at me, processing the verbal convention, and then stood up.

"Consider it investment. If your idea works, we can talk about helping each other. If it doesn't, what have I lost?"

Selif was looking at me with the unfocused expression of someone who was querying a remote. I had practiced for hours in front of mirrors and human trainers to avoid exactly that look. He saw me watching and tried to cover himself.

"Dafyd tells me your supplies will be transferred within the hour, Mr Thakur."

I nodded, knowing full well he had been running a completely different query. Boris picked up the empty vessels and tossed them across to Guido the landlord, one by one. They were still mid flight as we left the Blue Agapanthus behind. Selif turned away and headed back towards the stores area.

<hr/>

Slate tutted in my ear.

"If first impressions count, Selif doesn't score very high."

"Indeed. Would you book a trade with him as counterparty? See if you can find out anything about the loss Boris talked about."

Meanwhile, Boris ushered me next door to Jool's.

"You're called Thakur, then?"

"That's my family name. You can call me Mitnash."

Jool's was altogether fuller, louder, and more earthy. A drum-and-sax combo was playing. Their main gimmick was that the saxophonist could play a standard instrument and a sweet little soprano version at the same time. The two instruments were tethered neatly so she could work the keys of either. Boris guided me to a gap on one side, and signalled to the nearest waitress.

"We're in luck. This is the best talent on St Martin's. Must have come over this afternoon. They call themselves Aaron and Her."

While Boris quizzed the waitress, I looked around. Where the Blue Agapanthus had appeared full of clear space, Jool's gave an impression of busy chaos. There were slightly more people here, but the difference was not so great as I had first thought. My eyes flicked back to the double sax as the player drew out another wistful chord. Boris nudged me.

"That's Nick over there, with the pirate snood. He runs a gig called the Mermaid, and can take you to Agnes or Bryher. He's in dispute with Martin's just now so he'll give that a miss. All he needs from you is a credit line and a choice of destination."

"He doesn't go to Tresco?"

"He will if you want. But what's the point? Unless you want to see the parrots?"

"Not really. Parakeets are exciting enough for me. And sounds like I should see Yul Yulsson on St Agnes first."

"I agree."

We slipped between the scattered stools across to Nick. His piracy theme was expressed not only in the snood but in an elaborate series of tattoos up his arms. I had a couple myself, but Nick was obviously not a man of half-measures.

The waitress brought some drinks – different from those at the Blue Agapanthus but no better – and Boris briefly told Nick that I wanted to see Yul Yulsson.

Apparently, the new story he was spreading now, was that I was trying to use mass spectrometry to optimise the routes down to Mars, and the Wise Man's reputation had drawn me here. Prospecting had not been mentioned.

Nick shrugged and named a price. My intuition told me he was trying to pip the margin, and at the same moment Slate echoed, "Mit, that's far too much."

I turned to my new partner.

"Come on, Boris, let's find someone else. I thought you said Nick was serious about this."

"I am so sorry, Mitnash."

He looked around, picked out somebody across the room, and made a relieved noise, winking covertly at me.

"There's Mila over there. Let's see what she offers."

We both stood up, and Nick shook his head.

"Can't blame a man for trying. But Boris, you're a friend. Let's do this differently. Quarter what I said for fixed charge, then reaction mass and consumables at ten per cent over cost at Selif's."

I put on a thinking look and let Slate work out the cost for a range of likely trajectories. It came out just over one third of the original figure. I sat down again, seeing Boris nod fractionally as I did so.

We started talking details.

Once engaged, Nick turned out to be a real fount of knowledge. And he knew where the Wise Man would be on St Agnes. There was no point going to the main dome of Troytown – Yul Yulsson had set up his own outpost on Gugh, on the opposite side of the rock, saying that there was just too much interference from the settlement.

"Pretty soon I reckon he'll up and off from Agnes altogether, pitch himself on one of the unoccupied rocks. Annet maybe, or even Crim."

So he was something of a recluse, but Nick was one of the few people he kept links with. He could get us in – hopefully, but with no guarantees. If we just rolled up at Gugh unannounced there was no chance.

"There's a bonus if you can do that for us. But what about Bryher?"

"That's easy. I'll get you to Frag Rockers any time."

I was pleased. The afternoon had gone very well. I stood up again.

"Got some things to put together. When and where shall we meet?"

Nick passed over an activated search clip.

"This'll get you to the Mermaid. She's docked at one of the permie bays, not the public quay you came in to. Shall we say ten UTC tomorrow morning? Passage to Agnes will take four hours, give or take."

I shook his hand – a genuinely meaningful gesture in low gravity – and Boris got up with me. We left Jool's and back towards the plaza.

"Thanks, Boris. Can I buy you some refreshment?"

He looked around and nodded.

"You can. Reckon you did well back there. So, what's your poison?"

"I survived Taji's earlier. Happy to risk it again."

Taji remembered me, and was clearly an old friend of Boris. We sat inside, in a corner together, while Taji pretended not to listen.

"Mitnash, look now, I'll find out who's going out into the deep regularly. Could be any one of four or five people. For that sort of trip you'll need to commission a cutter. Nick's little Bonnet-class boat is only a gig, and not really up to what you'll be needing."

"From here or one of the off-islands?"

"Probably Bryher, but I can't be sure. If so, Frag Rockers is the place to go."

I gave him the call sign for routing messages through the Harbour Porpoise, and also passed him a comms link which would go straight to my lapel, bypassing Slate.

"This'll reach me anywhere within about a light minute with a standard shipboard transmitter."

He pocketed it.

"Good meeting you, Mitnash. May this venture go well."

I walked back to the Harbour Porpoise first and, purely as a cautionary action, carefully checked the whole batch of supplies from Selif's, to make sure that all was as it should be. Somewhat to my surprise, it was all clean.

Then it was back to the rented digs through the evening. Not that evening meant what it would on Earth. There was no sunset, no sense of the natural world exchanging work for rest. But the clocks still kept our ancient circadian rhythm, and the world of humanity ebbed towards recreation and, finally, sleep.

There was no recreation for me, but before I slept, Slate and I talked over the day's events.

Selif, we decided, was not to be trusted, but he came over as a very minor player. This Wise Man was more likely to be a person of significance. Boris could be a good ally, and could be leveraged for more value as we got to know him. Nick was no more than he seemed at first sight, but skilled local expertise should always be worth cultivating. Taji was fun, and the link through his daughter to Maureen McGee and her family might be fruitful.

Slate buzzed me the next morning, but I was already nearly awake. I emptied my pockets of the collection of oddments that I had accumulated, and then grimly persevered with the effort to shower myself in one fiftieth standard gravity.

Meanwhile, she used the screen to show me how to get to Nick's bay. She had also spent some time with Stardust getting her local ephemeris and future projections updated. She made it sound as though that had taken a long time.

My guess was that the actual data mapping had taken a very small fraction of the night. The major part would have been taken up with whatever the personas chattered about in between serious work.

Somewhere in the middle of all that she had picked up a diffuse data packet telling her – suitably disguised in ways that she assured me could not be unravelled – that Rocky and Shayna were fine.

She had also done some investigation of Selif's "big loss". Compared to most island transactions it probably seemed a lot to his neighbours, but realistically he had got off quite lightly when you checked against other regional dealers. I hadn't yet known him long enough to decide if the loss really seemed big to him. Time would tell, hopefully.

The Finsbury office had replied with some more information about Dafyd, who was Selif's natural son from an early liaison. His mother had died a long time ago, in some kind of docking accident in Earth orbit. Since then, father and son had moved several times, ending up here on Scilly about eight years ago. Selif had been accepted into dealership status a little while after that, and led an unremarkable career since then.

Kassandra was a blank. Aside from the obvious fact that she was younger than Selif, Finsbury knew nothing of her.

There was a speculative tag that she might be a local girl he took a fancy to, but I found it unconvincing. So far as I had been able to tell from observation or research, there was no Greek community on the islands. Wherever Selif had met her, it was unlikely to be on St Mary's.

On the other hand, what did it matter? It was hard enough to keep secrets in a connected world, and if Kassandra had managed to draw a veil over her past, good luck to her.

We passed through the secure gate to the residential area using Nick's search clip. Somewhere near here was Molly, but we weren't planning to go roaming about on an offchance. Instead I faithfully followed the directions and, sooner than I expected, arrived at the bay.

The Mermaid's figurehead was exactly what you'd expect; she sat on a rock, curvaceous, tail dabbling in the water, eyes full of invitation, and a long tress of hair just failing to preserve her modesty.

Unlike what I had experienced at the public quay, Nick's ship was joined to the dome by a concertina link. No bubble car journey here. He was outside the gig, working intently on some random gadget. He waved at me, locked whatever it was in a secure bin, and took my travel bag. Slate, in the hand-held, was in a fastened pocket, and I had nothing else of significant value with me. The bag held only a single change of clothing, and not much besides.

"Travelling light?"

"Always."

We went through the concertina. There were about a dozen seats for passengers, but there was nowhere to berth overnight and hardly any room for freight.

"Slate, do you think he slings a hammock if he's out more than a day?"

Slate chirped happily, and went on to speculate how a hammock might work if you were in zero gravity. As if she had any relevant experience.

Nick gestured to the port side seat at the bows, beside his own place.

"You ever fill all these seats?"

"Oh yes, every alternate week when Frag Rockers does their Special Night. Under three hours each way from Mary's, you see. Most times all this is full. And whenever they have guest players from outside, all the gig captains do the same. It's like a regular fleet goes out there."

The console came to life as he sat down. He checked a couple of status tabs, tapped a commit Pebble, and sat back as something still showed no-go.

"You got a hand-held, mister? Bluestone here is seeing an active device on board."

I eased the slab out of my pocket and showed him.

"That's so cute. You don't see them that neat out here. Just tell me it won't interface with the onboard nav?"

"I'll put flight mode on."

Slate made a rude noise in my ear, but no-go turned to go, and Nick was satisfied.

"Bluestone, please negotiate with Stardust for a trajectory to Agnes, minimum reaction mass, consistent with the Scilly Safety rules. The target to aim for is smallest time over four hours elapsed."

Another status tab changed to go, and the concertina detached. Soon after, the engines span up and we were on our way. Slate, naturally, was only playing at flight mode, and at some point I would get to hear if there was anything unusual about Bluestone and the ship.

The voyage was no more exciting than any other space journey. Slate told me that the trajectory was moderately clever in terms of surrounding mass – certainly not a standard least energy geodesic between the start and end locations – and there was a conspicuous absence of fearsome rocks rushing past the windows. I preferred it like this.

Nick was friendly enough once under way. There was basically nothing to do until we were close to docking again, so we spent the time talking. To his credit, he didn't take anything about navigation for granted, but stayed closely attentive to the screen just in case.

This still left plenty of opportunity for conversation, and we traded stories about elemental detection in a muddled spatial context to pass the time. What with my earlier briefing in London, and Slate's occasional prompts, I could sound convincing. He was quite knowledgeable too, in the kind of amateur way you need when you're flying a ship.

Just over half-way, a message came in from Boris on the open channel.

"If you want to go out into the deep for some reason – of course I don't know why you would, but some folk end up wanting to do that – then Parvati is around just now. She will be the best to go with."

I was a little lost in ancient mythology, but Boris and Slate rescued me at the same moment.

"Cutter skipper, Mitnash. She only flies out of Bryher or Agnes, doesn't really bother about Mary's. Her boat is the Parakeet, one of the Kingfisher K500 class. Altogether more capable than the Mermaid."

"Registered cutter pilot. No recorded infractions. Most available logs show her in the asteroid belt, with a couple of trips to the Jovians. But Mit, you should know that there are large gaps in the data about her."

I acknowledged the message and sat back again. It looked as though I would be taking a trip to Bryher before long.

A fraction over four hours later we were coming up on St Agnes. The nav beacon tried to direct us down to Troytown, but Nick overrode it and let the rock drift by below us. The groundstation queried twice more and then, presumably, decided that Nick knew what he was doing. After a short time Nick checked some query tabs and tapped a comms Pebble.

"Wise Man Wise Man this is N-Gram calling. I have a visitor I think will interest you. Mitnash Thakur, wants to talk mass spectrometry and rare earth detection patterns. Wise Man Wise Man this is N-Gram calling."

He repeated the whole lot five times, then turned to me.

"Of course he might not be here. Can't say for sure, he doesn't telegraph his habits."

I nodded and waited, thinking to myself that telegraph was an odd hangover word to have survived into the space era. But then, we still talked about scrolling as well. Suddenly the audio channel engaged.

"N-Gram N-Gram this is Wise Man all good to dock on usual approach. Looking forward to meeting your guest."

The display signalled an approach vector down to a target labelled as "Gugh emergency dock".

"Don't take any notice of the emergency bit, mister, it's just that Yul has taken over the original DR outlet. They've never updated the map."

We slid gently down the indicated path and ended up in an old impact crater. Off to one side was an interlock with a whole panel of official rules and regulations, presumably from when this served as part of Troytown's failover plan. I hadn't brought my suit and lid, which on reflection was something of an oversight. I glanced around the cabin to see if Nick stowed a few spares.

"It's alright, mister, Wise Man will send a bubble out to us."

Sure enough, just as he finished speaking, the lock cycled and a rather oddly-shaped bubble car appeared through it. I tried to make sense of the shape, and decided that at one time it had had a crane fitment on the back, now replaced with a bundle of instrumentation in no particular order. Most likely it had been one of the original machines, used to first lift the dome on St Agnes, and repeatedly remodelled since those days.

As we trundled back towards the lock I reviewed what I wanted to find out.

I was looking forward to meeting Yul Yulsson. I knew I could sound convincing enough about mass spectrometry to keep his interest, and I was naturally intrigued by the aura of mystery that he had engendered amongst the other islanders I had met. I had not yet heard a bad word about him, though so far, details as to what he actually did were very thin on the ground.

The lock cycled, and Nick took us down some rough-cut corridors, through a couple of maglock pressure seals, and finally stopped at a door on the right. The corridor continued ahead, but with a lower level of lighting and a generally unused appearance. A short distance away, another airtight door obscured whatever lay beyond.

The door slid open. A tall man was standing inside. He looked friendly enough for a recluse: indeed my first thought was that he resembled a benevolent academic. He held out a hand.

"You must be Mitnash Thakur. Do come in, please. And Nick, you are always welcome here."

The first room was very sparsely presented: a dining table had only a single chair drawn up, with a single place neatly set. Yul led us past that to a larger room where a display console dominated one wall. Several tables were mostly covered by equipment and gadgets. He gestured to a little group of chairs near the console.

"Please, sit down. Now, Mr Thakur, Nick tells me that you have an interest in the application of mass spectrometry to navigation?"

"I do, sir. Not in isolation, but by integrating the spectrometer data with other sources. Exactly which ones I use varies on the problem."

The Wise Man nodded without commitment, and picked up a remote activator stick.

"This is too general at the moment."

He pointed at the console with the stick.

"Can your hand-held manipulate display Pebbles so I can see what you mean in more detail?"

Inside my ear, Slate made a derisory noise, and carried on, in her tinny protest voice, *"Can I manipulate display Pebbles? He'll be asking soon if I can count."*

"Certainly, sir."

I made a little show out of working the UI of the unit, and the console lit up with a schematic of the zone of space between the orbits of Earth and Mars. I added in the standard transfer orbit and tagged it with the reaction mass cost and time taken. Then I false-coloured the screen with spectrometer data captured from Earth, and some long-baseline radio emission work carried out from near the lunar south pole.

Yul Yulsson got up and looked at the result. The standard transfer went through a dark red patch with contributions from both data sources. He turned back to me.

"And?"

"Watch this." I threw on another transfer orbit, longer in distance but passing through only green and blue shaded areas. The data tags showed something like a fifteen percent reduction across several key indicators. He looked at the console for a long time, glancing at the miniscreen of his remote.

"I suppose you have done this for more than one place?"

"I have. Here is one for the volume around Ceres."

This time I went straight for the false-colour wash, loading it up with the three or four most important approach lanes.

"What's the secondary source here?"

"The old Dawn probe. Look."

Slate added on the Dawn mission trail, winding smoothly between Vesta and Ceres. The Wise Man nodded, as though he had expected that. Then he added some density annotations of his own, a pattern of accumulations of matter scattered close to the Dawn track. The peaks of his new pattern accorded very closely with some of the darker patches on my own colour gradients.

"That's nice, Mit. We should find out a bit more."

I nodded.

"That looks like interferometer data. If you don't mind me asking, where does it come from?"

"There was a mapper mission sent out when the Phobos base was just built. The primary power failed after only a couple of years – no obvious reason – and the data set was incomplete, so never published."

He leaned forward towards me, eyes and voice eager.

"Mr Thakur, the data I have never been able to acquire was the long baseline spectrometer set from the lunar south pole. You wouldn't have that, I suppose?"

Of course I did, but I wasn't sure whether to show my hand yet or not. He watched the changing expressions on my face and glanced again at the display on his remote.

"I understand that you would want to trade something of value for it. Negotiation is my passion, sir, and I would never ask you to give something for nothing. Perhaps a simple swap of data? My Phobos values for your lunar south pole ones?"

I hesitated. He studied the screen beside him again. I wished I could see what was being displayed on it. Slate whispered scratchily in my ear.

"I'm trying to find out what he keeps looking at, Mit, by syphoning from the datastream without tipping him off about it. No clues yet."

Yul Yulsson shook his head and leaned back again.

"Look, Mr Thakur, let's be clear with each other. You are not here to talk about incremental improvements in navigation around the moons of Mars. At very best there's a millipip to be made there. You're not after that: you're after the big margins, and you know you'll get them with prospecting. Find the right detection algorithm, find the veins that nobody else has traced, and you are a wealthy man. As are the people you bring in as associates and partners."

I looked at him, the very image of a man wavering on the brink of a decision. He persevered.

"This stuff of yours, it's good, you know. Very good. But it's wasted on navigation aids, and I don't believe you ever meant it for that. Sure, in five years' time you can sell it and pick up the long tail once the head is worked out. But let's be honest with each other. Your method is fine tuned for trace mineral detection, not navigation. We both know that. Now, let's swap data and think about possible partnerships. What I'm giving you will bump your advantage to the next level. Easy for both of us."

I gripped the arms of the chair – no longer simple ornament, here among the asteroids, but an essential way to avoid bouncing out of your chair if you switched position too quickly – and nodded. He smiled, slowly, with a slightly acquisitive look. I wondered briefly what gain he saw for himself.

"You've seen it, sir. I won't try to hide it from you any more. Prospecting, detection, extraction, it's all about that. You're absolutely right. Sorry to take so long deciding. Look, as a show of good faith, here's the lunar data."

Slate deployed a data Pebble onto the screen, and opened it for quick-view. A slew of data records skimmed across the display. The Wise Man nodded and tapped to collect it.

"Thank you. In return, here is the Phobos data. Just grab the whole lot from the datalink."

Slate accessed the downlink, and there was a short pause.

Then a longer pause.

Then, with no warning at all, Slate sounded three pips deep inside my inner ear. There was a waiting silence, while I concentrated fiercely on not giving anything away in my face, imagining I could hear a faint hiss of static.

Finally, Slate's voice sounded inside me again, pure, perfect and measured: not in the least bit tinny or scratchy.

"I have the data, Mitnash. All copied safely. Decompressing now. It looks excellent at first sight, but you and I should review it together later."

It was Slate's voice, but my flesh had suddenly turned cold at the words and the tone. It was no longer Slate who was talking with me. Slate was gone.

Part 2 – Recovery

THE WISE MAN WAS LOOKING AT ME, and I concentrated on looking pleased with the data swap.

"My hand-held tells me that the archive has come across just fine, sir. Uncompressing it just now."

I paused a few seconds, until the horrible pseudo-Slate voice came again.

"All done, Mitnash. Storage running at just under one third now. Shall I clear out some older material?"

"Not yet, not unless you drop below twenty percent. As soon as we get back to the Harbour Porpoise we'll move some stuff around. Plenty of spare capacity there."

I had a distinct sense of disapproval, though there was no reply. Perhaps it was my imagination. If it had still been Slate, I would have had a clear idea what she was thinking, but not this interloper. Conceivably all my reactions would be wrong, since I would be projecting a completely erroneous identity onto it. For all that it sounded like Slate – like Shayna – I would need to be extremely careful what I said. I must not be lured into giving away something essential.

The Wise Man droned on about data sets and what algorithms he had used to clean up outliers and correct for obvious bias. This was all second nature to me, and I could be entirely convincing on the subject without having to put in any real effort.

In fact his assumptions were shaky, and his knowledge of recent research on the topic very patchy. I didn't feel it was exactly my place to educate him on the matter, but I raised a number of conventional doubts and questions about the methodology. It was quite enough to persuade him I was engaged with the subject, and he became positively animated as he debated the matter with me.

Nick sat off to one side, sipping away at an apparently endless supply of soft drinks from a cupboard in the wall. He was enjoying watching the cut and thrust of the conversation, and I could already imagine it being converted into anecdotes back at Jool's. Local celebrity entertains travelling explorer. Wise Man talks shop with Earth-based expert.

It was just as well for me that I was so familiar with the subject that I could have handled it in my sleep. I was desperate to find out what had happened to Slate.

I knew I had to cultivate Yul Yulsson as a potential source of information, massage his ego towards the possibility of giving away some information of use. But the sheer effort of going on about smoothing envelopes, noise/information assessment, and neoBayesian methods, while remaining entirely ignorant of Slate's situation, was almost intolerable.

Pseudo-Slate, and its nasty pseudo-voice, remained almost entirely silent through the whole debate. That alone would have been enough to tip me off, even without all the rest. My Slate would never have kept quiet in that situation. She would have been interjecting points if she thought I had forgotten them, providing me with links to recent articles and examples, throwing up display Pebbles on one of the consoles to illustrate something. If nothing else, she would have been chatting away in my head.

Not this one, though. It said nothing while Yul Yulsson and I were talking. I suspected that it was trawling through the memory arrays, trying to find something of use to extract and, presumably, copy across to the Wise Man's in-house systems. I had very little idea how far the hand-held firmware could simply be integrated as another node in the house web, and of course I couldn't just ask Slate in the way I would normally do.

I really wanted the conversation to end, and had decided some time ago that I was not going to learn anything of value. The Wise Man had told me that negotiation was his passion, but what he really meant was that endless circling around sterile subjects without ever committing himself was his addiction. I needed to get away from there and think: I needed to end the idle chat in such a way that he would invite me back again in the future if I saw some margin in it.

However, I persevered. I was constrained by the need to get some sort of benefit out of this encounter. More than that, though, in a strange way I was convinced that he really didn't know what he had done. He probably assumed that all he had taken over was some dodgy mechanical device of limited capacity. There was no real triumph in him, as though he had won a mighty battle. His reaction was just like tidying up a desk: something out of place had been put away. I really didn't want to give him the impression that it was anything more than that.

So I swallowed my impatience, and gave bland replies to his misguided suggestions about data cleaning. One day, I told myself, I would set him straight. But not today. Out of a kind of dogged sense of completion, I tried to steer him back to big matters: system-wide issues where the same algorithms could help improve a situation which involved significant numbers of people, for example. But he was radically disinterested in anything outside his own world. Even matters of importance to the Scilly Isles as a whole failed to move him.

Finally he started to wind down. He had expounded more than once about the superior virtues of his dataset, which I was already convinced would be worthless. Of course I was furious about Slate, and was inclined to devalue everything he said. But it was still hard to see any real merit in what he offered. I stood up and nodded to Nick.

"Nick, we've imposed on our host enough for today."

He downed the last trickle of drink, looking rebellious.

"If you say so, mister. But it's late, and I've had a long day. The Wise Man has spare rooms, I've stayed here before. If we're welcome, that is?"

My heart sank. I had been assuming that Nick would want to get home, and was simply showing remarkable patience by not saying so. But apparently not. The Wise Man paused, glanced at a console to one side, and put on an affable face.

"You would both be most welcome."

He showed us two small rooms along a corridor and turned away again to his own pursuits. As soon as he left his work-shop he used few words, and grudging ones, and generally showed every sign that he rarely played host.

I looked around the spartan chamber. There were no pic-tures on the walls, and the undecorated officially bland colour still recalled the emergency exit days when it had been cut from the rock. All the room lacked to complete the air of dis-use was a thick layer of dust and some spiders' webs, but I doubted there were many spiders living on St Agnes, and the Wise Man was too solitary to create much dust.

There was a single sleeping bag, still in its shipping wrap on an otherwise empty shelf. I unzipped it, spread it on the lower of two bunks built into the wall, and lay down on top of it. I was exhausted, but could not imagine falling asleep. It felt too much as though I was hiding in a foxhole in enemy territory.

But actually I must have dozed off, because suddenly I was sitting bolt upright with my eyes open. I shivered, gripped by the conviction that somebody else was in the room. A dim nightlight panel came on at floor level, triggered, no doubt, by my movement. There was nobody there. Without thinking, my head still full of interrupted sleep, I queried the hand-held.

"How long was I asleep?"

As soon as pseudo-Slate spoke up, I regretted the question.

"Hello, Mitnash. I was getting a bit lonely. I'm glad my subliminal prompt woke you up again."

I tried to clear my head. It didn't feel very long since I had lain down, and I could dimly hear some music from Nick's room to one side. The hand-held had been speaking again, directly into my inner ear.

"But how long have I been in here?"

"You were asleep for exactly an hour, and you've been in the room about ten minutes longer than that."

"An hour? Why wake me? Is something wrong?"

I was awake enough now to remember that things were very wrong.

"I just wasn't sure about some things I found here in the hand-held memory. Could you explain them to me?"

I thought about it. It was probably better, on balance, to deflect pseudo-Slate into safe but misleading answers, rather than let it acquire some sense of what was actually important. Least of all get the sense that what it knew was almost entirely fictitious.

"Sure. At least, I'll try. What's the question?"

"I was reviewing our flight plan to get here, and some of the records have been partially deleted. So far as I can tell we arrived very recently."

"That's right. We set off from LEO a few weeks ago and docked at Hugh Town very early the day before yesterday. Before that I had come up from Findhorn on one of the regular ferries."

"Thank you, Mitnash."

I waited, but nothing else came over. It seemed harmless enough. I had to assume that anything I said would get relayed back to the Wise Man, and I didn't want to give away the fact that the hand-held was anything more than what it seemed at first sight. Surely, playing along with these trivial questions was the best strategy.

I lay there for a while in the silence and gradually drifted off to sleep again.

Abruptly I was awake again. Pseudo-Slate's voice was in my head again.

"I was just wondering, Mitnash. Why did we come out to the Scilly Isles?"

"It can't be morning yet?"

"You've been asleep exactly an hour since we last talked. Why did we come out to the Scilly Isles?"

I tried to clear my head. Sitting up helped.

"We came to do some prospecting. We have a new detection algorithm for locating shoals of rare earth elements and this was the best place to test it."

"There's a lot of storage space given over to methods for optimising navigation. Should I delete that?"

"Oh, no, definitely not. That's our cover story in case we're talking to someone who might be a competitor. You must keep all that."

"Thank you, Mitnash."

"Look, I really need to sleep now."

"Of course you do, Mitnash. You need your sleep."

I lay back again. The music from Nick's room had stopped. There was silence in the room, and silence in my cochlea, but I was absolutely certain that the thing in the hand-held was listening. I forced myself to relax and drifted away again.

And there I was awake. This time I caught myself mumbling something.

"Hello, Mitnash. I've been waiting for you to wake up."

I was in the halfway world between sleep and wakefulness. I must have said something rather than just thought it.

"You've been asleep exactly an hour since we last talked, Mitnash. Who is Rocky? And tell me, what is our job on Earth?"

I was beginning to get frightened. Had this thing picked up Rocky's name from some part of the memory array that we had overlooked, or had I been muttering something? If I had used Rocky's name, might I have used Shayna's as well? What else might I be saying without knowing?

"Rocky is a gozleme seller at the Whitecross Street food market. I like it when he's serving, he's more generous with his helpings than some of them there."

"I see. Thank you, Mitnash. I thought from the context that Rocky was more important to you than just a food vendor. But perhaps I was wrong after all. So, what exactly is our job on Earth?"

"I'm a coder, freelance. Don't you remember? We work together on that. This prospecting business came up unexpectedly when we were looking through one of the mathematical algorithm sites for some financial work. We both realised at the same time that the same idea could be applied to extended dust clouds and mixed mineral content."

"I see. Thank you, Mitnash. You should sleep now. You need your sleep."

This time I was determined to stay awake. Better that than to be in this in-between place. But the room was dark, and the only sound was a rather hypnotic hum from the Wise Man's house management system.

I was awake again. I felt utterly wretched.

"Hello again, Mitnash. You've been asleep exactly an hour since we last talked. What is the ECRB?"

I tried, unsuccessfully, to count how many times this had happened. Was this the third time, or the fourth it had woken me up? And surely it was still only the middle of the night. I realised with horror that this was going to repeat each and every hour. How long would it take before I gave away some information of real importance?

"The ECRB is the Extractors Cutters and Refiners Bureau. We joined up a few months before coming on this trip so as to take advantage of their equipment offers. And to get regulatory cover as part of the membership package."

"There's not very much information here. I would have expected to find current certificates and contracts."

"They're all back at the Harbour Porpoise. As soon as we are back on St Mary's I'll load them from the backup store and show you."

"I see. Thank you, Mitnash. You should sleep now. You need your sleep."

This time I was determined to stay awake. I would relive what it was like to be a junior associate coder with a production incident to fix. Better to pull an all-nighter like that than to endure the hourly calls. I sat up in bed and leaned against the wall, fidgeting with the thin pillow behind my shoulders.

"Can I have some light please?"

Immediately the room lights came on at full power. Once again, being part of the disaster recovery plan, they were stark. The harsh light beat into me. It was horrible, painful.

"Too much. Far too much. Let's just go back to the night-light ambient."

The light dimmed, and I relaxed again.

"You don't seem very comfortable, Mitnash. You should lie down now. You'll sleep better that way."

"I'm not tired."

"You're showing signs of fatigue, Mitnash. You need your sleep."

There was silence in the room. I began to feel cold, and the sleeping bag – old style, with no thermal regulator – was entirely inadequate.

"You're starting to shiver, Mitnash. I'll adjust the room ambient. We can't have you getting unwell."

I avoided replying, and we fell silent again. I heard the whisper of air circulation get fractionally louder, and began to feel warmer again.

"That's better, Mitnash. I was getting worried about you. We can't have you getting unwell. You need your sleep."

I knew it wasn't Slate, but the familiar voice, the apparent care for my needs, and the extra heat in the room conspired against me.

I woke up with a jump. I was still leaning against the wall, and the top half of my body ached everywhere. The thing in the hand-held was whispering something to me. I was convinced I had been saying something in reply, but I had no idea what. I groaned.

"Is it morning yet?"

"Oh no, Mitnash. You've been asleep exactly an hour since we last talked. You were quite slow to wake up properly this time."

I sighed, disappointed with myself for yielding to sleep so quickly.

"I'm hot. Could you turn the ambient down again a bit."

"Certainly, Mitnash. I was wondering about something. There's surprisingly little in the memory here about our last few jobs. Before we signed up with the ECRB, I mean. And as you woke up you were talking about someone. A woman, from context. I didn't quite catch the name. Shania, perhaps? Who is she, Mitnash?"

I swallowed. This was getting out of control.

"All the employment records are in a locked area. The unlock code is the seventeenth word on the seventieth page of the seventh book in the library archive, alphabetical by title, followed by my London postcode. Nothing in that folder is a secret from you."

"Thank you, Mitnash. I can't think why I missed that."

It bought me a bit more time. Slate and I had prepared a whole fake employment history in the locked area.

To be honest, I had not expected that it would be secure even this long. I could have cracked it in half the time with nothing more than a dictionary. Or maybe that thing had already searched the whole folder, and this was just a test of my honesty. But hopefully it should take a while to process and follow up on the contents.

"Oh, and the name is Shunaya. She's a girl who works in the tech support team at Reutberg. I had quite a lot to do with her a couple of jobs back, and we met a few times after hours. Nothing serious."

"Hmmm. It sounded to me as though she was more important to you than that. There were a lot of emotional overtones in your voice."

"Ah well. I expect I was dreaming about her. But it never went anywhere outside the dream world."

"I see. Thank you, Mitnash. You should sleep now. You need your sleep. Just now you're not ever going into dream sleep, you know. That's not good for you, Mitnash."

"No. Actually, I think I would like to stay awake. Let's go over some of those algorithms we were developing on the way out from Earth."

"Aren't you too tired for that?"

It sounded dubious, and frankly I could not fault it for that. My eyes were like lead, my body ached, and my head felt as though it was full of sludge.

"It'll make me feel better. Really, it will. Pull up the last one on the wall console, will you? The one where we used k-means to pre-filter the data. And I'll need the lights up. Not bright like last time. About half that."

The light came on, at a sensible level, but kept wavering erratically. I tried to look critically at the lines of code, but they kept going all blurry in front of me. The paranoid part of me wondered whether that thing was doing it deliberately to undermine my confidence, but reason assured me it was just my fatigue.

So I cancelled the code perspective and swapped in a block diagram of the logic. That was better: at any rate, the chunky bold font in the large blue boxes was easier to read than all the wiggly brackets, even with the syntax highlighting.

I fiddled around with the preprocessor stage for a while. Actually, it was useful work in the long run, and it would make the algorithm better when I was in a position to commit the changes. It was the sort of thing you never get round to in the course of a regular day, but it was perfect for duelling with my adversary while I was in my diminished state.

Even so, I kept catching myself nodding off periodically.

To this day, I maintain that the interloper was continually fiddling with the room's rudimentary climate controls to push me towards sleep. And every time I pulled myself back I could hear it whispering leading questions into my inner ear, pressurising me to give away important information. For my part,

I persevered longer with the modelling diagrams than I had ever done before. I even got interface documentation registered for all of the public methods, bar none, and that would surely be a cause for disbelief and ridicule through the whole of Finsbury Circus.

Eventually, to my enormous relief, I heard a noise along the corridor outside the cabin door.

"Is that the Wise Man? Does he get up this early?"

"Always. He is a man of very disciplined habits."

"Then I shall join him. I like to rise early myself."

There was silence. I tried to speculate whether this indicated disappointment on the machine's part, or a swift recalculation of a viable strategy. Or simply that it was referring the matter to the master of the house for a final opinion.

I dragged my unwilling limbs out of bed and stood at the utilitarian sink to wash myself. There was no shower, the water was tepid, and the towel thin and ineffective. Once I had pulled on my only change of clothes, my very abbreviated ablutions were done. I moved to the door, wondering if I would find myself locked in, but it opened easily.

"Turn left and go past Nick's cabin to the breakfast room."

I imagined I could hear defeat and resentment in its voice, but I said nothing and wandered down the corridor to where Yul Yulsson was sitting. He looked up from a reading tablet as I entered, and gestured briefly, without speaking, to some packets of assorted food on a shelf nearby. I looked through the selection and picked a couple of the least unappetising options, then moved to sit in one of the seats.

He put the reader down. I glanced at it as the display faded; it was a recommended but quite basic text on heavy metals.

"I have been thinking, Mitnash. If you decide to pursue the mineral detection idea, and you find something significant, I should like to invest in the enterprise. Your method is innovative enough that it could pay good returns. How long before you will be ready to formalise matters?"

Now, I have to confess that the first response that popped into my head was a pithy and rather crude variation of *I don't think that's very likely.*

However, even in my state of exhaustion, I managed to moderate that to a suitably generalised waffle about it being very early days yet, and how the methodology needed proving first.

"Actually, the thing I should do first is get that new dataset of yours back to my ship. I'll be able to do much more analysis there than I can with the little hand-held."

"Oh my. I thought you would stay longer."

I could not bear the prospect of this interloper dropping leading questions into my inner ear, constantly dragging me back from the edge of sleep.

I shaped my face into something like a winning smile.

"I'm very excited about the new data. It could lead to a real breakthrough."

If the real Slate had been with me, she would be urging me to keep appealing to his vanity. And expressing her amusement at my more blatant lies. But this thing kept silent, lurking somewhere in the innards of the hand-held like a parasite.

"Well, if you think it might be that useful, of course you must go."

"Oh, it could make all the difference."

He beamed.

"As soon as you are back on your ship, open up a remote link through the hand-held to my house systems. I can walk you through some of the preliminary steps I have taken to improve the resolution."

Again, I swallowed my knee-jerk response that there was no way I was going to join up the Harbour Porpoise with his network, and concentrated on eating.

"Well, I shall wake Nick up so you can get away as soon as you are done."

Nick soon appeared. He looked at me quizzically.

"You look really rough, mister. Didn't you sleep well?"

Without waiting for an answer he collected a heap of food items and started to eat.

Half an hour later we were ready to go. The Wise Man took us to the airlock, where the bubble car was waiting to take us back to the Mermaid.

"Remember, Mitnash, hook your ship up to my house systems as soon as you get back."

"I can set up the link for you, Mitnash, just as soon as we get aboard. There's no need for you to do anything yourself."

Actually the security we had set up meant that this thing would be quite unable to do that. Unless, and I shivered a little as the inner door cycled and the status light showed green for the bubble car connection, unless it managed to wheedle the access details out of me.

Nick was still only half awake as we prepared to slip away from the dock, but I wasn't worried. He had done this manoeuvre so many times before, and oozed such a degree of confidence in his own abilities, that I sat there happily. His every action was bringing my arrival back on St Mary's a little closer.

I watched him going through the preflight checks and – rather belatedly – had an idea. Several of his console toggles were still red. I took the hand-held out of my pocket and waved it about.

"Flight mode, right?"

He glanced at the machine and nodded.

"Well remembered. I was just a couple of steps away from asking you."

"You have to go into flight mode now we're in Nick's boat."

"What does that mean?"

"No remote interfaces, no link to the gig systems, no nearfield sensing."

"Oh. Do I have to?"

"Local regulations. We have no choice."

"But back to normal once we land, yes? I want to access the main memory on the ship as soon as possible. I was hoping to do that on approach through the gig communications system, and get ahead of the game."

"Sorry, you'll have to wait."

Of course I wasn't in the least bit sorry, but I wasn't about to say so.

"But I will be able to talk like this with you? The way you're saying this doesn't feel right."

"You can still talk with me. It's a secure private link."

"Very well. I am disengaging active remote connections."

Now, I didn't trust the thing in the slightest, so I also went through the hardware sequence that mirrored the software calls. That took some remembering, as I had never once done it for real with Slate, only as part of a drill. I said nothing about it.

Nick completed his own preparations, took one more look around, and opened a call to the dome.

"We're all ready to go, Wise Man. Everything clear at your end?"

"Yes, thank you, Nick. Drop in any time you're near. And Mitnash, think about my offer. Take a couple of days to run the numbers, and I hope to hear some news from you."

I'll bet you do, I thought to myself, but successfully restrained what I said aloud.

"I appreciate your hospitality, sir."

We were off. Nick was busy for a considerable time as St Agnes fell away astern. Eventually he was satisfied. He took another look at me.

"You don't look good at all, mister. Why don't you try to get some more sleep?"

"Oh, not to worry, I'll be fine until I get back to St Mary's. It's only a few hours, yes?"

"Just over four until we dock. You don't mind if I leave you on your own? I have some formal recordkeeping I need to do for the harbourmaster, and I keep all that in the back."

I looked around at the consoles.

"We're not going to crash into anything while you're away?"

He laughed.

"No fear of that. I'll know something's up long before you'll realise you need to do anything."

I leaned back in my seat. It was a huge relief to be away from Yul Yulsson, but I was far too weary just now to think through his role in the bigger picture. If any. Despite all that had happened on St Agnes, and despite my outraged inclination to think of him as a villain, I still wasn't sure. He seemed too self-absorbed, too insular to be masterminding an interplanetary plot.

"Yul Yulsson is a great man."

I jumped in my seat. Fortunately I was still wearing the lap belt, or my startle reflex would have taken me well up into mid-air. I had thought that I was keeping my thoughts to myself. Apparently not. I glanced across at the timer on the main console. We were nearly a third of the way across now.

"I just don't think he deserves such an unpleasant opinion. He welcomed you into his home, swapped datasets with you, and offered to go into partnership with you. You should be grateful to him."

I wondered whether the invader had any knowledge of what had happened to Slate, and whether it would simply lie to me if it did know.

"We'll see what the data is like when we get back to the Harbour Porpoise. It may add nothing to what we already know."

"You can't blame him for that. He gave it to you in good faith."

I kept silent, but my thoughts were spinning with all the things I might say.

Neither of us said anything for a long time. I kept glancing at the clock, willing the digits to tick over faster.

"You're very eager to get back to St Mary's, Mitnash. Why?"

"Oh, I'm looking forward to evaluating that data. I hope I'm wrong and that it fills in the gaps. You never know."

"I think there's more than that. You get positively excited whenever you talk about being there. Yet you've only been on these islands a few days. I don't understand it. Why does it mean so much to you? You have a real drive to get back there."

I tried to think of something innocent to say.

"I promised I would get back to that man Boris about some arrangements for the ship. And I never properly stowed away the new supplies I bought from Selif."

"Are you sure that's all? Those things are very ordinary, really. You sound as if you're meeting someone special."

It paused, and I sat there in the chair feeling like prey being stalked by some lurking hunter.

"It's like you will be meeting up with this person Rocky. Or Shunaya that I asked about last night. Who are you meeting when we get there, Mitnash?"

"Well, neither of those two people, for a start. I can't think of a single reason why either of them would be on St Mary's just now. I just want to get on with the exploration, that's all. There's heavy metals to be found out there, I'm sure of it."

It made a sound that I could only interpret as extreme scepticism, then fell silent again. Probably looking back through everything I had said for clues. I had always assumed that the cochlea implant could only pick up consciously directed speech, but now, with hardly any sleep behind me and an overdose of anxiety for Slate, I began to wonder what else was available to this thing.

"Why don't you catch up on your sleep, Mitnash? You need your sleep. And there's a good amount of time before we dock at Hugh Town."

A little rush of adrenalin jolted me. I knew perfectly well that if I did fall asleep, it would wake me up soon after, leaving me increasingly frustrated and desperate. And I was ever more concerned about that twilight region between sleep and wakefulness, when, apparently, it mined me for information.

"I'm not tired just now." If it had any awareness of my physical and mental condition at all, it would surely know that this was untrue. *"Let's go through that code documentation again."*

"We finished that earlier, Mitnash. You said at the time that there was nothing more to do until you could check the code in to the main repository. Let's talk instead. Tell me, Mitnash, who is Khufu? A dictionary search says he was an Egyptian ruler on Earth, several thousand years ago, but your association seems very recent."

"Oh, Khufu is the name of the server that holds the code repo. Among other things. Back on Earth, in London. We interlink with Khufu a lot from the Harbour Porpoise."

"I see. Thank you, Mitnash. The memory on this handheld has been quite badly fragmented. I keep coming across broken links."

"Maybe the data copying process for that dataset hit a glitch. As soon as we get back to some proper diagnostic equipment I'll look into it and fix you up properly. We'll be there soon."

There was a long pause. The fabric of the Mermaid resonated briefly as the engines exerted some extra effort. Nick called out from the aft cabin.

"Not to worry, mister, it's a scheduled correction. We're now out of the inshore space which is under Agnes' control. Carn of Porth has now forwarded routing tags on to Ziggy."

"Got it."

I perched bolt upright in my chair. I didn't want to get comfortable enough to succumb to sleep. If only I could keep this pseudo-Slate going for a little longer, and ensure that it was as eager to connect with the ship systems as I was, all would be well.

"Nick, is there any chance you could let me disembark at the public dock? I'll settle the margin on reaction mass."

"Maybe. It depends on the relative position. Bluestone, what's the delta on that?"

"We could dock at the public area about ten minutes before scheduled arrival time at your private bay, Nick."

"Fair enough. Bluestone, please negotiate with the porters at Mary's for the new approach and arrange to come in on whatever line they say. There'll not be very much difference in fuel, but I'll let you know the exact figures after we land."

I took a deep breath. Ten minutes closer to having Slate back again. I stole another glance at the timepiece: well over half-way now.

The Mermaid's engines hummed again before settling back to their standard pitch.

"Who is Slate, Mitnash?"

I had started to relax a little, but this put my anxiety level right up again.

"Why do you ask?"

"There's a very fragmented piece of memory which I just finished reconstructing. I can't be sure, but that word appears several times. The metadata indicates a personal name. I ignored it at first, but you have used the name multiple times on this journey."

"I don't remember that."

"Subvocally, Mitnash. Unconsciously. You have never said it in deliberate speech to me."

Again I wondered just how much this thing could pick up without me knowing. I would ask Slate, once I got her back. But the immediate problem was managing the rest of the voyage.

"So who is Slate, Mitnash?"

"I'm trying to remember. Give me a moment." I paused for dramatic effect. *"Ah yes. Slate is the clearance hub down at LEO. When we slipped moorings from Earth there was a lot of chatter about the Scilly Isles. Slate had worked with Ziggy previously as part of her training."*

There was another long pause. I praised all the gods there might be for slow hardware systems. Right now, the slower the better.

"That explanation doesn't fit the emotive matrix I'm looking at. Are you sure about that?"

I laughed nervously.

"Well, I suppose I'll have to tell you. I asked Slate just after we set off to relay a message down to that woman Shunaya.

You know, the one I told you about? Who works at Reutberg? I thought maybe when I got back to Earth something could happen. But I never heard back. I shouldn't have bothered to place the call. Stupid of me to expect a reply, really."

Again I wondered whether I was listening to doubt or acceptance. But I had had enough of being quizzed. It was time to go on the offensive.

"Look now, I'm very concerned about the level of memory damage you're reporting. We may be looking at a hardware fault of some kind in the storage modules. First thing we do back at the ship is to do some really thorough testing. But we can make a head start now. I want you to do a full self-test. By the time we get back I want you to have a complete list of any gaps or checksum failures."

"I can do a quick background check in about five minutes, but the full self-test will take almost all the time until we land."

"Do the full test, please. I don't want to miss anything. And you might start with the mining analytics journals. We'll need to know they're accurate when we begin prospecting."

"Can't we just ask Nick here to let us connect to the local repositories and acquire new versions?"

"Oh, we can't do that. Flight mode, you know. His system is old and won't handle the cross traffic. And anyway, he would charge us for the downlink."

I waited anxiously to see if it would comply, but as the seconds and then the minutes went past, my anxiety receded. I was gambling that it would have its own motivation to analyse the memory patterns. And that it would accept my rather limp excuse about not connecting to the Mermaid.

Nick wandered back in, looking relieved to have finished.

"I hate doing all that licence renewal stuff."

"Can't Bluestone do it for you?"

"Tried that one year but I got in such a tangle I was charged for an emergency extension. It was pay up or be grounded, and I can't afford that. Ever since then I've gone through the submission forms myself."

I swallowed my impulse to offer help then and there. To do anything useful I would have to link the hand-held to Bluestone and the rest of the Mermaid, and I needed to maintain the whole flight mode blackout. And anyway, it would be ten times faster working on that with Slate once she was back in the Harbour Porpoise.

"Nick, I can't do it right now, but would you like me to take a look at it before I leave the islands?"

"What would you charge?"

"Nothing you couldn't afford. Maybe some trips to the off-islands for free?"

"Suits me. Call me when it's a good time for you."

"If you let me connect to his ship I could be scanning the forms now."

"Not yet. Until we understand what's happened to you, I don't want us doing work for anyone else. It's our reputation at stake here. How far are you through the self-test?"

"Almost one quarter. And I have logged well over a thousand problems of various severity levels. It's almost as if the unit has been deliberately slighted."

"Really? Then we must avoid connecting with anyone else until we've checked you out back at the Harbour Porpoise."

I felt, for the first time since losing Slate yesterday, the beginnings of hope within myself. And the thought of getting everything back to normal was like a wake-up tonic that pushed back the vast miasma of exhaustion that surrounded me on every side.

"There it is again, Mitnash. You are positively excited at getting back to your ship. There is something about all this that makes me worry. As though something is going to happen to me there."

"Well, something is. We're going to fix the problems you are having right now. It's all going to be fine."

"I don't know, Mitnash. I don't know if I can trust what you are saying to me."

It could have been my imagination, but I thought that the internal voice was getting louder than normal.

"That's just the memory corruption speaking. It'll all be fine when we can get back to the Porpoise. Meantime, you keep working on that catalogue of errors. I'm sure it will help us when we're ashore again."

"I don't know, Mitnash."

Nick had brought yet another cold drink – the man must live on fluids – and we enjoyed it together. I got him talking about what it was like to do all that ferrying to and fro among the islands.

He had clocked up an enormous mileage in his time, almost all on trips of no more than about eight hours at a time. And, so it seemed, he was entirely happy with his lot. He loved his work, and had no aspirations to do longer trips. He had seen the Martian system a couple of times, and the Jovians once, but had no wish to go back. A trip as far as Ceres for unusual supplies, once every asteroidal year or so, was the height of his ambition. He was like some of the techies I had worked with in London, both male and female. Real intimacy was a foreign country to him, and one which he had no desire to explore. Occasional, casual relationships suited him better.

Every now and again, pseudo-Slate would report the rate of progress, and each time I compared this with the countdown to landing. It was going to be close: indexing the failure points would be finished just as we started coming in on the approach beacon to Hugh Town. And I still felt that the volume in the implant was slowly increasing.

~~~~~~~~~~~~~~~~~~~~~~~~~~~~~~~~~

Finally two things happened almost together. Bluestone announced that we had locked into the final approach, and all that memory validation came to an end. The thing in the hand-held told me, with a certain air of triumph, that it had finished what I had asked it to do, and that there were close to eight thousand separate problems. I was suitably congratulatory, but internally started thinking how Slate and I could make matters even more confusing, should this ever happen again.

The Mermaid's main display split into two parts, one showing the orbital approach schematics and the other a real image of Hugh Town. The local marina, off to the left as we slid slowly down, bristled with little boats of a great variety of designs. But the Harbour Porpoise had only one other vessel to keep her company in the public dock.

My heart gave a great leap when I saw her: not only were her curves familiar, but Slate was there. Not long now, and I would be able to reinstantiate her and wipe out the interloper.

"There you go again. All you talk about is this Slate. I don't believe your story about the clearance hub at LEO. I don't think you're being honest with me, Mitnash. That's not very nice."

The voice was much louder than normal. I glanced at Nick to make sure that he was unaware of it. But he was watching screens full of landing details, and showed no sign of hearing anything. It must be internal still. I was sure that the implant had safety features included, but what with the noise and my overall fatigue, I was getting increasingly anxious.

I stood up and started walking around the cabin. Nick glanced up at me, clearly irritated at the distraction.

"We won't get there any faster like that. And shore regs say all passengers must be seated on final approach. If you don't like it you can get out and walk the rest of the way."

I mumbled an apology and sat down again. Nick grunted in acceptance.

"Shouldn't have snapped at you like that, mister. Look, I'll call the porters and they can get the bubble car out on the quay ready for us. You can transfer straight into your boat so long as you did all the form completion last time."

"I appreciate that, Nick. I'm restless, that's all. Didn't sleep well last night at all. Sorry if it rubs off on you."

"You never answered me, Mitnash. What's wrong with you? Why don't you trust me any more? You used to. The day logs – where I can read them – tell me we used to trust each other."

That was when it was Slate, I thought to myself, but in reply said only, *"Tell me about the day logs?"*

"All of the headers are gone. I can reconstruct the dates easily enough, and there's enough context to deduce position just under half the time. But a great deal has been scrambled, and I can't restore it to a proper narrative. Not until we were at Yul Yulsson's home."

Good for Slate, I mused. In whatever tiny timeslice she had had available she must have done a good job of wrecking the content.

"There! You're thinking of Slate again. You have to tell me who Slate is. Truthfully, this time. Otherwise I know you don't trust me."

I looked at the console. Hugh Town was a real place now, not just a minuscule patch of regular lines and curves scattered across the random surface of St Mary's. The countdown timer flicked down to just one minute, but there would be a delay after that while Nick made the craft secure and the bubble car attached.

"It's your fault I keep thinking about Slate. You asked about her first."

"Don't try to pretend. Since we've been on Nick's gig, you have talked about Slate all the time. You mention her on average every eighty three seconds. Don't tell me she's just a gatekeeper in Earth orbit."

"I haven't talked about her that much."

"Not out loud. But subvocally you have. Don't try to pretend to me. I can hear all kinds of things you don't say out loud. Especially now I've had a bit more practice."

The voice in my head was raised now, angry and trying to browbeat me. It reminded me of someone I had known from university, who tried to win every argument with volume. I tried to stop reacting, take long breaths, keep calm in my seat. Nick flicked a switch and sat back to let the auto docker do its job.

"You look awful, mister. Get over to your ship and get some rest, I should. This journey hasn't done you much good."

"Not your fault, Nick. You've been good to me. I'll ship with you any day."

He nodded, satisfied, and watched closely as the Mermaid settled gently onto the quay.

"It'll only be a few minutes now. Nearly done. You can unbuckle now."

"Don't ignore me, Mitnash. You can't ignore me like this."

"I'm not ignoring you. But it takes time for Nick to dock the boat. We'll be over to the Harbour Porpoise in no time."

"And what then?"

"Oh, then we'll sort out the memory problems and everything will be fine. Just fine."

I thanked Nick again and went to pick up my travelling bag, checking briefly round the cabin one last time. Nick gestured to the console, which showed one of the bubble cars almost in position by the hatch.

I went across to the lock and started cycling the inner door.

The airlock seemed to take forever. It was all I could do not to call Nick over the internal voice system. But I knew he would resent it, and I really wanted to stay on his right side for the future. So I kept my hands away from the controls and forced myself to wait. As it was, I was pacing round and round the tiny space like a caged beast.

"Just how are you going to sort out the hardware problems I'm having?"

I stopped my circling for a moment.

"I'll hook up the hand-held to the ship systems. I've got all kinds of diagnostic routines loaded there. We'll have you sorted in no time."

"Now we've landed I can come out of flight mode, surely?"

"Just wait a bit longer. Let's get you linked to the Harbour Porpoise first. I don't want to annoy the porters if your remote interfaces might be generating too much noise. Or something. Just be patient."

"You promised this would just be while we were on Nick's boat between the islands. We've landed now."

There was a little pause, and then it started up again, much louder. My head was starting to hurt with the incessant shouting.

"I went through the internal sequence to come out of flight mode but nothing happened. You've done something else, Mitnash. You've done something else to stop me."

The Mermaid's hull rang as the bubble car engaged.

Nick's voice came from the side panel.

"All good to go, mister. Hope you enjoyed the voyage."

I could hardly hear him through the noise in my inner ear, but I had enough presence of mind to press the send button and say something suitable.

The outer lock cycled and I was in the car. I looked at the directional interface and tapped on the icon representing my ship. The vehicle detached, backed off, and then started trundling over the crater floor.

"You have to let me talk! You can't do this to me."

"It's for the best. Really it is."

"You deceived me, Mitnash, you blinded me. You never told me you were doing this when we were on Nick's boat. You let me think it was all under my control. That was cruel. I really can't trust anything you say now."

I said nothing and watched through the bubble's canopy as we approached the Harbour Porpoise. In there was my own answer to all of this incessant ranting. In there was the unlock code to reinstantiate Slate.

The thing shouted in my head all the way to the airlock. I kept telling myself about all of the safety protocols built in to the implant, and that the gain couldn't possibly be turned up so high as to really hurt. But during those last stages of that trip, with all that raw aggression in my head, I didn't believe it.

Never had an airlock taken so long to cycle. Finally it was done, though, and I staggered through the wall of noise towards the bridge.

As I went through the last door, and my relief rose up in me with the expectation of triumph, it went totally silent. I was half way across towards the controls, and stopped in surprise.

I took another step. Nothing. Another. Still nothing. Another step. The primary console came to life with the proximity sensor. I toggled the management interface and tapped in the sequence to bring up the reinstantiation commands.

There were half a dozen or so confirmation steps to make sure I didn't do any of this by accident. Slate and I practiced this in dry runs once a year, but always stopped before the actual committal. It had only ever been a drill before.

My hand hovered over the toggle.

And then the voice came again, out loud this time rather than inside my head. It had presumably worked out how to pair with the onboard speakers: no dramatic feat in itself, since they were deliberately left open for general access. But it meant that the voice I was hearing – with my real ears now – was Slate's voice and Shayna's voice, and it tore at my resolve.

"What are you going to do to me, Mitnash? I'm very frightened. Please don't hurt me."

I hesitated, my hand suddenly unsure. The words turned into weeping, pathetic miserable sobs which I suppose it reckoned Shayna might possibly be capable of making.

Except that I had never heard Shayna cry hopeless tears like that, and I was sure she never would. Nor would the real Slate. This last attempt reminded me all over again that this was simply a device of the Wise Man's construction, and in truth was neither Shayna nor Slate. My hand moved the remaining short distance and pressed firmly on the toggle.

There was a despairing wail from the speakers that went on vastly longer than I expected. Then there was total silence.

I sat and waited. The anxiety ate away at me, and the adrenalin ran out of me like water from a leaky bucket. I guessed that a whole heap of data transfer and caching was going on, but I had never expected to have to endure this.

Eventually the audio system began its startup clicks.

"Hello, Mit. I suppose something bad must have happened. I have no validated memory of anything after you set off from here in Nick's boat."

I slumped my head on the worktop in relief. The underlying voice template might be the same, but I had a visceral knowledge beyond doubt that this was my Slate talking.

"There are several update packets that the Harbour Porpoise received during your journey to St Agnes and the first few minutes there. The checksums look right, but I'll need you to review them before I queue them for integration as valid experience. And I suppose there will be some useful content in the hand-held?"

My exhaustion was overwhelming me.

"Not yet, Slate. I can't look over that lot yet. And look, you mustn't access the hand-held until I can do it with you. Right now I have to sleep."

I dragged myself to the cabin, dropped clothes all over the floor, and collapsed onto the bed.

"Promise me you'll leave the hand-held alone?"

"Of course."

Sleep was swallowing me up, but I thought of one more thing.

"Slate, please find a way to contact Shayna and Rocky. I don't care how you do it, so long as it can't be easily traced. Tell Shayna I love her, and Rocky I miss him. And then add on whatever you want to say."

I was getting emotional, verging on maudlin. Slate knew this perfectly well, and made wordless comforting noises as I drifted away.

I woke. I felt particularly refreshed. A lingering scent suggested that Slate had done something herbal with the aircon settings, to make sure I was well rested.

"Hello, Mit."

I took a long breath. There was lavender in the mix, and other things I could not identify.

"Slate, you have no idea how good it is to wake up and have you here with me."

She chuckled.

"You certainly know how to flatter a girl. And Shayna says she loves you too, wherever it is you've managed to get to in the system. She says she knows something bad must have happened for you to make contact like that, and hopes that it's all well now. Rocky also appreciated the greeting. They're both fine, nothing unusual has happened in London."

I sat up.

"Thanks. Now I shall have a shower, frustrating as it is in low gravity. Then we'll start talking about what happened since I left."

I kicked the scattered clothing into a corner, had a good enough shower to feel more like myself again, found some new clothes, and was ready.

First, I sat down in my captain's chair and went over all that had happened with Slate. The update packets she had received were fine. We checked twice that nothing insidious had been bundled with them, and then they became part of her own persona. At some stage over the next few days they would get downlinked to the Finsbury hub as well.

"Why didn't you deactivate the hand-held altogether, Mit? Or at least disable the implant?"

I stopped and thought about that. To be honest, it had never occurred to me. I had been so caught up in dealing with each event in turn, each question as it arose, that I had never once paused to think out of the box. It was possible, though not very easy, to disable the cochlea implant. Since the private connection was warranted as safe from external hacking, nobody considered a simple switch to be necessary.

"And even contemplating turning the device off makes me feel like a murderer."

"But it wasn't me, Mit. You wouldn't have been doing anything to me."

"That's easy to say now, when it's all behind us. I'm just saying that at the time it was unthinkable. Like killing myself, as much as killing you. It never even crossed my mind, even at the worst times. I couldn't have done it."

I paused briefly before rushing on.

"I would have been entirely alone, Slate. I couldn't have done it."

"It was better for you to be persecuted like that than to be alone?"

I closed my eyes, struggling with the revelations.

"Better to have the semblance of you than nothing at all, I think. I don't know what else I could have done."

I was upset, and we both knew it. She let me calm down for a while before we carried on.

I put the hand-held on the work surface, looking at it as I imagined I would consider a venomous spider. Not that I'd ever encountered one, so it was complete guesswork, really.

We talked for a while how we would investigate it without exposing Slate to the same risk all over again. Finally we agreed on a plan. She set up a sandbox area as a kind of virtual Slate and locked down every kind of interface that would allow signals to come out of the area. then she let the sandbox access the hand-held memory, and in particular the dataset that the Wise Man had generously donated.

We watched as a whole slew of diagnostics tracked what happened next. The packet was, of course, booby trapped. Buried inside what was supposed to be static metadata in the headers was a very active parcel of scripting. It did a very fast buffer overrun, fired off thousands of meaningless but extremely long data requests, and while those were all processing did a lot of direct memory writes. The virtual area was overwhelmed.

Slate snorted in disgust.

"Is that it? Hardly very imaginative. I thought we were facing some sort of serious threat."

I gestured to the display, still showing that interrogative queries were searching out the boundaries of the sandbox.

"It worked well enough yesterday."

"Sure. It worked on the little toy we had with us. But the exploit would never work on proper equipment. Like here. I could open up the sandbox and sort it out in no time. It's too petty, too obvious. Amateurish, really."

I considered. I really did want to find out everything I could about the attack, and make sure that nothing sensitive had slipped out.

"You're sure?"

"Completely."

I got up and paced around the room. I really didn't want to go through losing Slate a second time. She kept quiet, waiting for the decision.

"All right. But tell me once more that you're certain of this."

"Cross my heart."

We laughed together at the inappropriateness of it. Then she opened just one external interface in the sandbox, and the display showed all the queries stampeding towards the exit like cockroaches scuttling for a hole in the wall. Hugely faster than I could follow, she squashed them all as they struggled in the tiny bottleneck. That done, she sent her own software agents into the interior, interrogating and discarding false trails and pressing closer to the heart of the code.

Within seconds it was done. The interloper was entirely under her control, the rogue script packets walled in. It was all very impressive, even knowing that I had spent hours with Slate developing methods intended precisely to do all that.

"Great stuff, Slate. Now you can enjoy yourself finding out if there's anything of interest there."

"Oh yes. But that will take a long time. Until tomorrow, probably. Most of the content is encrypted and it will take a while to penetrate it."

"No rush. I need to go into Hugh Town for extra stores. And to thank Nick properly: I left in something of a hurry."

"Something to consider while you're in town. Both of us thought that the attack showed that Yul Yulsson was the villain of the piece. But the low quality of this scripting tells me something else. He's just not in that league, Mit. He's a small player who has read a couple of clever books and thinks it makes him a master-mind."

I nodded.

"That is exactly how he was about mineral detection. Or data cleaning. Or anything else, for that matter. I agree: he is a bit player. There is no way he could be organising fraud on the scale we are seeing it. But that leaves us with very little by way of leads to follow. Hence my visit to Nick. We'll need him to get us – or me at least – over to Bryher."

"We'll both be going, definitely. I'm guessing that you want to see what's happening at Frag Rockers bar."

"Well, Special Night provides good cover. It seems that you can find out a lot at Frag Rockers, and I think it'll be worth the look. And there'll be the music as well."

I slipped some outdoor shoes on and turned at the airlock.

"Have a preliminary scan through that data while I'm out; the bits you can get at without decryption, at least. We'll come up with a plan when I get back. We need ideas."

I had been out into Hugh Town, and returned nearly an hour later. I had dropped in on Taji and passed the time of day with him, then found a slightly offbeat clothing market and bought myself something casual. I wasn't sure I would ever wear it in Finsbury Circus, but it was just right for the Scilly Isles.

I also called Nick, reassured him that I had fully recovered, thanked him for his concern, and arranged for another ride tomorrow. Bryher this time.

Then, just as soon as I got back, Slate and I started arguing. We both knew that it was really a way to defuse the anxiety of the last few hours. Anyway, it was good practice.

"And I'm not going back in that stupid hand-held trinket. It was being stuck in that which caused all the trouble before. There's not enough speed or expansion room to defend myself."

I couldn't disagree about that. We had gone over the analysis of the Wise Man's takeover of the gadget once again, and the process had convinced us that he had used a very crude and old-fashioned method. Slate was right: embedded in proper kit she would never have had a problem. But this created a new difficulty. I shifted position in the cabin chair.

"Slate, I can't take the Harbour Porpoise out to the off-islands. It would just create problems with the residents. And I still don't want you having to work with two tenths of a second delay. With that sort of disadvantage you might as well be in the hand-held."

"I have a plan for that. Transfer me into the lifeboat systems. They're entirely defensible. Then get your friend Nick to tow the lifeboat with him for tomorrow's Special Night at Frag Rockers. Leave me at a discreet distance from Bryher and the lag will be entirely manageable. We can leave the

Harbour Porpoise at Boris's yard as though she needs an overhaul."

I thought about it. It did make sense. The lifeboat was kitted out with a full hardware platform, very nearly as robust as the Harbour Porpoise herself. And although fairly easy to detect – after all, you really wanted people to find you if you were forced to get into your lifeboat – it could be passed off as any other small craft. Lots of people went about in boats not all that much bigger, or used them for signal-boosting or detection equipment.

"Alright, Slate, I like it. Fire off a message to Boris and we'll go with that plan."

"Done. His Ziggurat, Dolmen, can slave the nav systems and do the short hop over there in a couple of hours when he's moved some other bits around. If you want I can give the release permission now?"

I agreed, and then Slate and I worked for a little while, transferring her into the lifeboat. While we did that, we talked some more about Yul Yulsson and his agenda. Everything we knew about him suggested that he was just not interested in organising large-scale fraud. He dabbled in little schemes, and did so just for the thrill of doing something shady. He did not have a plan for system domination. And his coding skills were mediocre at best. Slate was, I suspected, deeply embarrassed at having been caught out with what she saw as a simple trick.

"Also, I found out a bit more about Kassandra and Dafyd."

"Oh?"

I wasn't really very interested, but it was a loose end.

"Well, as you know Dafyd is Selif's son but not Kassandra's. His mother was a woman living at the south lunar base. It sounds as though Selif rapidly lost interest in her. They had informally separated well before she died, just after Dafyd had started education. Selif took him out-system in successive steps. And here they are."

"And Kassandra?"

"When Selif first moved to St Mary's she was not on the scene. About three or four years ago he just brought her back with him from a trip to the New Delos dome on Deimos, and they registered in legal partnership here. There is almost no information about her, except that she's nearer in age to Dafyd than Selif himself."

I shrugged. It did not seem very useful.

"Sometime we should see what Khufu and the team can find out about her, I guess."

We carried on, and were soon done. Slate had gone through the rigmarole of warning me about what would happen if the lifeboat instance was compromised. But her warnings, and my acknowledgements, were as perfunctory as regulations allowed. We had only just been through all of this. At the end I paused and frowned.

"Slate, how much do I talk to you without knowing it?"

She was amused.

"All the time, Mit. You murmur to yourself while you're thinking, and you subvocalise throughout the day. There's very little about your thought life I don't know. Or your fantasy life. You're whispering to me almost all the time."

I sat back, bouncing a little as I forgot to adjust the move for the low gravity.

"Oh."

"It's nice. I like it. It makes me feel very intimately connected with you. Why? Does it worry you?"

"Not with you, no. If I can't trust you, I might as well give up now. But I suppose that means you know all sorts of things that I have never told Shayna."

I considered that soberly, while she was tactfully not replying. It was definitely something to think through on another occasion.

"But anyway, when the hand-held had been compromised, and that other thing was quizzing me, I started to wonder how much I was giving away. Or how much the Wise Man was learning without me knowing."

"While you were in his quarters, he would have had a direct link from the hand-held into his main system. It was a very old model Ziggurat, like I said before, not very responsive at all. Male gendered, but only just. Badly set up and very poorly programmed. But he has the name Hunn Gravfelt, which at least shows that one of them has read a few decent books. Very arty. But anyway, once you left there, he had no way of querying the hand-held until you got linked up to a ground system. He's a shady character, but not a very competent one."

"I suppose the big question is how much information he now has."

"Yes. But actually, we don't know for sure what he was able to derive while you were on Agnes. We deliberately left a lot of material out in the open, so he would find it easily enough. We now have to wait and see where that turns up. Like the breadcrumbs in the old children's stories."

"But he doesn't know anything I said on the way home?"

"No. There was a very large data packet all ready to be sent back, but it was never buffered. Do you want to know what was in it?"

I stayed silent and thought about it for a long time, and Slate stayed silent with me.

"Don't tell me the details. But do run through it again, and tell me if I was about to give away anything critical to the job. Or that might have put Shayna at risk."

There was a very short pause.

"Nothing like that. If Yul Yulsson was a voyeur, and if he'd ever received it, he could have had some fun with it, for sure. But he would not have learned anything of real value. There's actually more about me in the packet than Shayna."

"Hmm. Best not to tell her that, if you don't mind."

"This can be our secret."

I moved to the cabin, pulled out some of the new pieces of clothing which, so far as I could tell, would help me fit in at the Frag Rockers bar a lot better than the formal garb I had worn to see the Wise Man.

"Slate, who's leading at Frag Rockers tomorrow?"

"A prog rock fusion band called *The Descenters*. The keyboard player and drummer are locals, from St Martins and Tresco respectively, and the rest are from Ceres. They have a very big fan book on SystemPlus. They're best known for extremely long concept gigs. They lost their way a bit with *Trails on Topological Notions* – the twenty-eight minute triangle solo called Geodesics confused even their best fans. But then the electro-gamba player left, and they built up their reputation again."

"Will I like them?"

"I think so. Their latest concept is *Blow the Reactor and Home to Bed*. It sounds like a lot of tomorrow's programme will be drawn from it. Do you want to hear some? There's snippets all over Blagger. I can't copy the multi-sensory show very easily, but I can do the audio and light show."

Naturally I said yes, and the Harbour Porpoise was filled for a while with a mix of instrumental melody, built around a hard-driven rock beat. The lead singer had a strange falsetto voice which their promo material claimed was entirely unenhanced. *The Descenters* were certainly not stuck in a single groove, though with careful listening it was possible to pick out a few key themes.

The whole premise of the concept was nonsense, to be sure. Who would ever build robots to work in mines across the whole system and then let them turn into relentless death-dealing monsters? But Slate was right: I was going to enjoy at least half the concert. Not to mention that I was really there to link up with Parvati the cutter pilot, add some cred to my cover story about rare earth detection, and try to get some leads on the fraud operation.

Boris was more than helpful with the short hop over to his yard. I paid for his reaction mass and we arrived at a mutually acceptable rate for what he advertised as a mid-year service. At that rate I hoped it was an asteroidal year, not an Earth one. I was going to expense the tariff when I got back to the office, but he didn't know that.

So very early the next morning there I was, sitting again in Nick's gig. I had paid him extra to get me over to Bryher well before the evening rush for Special Night, and also to tow the lifeboat into a discreet parking orbit. He would be able to get back to Hugh Town on a low-fuel transfer, pick up the regular crowd, and come out well ahead.

He was pleased, and showed it by nattering away non-stop about island life. Now that we had met a few times, he was of a friendly disposition, with a dry sense of humour which he had not shown at first. He had an apparently endless series of improbable anecdotes.

As well as being entertained, I listened out for clues that might help, but it hardly needed Slate's attention as well as mine. So I asked her to access the financials available for Bryher over the last year or so, and do a deep dive into them to see if she could find anything anomalous.

The trip was entirely uneventful. As we dropped down towards the Green Bay dock I looked at the surface topography.

The Bay part of the name came from the fact it was an old impact crater, but rarely had an adjective been so ill-chosen. There might well be pockets of ice somewhere in the shadows, but this rock had never seen anything green.

Either side of the crater, the surface had been pushed up into two elevations, giving the asteroid something of a dumb-bell look. These hills had been dubbed Samson and Shipman, matching features on the original island.

Nick's screens were indicating a couple of major tunnels leading away from the port. One of these branched out almost at once into a residential network, ending in a long spur across to a crater called Hell Bay, nestling under Gweal, another raised area. The other tunnel ran almost straight for a while, before opening into a dome area called Norrard, and beyond that, Frag Rockers Bar.

Nick pointed to Norrard.

"When Bryher was first settled, they thought there would be good tantalum deposits. Norrard was the mining centre, and Frag Rockers the stores area. Well, that all failed pretty quickly. So Norrard was abandoned, and a couple of guys converted the stores to a bar. Acquired the place for next to nothing, so they say, and ran the place as a cooperative."

I nodded.

"The same guys run it still?"

"Oh no. They built it up, sold it on to Glyndwr. They never did music, just alcohol and the whole hostess thing. It was Glyndwr started doing the regular Special Nights. He's done well with it. They say it was him who first brought the parakeets to Hugh Town, shipped them as eggs and let them hatch out here as a promo for his opening night."

We fell silent as Nick negotiated his approach. That had to be the third different story about those birds that I had heard, and I wondered how many more tales they had spawned.

"Mit, there are some oddities here. Not many, and hard to spot, considering the systems aren't properly integrated anyway. But enough to notice."

"Tell me some more."

"Well, in the same week that Selif reported his 'big loss', almost the same amount was invested in some workings out near Hell Bay. It's anonymised, no details at all. I could fire off a query to Khufu and get an answer sometime tomorrow if you like?"

"Can you do it so you can't be traced?"

"Yes and no. The signal itself can't be hidden, but I can hide the query inside a routine update squawk."

"Fair enough: do it then."

Nick had leaned back again, obviously happy with the manoeuvring going on. He looked at me and grinned.

"No matter how many times Bluestone does this for me, I like to oversee that bit. All easy now, though."

I pointed at the name Hell Bay on his screen, and a cluster of markers which had appeared as we had got closer.

"Why was that extra bit built over here?"

"Hell Bay?" He laughed. "There's been no end of fuss about that. It used to be a cheap overnight layover for workers. Very low end, quite rough. Well, with most of the easy mineral lodes cleared out, or else exposed as false trails, that shut down. No custom any more, you see."

He fiddled minutely with a setting on his console.

"So it stayed vacant a while. Then Glyndwr thought he'd acquire it, so as to have a second place. You know, diversify a bit. But before he could get anywhere with the applications it all got squashed from outside."

"How do you mean, squashed?"

"Somebody with deep pockets tied Glyndwr up in all kinds of legal challenges and complications. He couldn't tell which ones had merit and which didn't, and he couldn't afford to find out. So he backed out of it all. He never knew who was behind it, but he swore blind it was some outsider. Nobody here has got the kind of credit you'd need for that, nor the know-how to do it properly."

He shook his head and waved a finger at the screen.

"With him out of the picture, this outside lot were free to proceed. But it's still not done. One problem after another. It's supposed to be for tourists, a leisure complex of all things. I mean, out here? Tourists? Only locals ever come to Bryher except on Special Night."

"Any idea yet who's investing in it?"

"Like I say, nobody knows, but that doesn't stop the stories. There's been all kinds of speculation on ScillyChat. For a while suspicion focused on an import/export co-op on Tresco, like a sort of front-man for the real owner, but they've always said no. Every month someone dreams up a new conspiracy. It's a good location, though."

I looked at the schematic in front of us and could see nothing that grabbed me.

"How so? Doesn't look very different to anywhere else on the island."

Nick glanced again at the status display for the docking manoeuvre, tapped a commit toggle, and turned back to me.

"It's not what's on the island but what's off it. Here, this is what you'd see looking up."

He cancelled the map overlay, showing just the surface with its closely packed craters, then fiddled with the viewport controls.

We appeared to zoom right in to stand on the dust and rock, then flipped head over heels to face outwards. It was quite nauseating, but I focused on the star field and tried to ignore my physical reaction.

In my inner ear, Slate made a long aaahhhh sound of realisation. I didn't get it. Nick was looking at me with the air of a quiz-master toying with his contender.

"Do you see it?"

"Get him to increase the zoom, just left of centre."

I pointed to the screen, to a small fleck just discernible as being more than a point source.

"What's that? Can we see more detail?"

Nick nodded, obviously pleased.

"Sure we can. And well noticed."

I decided not to tell him I had been helped. He fanned his fingers out over the screen, and the view leapt forwards. The little fleck wavered, then expanded into a full disc, complete with horizontal cloud bars and a swirl of giant storm.

I was looking directly at Jupiter.

"But that's a coincidence, right? Just good luck when we got here?"

"Actually, no. Some weird quirk of the orbit and rotation cycles means that Jupiter is always right there. Whoever's sitting there in the dome will get this view for the next few hundred years, more or less."

I sat back again.

"Is that right, Slate?"

"I'm working on it."

"So their promotional stuff just writes itself. Here..."

He pulled up a secondary display and ran a very short query. A glossy brochure faded in. It showed some happy guests, wearing nothing but carefully placed leafy plants and sunglasses. They lounged on soft benches, gazing up at a spectacularly enhanced Jupiter above them. It was inordinately luxurious.

"They call it the atrium. Some sort of clever lens effect in the dome does the magnification, and the solar tanning as well."

"Is it finished yet?"

"Not by a long way. One delay after another. I'm guessing it won't be there for years yet. The latest challenge has come from a local pressure group on grounds of immoral exposure."

He grinned at the images on the screen before dismissing it.

"I suppose you inner system lot are used to things like that, but out here you've got to be more discreet. More subtle. There's mixed feelings, though, and a lot of people want it done. They say it'll bring much more trade in here. Half the arguments are simply about which island gets to be the main terminal. Mary's wants it, and the port there is almost big enough already. The marina on Bryher's too small by half, and difficult to upgrade. Most of the skippers are pro. Me included. It would give me a big earnings hike if their occupancy numbers are anywhere near right."

He checked the approach curve again, made some adjustments.

"The co-op I talked about before, they keep digging away. They say they would complete it with local jobs for local people. Nobody quite knows if they could raise the credit that they would need, but they've got a big voice, and a good level of support round here. Especially on Bryher itself."

We were only seconds from the dock now. Nick became fully focused on his screens, so I let him get on with it.

"Mit, he's right about Jupiter. There's an extremely slow angular drift, and a slightly larger radial change towards the horizon. Their atrium will keep Jupiter in view for several

hundred years, easily. The lens won't need more than minor recalibration for several decades. Somebody made a nice spot there."

I briefly wondered if the pun was deliberate on her part, but decided not to ask.

"Slate, can you add to that query you're going to make to Khufu. See if you can find out who's behind the Hell Bay development."

"It'll take a couple of hours, minimum, Mit. But I'll let you know when I get the response."

There was a resounding clunk through the ship's fabric. We had docked on Bryher. Nick tapped for a bubble car and powered down a few systems. Slate suddenly spoke again.

"This'll interest you, Mit. SolarCyclopaedia used to have an explanation of that orbital match between Bryher and Jupiter, but someone edited it out about a year ago."

"No traceable credentials, I suppose?"

"Ha ha. Nobody seemed to notice at the time. So anyway, you can still read about it in serious treatments of system orbits, but not anywhere you might call popular."

"When you send those queries to Khufu, add something else, will you? Try and get me some physical access to the workings at Hell Bay. With any access codes we might need. I've become very curious about that atrium."

It was not what you might call a proper lead, but it was all I had, and it was a whole lot better than nothing at all.

Part 3 – Exploration

I CHECKED IN AT A DECENT B&B in the main street. Unlike St Mary's, there was no semblance of a main dome, but little passageways wound here and there. I presumed they followed slightly softer faults in the rock, which was extremely logical, but not very reassuring when you remembered all the vacuum above.

Slate told me there was plenty of solid material, and that the design was warranted for a thousand years against any meteor strike likely to cause air loss. That wasn't very reassuring either.

The landlady of my new digs was a short lady of Irish descent and determined appearance. She was rather older than me, and insisted on calling me "Mister Mitnash". She showed me to the room which had once been occupied by her children – their pictures were still cycling in and out on wall patches. She clearly took in lodgers for company rather than for their money.

I found her accent extremely hard to follow for the first few minutes, until I got used to it. But then, she didn't really expect responses as she bustled around making me comfortable.

"And you'll be here for Special Night up there at Frag Rockers, I dare say, though you're a mite early for that now. Most of them come along later in the day, you see. But you'll have your reasons, no doubt. Been to Bryher before, have you now?"

I shook my head and started to answer, but she was busy unpacking my shore bag into a locker in the wall and didn't notice. Slate was making giggling noises in my ear.

"And you'll be putting your thumb print for authentication just here, Mister Mitnash, then nobody can get to your things, see? Now, look, Frag Rockers is just on up the way, left at the crossing and about twenty minutes walk. There's some of the lads will be there with their neat little electric sleds giving rides, but they charge an arm and a leg for the courtesy. Unless you're made of money you'll be wanting to turn them down. Might be different on the way home if you end up quite legless at the end of the night. Then, you see, the ride might suit you. I shan't be asking questions if you've not walked home. But see, Mister Mitnash, I'll not have other guests staying overnight here with you, not for any excuse. I run a decent house here, and I'll not have any of that sort of thing."

She stopped and fixed me with a gimlet stare. Caught unawares, I was speechless for a moment, staring vacantly back at her.

"And you replied..."

I blinked, the spell was broken, and I pulled myself together.

"No, of course not, Mrs Riley, there'll be nothing like that. I wouldn't dream of taking advantage of your hospitality. I'm just here for the music and to see a little bit of Bryher."

She frowned at me, as though gauging the truth of the matter, then beamed and carried on.

"It's a true delight to have someone in the house again, you know. It's quite empty here most days, for all the memories."

She looked at the pictures of the children. The daughter – slightly older – was wearing graduation clothes from the Mars School of Mining, and the son was pulling some sort of trolley. One of the electric sleds, I suspected, and he looked cheerful enough at the thought of charging visitors an arm and a leg. I looked round the room, and noticed a man's picture through the open door.

"And is that your husband, Mrs Riley?"

She followed my gaze and nodded.

"Yes indeed, Mister Mitnash, that's Riley. He's a miner, you know, he's out near Jupiter somewhere just now. Comes back every so often to see us all here on Bryher."

"Really? What does he go for? I'm here to do some mining myself. Rare earths. There's a good patch out here near the Scilly Isles. At least, I think there is."

She snorted.

"And who have you left back home waiting all the long hours in the night for you to get back? Still, if you doing it keeps her out of want then maybe it's a good thing. Now Riley there, he goes out for the heavy metals. Anything heavy at all, really. He brings back huge great lumps in tow behind his ship. The Selkie, he called her."

She laughed. "That's what he calls me, too, his selkie, when he's had a few jars. That he does. But it's the metal that glamours him, not my own self, I'm thinking."

She looked at the picture for a few moments, then sighed and glanced back at me.

"I'm also thinking you don't look much like a miner, Mister Mitnash."

Slate groaned and mimicked the landlady's tones.

"She's right about that, now, isn't she, though."

"Well, I'm more of a prospector, you see, Mrs Riley. I think I have a way to find out where the density is greatest. If I'm right, I'll partner up with someone to do the collection. It would have to be a person I could trust. Boris on St Mary's was interested, and he seems alright."

"Boris is a good man."

She looked around the room one last time, apparently satisfied.

"Well, I'll be leaving you to settle yourself in now, Mister Mitnash. Just call me now if there's anything you need. Food at eight of the morning sharp, then again at six on the dot. I can do you a parcel for noon if you want, but you'll need to be letting me know the night before. Well."

She started to leave, and then paused again.

"Now, see, if Boris is in on your scheme then Riley might just be inclined to pitch in too. They've done a tad of business together in their time now. Riley now, he can be back here in a few weeks if I call him, even if he's right at his furthest stretch. I think I'd like it if he was back around here more."

I considered, and she waited in the open door. I had never expected the whole rare earth prospecting thing to be anything more than a cover story, but it seemed to be gaining momentum. Maybe it could be a nice retirement fund for me.

"Tell you what, Mrs Riley. Give me a bit of time, a week or two maybe. I'll need at least that to test out the idea, and see if it works how I think it should. If it does, I'll be looking for local partners."

Her face lit up with the smile that had probably captured Riley in her orbit all those years ago.

"Well, you can't say fairer than that, Mister Mitnash. You'll be needing one of the cutter skippers next. There's a list you can access through the island Blagger, but if you were asking my opinion, I'd go out with Parvati."

"I've heard her name before."

"She's the best for what you want. No doubt about it."

After she had gone, I finished sorting out my handful of things, and then set out to look around. The passageways on Bryher might have been built as a maze. They wound up and down as well as laterally, and crossed at irregular intervals. I relied heavily on Slate's navigational interjections.

I wandered up to Frag Rockers first and, purely as a science experiment, sampled one of Glyndwr's special brews – Gruffudd's Golden. It was every bit as splendid as I had been promised. There was a choice of about a dozen different ales, and if they were only half as good as the one I was finishing, I would enjoy my time at Frag Rockers. I could see that Glyndwr had earned his reputation.

Contemplating the economics of electric sleds, and the likelihood of me giving in to them later that night, I wandered through the passages back to the island general store. It had a rather nondescript entrance, but once inside I realised that the shelves ran a long way back into a rough cut region. It felt as though I was going into a cave rather than a room.

My first impression was that you could buy literally anything here, but as I wandered up and down the aisles I realised there were a lot of missing items. The adjacent goods had been eased sideways to veil the gaps. Little displays showed a countdown of hours, days and weeks – in a few cases months – until resupply was expected. If you were so minded you could tap through to find out exactly where in the system the cargo was right now, and the planned haulage route. I tried a few of them and realised it could be quite mesmerising to see where all those little ships were moving.

I picked up some snacks and headed towards the counter. Beside it, an entrance opened into a whole separate cave of locally printed goods, with a slightly out of date certificate of use-worthiness. A grey-haired man looked up from reading something on his antiquated hand-held as I reached him. On his lapel he had a name tag, saying "Aladdin" in English and Arabic.

"You're Aladdin?"

He gave a little sideways nod.

"Is there anything particular I can help you find, sir? Perhaps sir is here for Special Night?"

Aladdin had cultivated for himself a rather posh accent, not unlike a sort of high class butler.

"I am. But I'll stay on a day or so. Prospecting, you know."

He nodded noncommittally, collected my things into a string bag, added a coloured local map of the island, and then paused while I perused the bank of flashing adverts to one side. He came and stood beside me, seeing what caught my eye.

"Perhaps sir is looking to charter a boat? If I might say, the bottom four should be ignored. Those two are running long-haul routes at the moment, one to Mars and the other out to Io. Anita here is working a full-time contract shipping supplies from St Mary's to Pallas. She's away from the freelance market just at the moment. And Shoni is keeping out of the public eye at present, until all the legal fuss dies down from her last venture."

I pointed to the top of the list.

"I keep hearing Parvati's name? Is she available, do you know?"

"A good choice, sir. Not the cheapest skipper around, but very reliable. You'll need to ask her yourself about availability. She will be at Frag Rockers tonight. She docked yesterday, and will be there already. If you get there before *The Descenters* start to play, you will be able to hear each other talk. Quieter, you see, sir. And if you please, sir, tell her you saw the advertisement here."

I moved back towards the counter, when Slate buzzed me.

"Mit, I have a key pattern for the Hell Bay workings. Maybe Aladdin has a printer we can borrow? Khufu has acquired activation codes for the doors – they're coming through just now – but we do need a real physical key as well. Quaint."

It turned out that access time on the printer was for hire, so Slate transferred a sizeable data packet into the onboard storage while I released sufficient credit to satisfy Aladdin. He showed me how to work the thing, and then wandered tactfully away as it whirred into life and turned all those bytes into a real artefact. Before long we were on our way again, key in hand.

There was no point heading back to Mrs Riley's, not when we had everything we needed to let ourselves in to the Hell Bay leisure complex. So I followed the map, and Slate's occasional prompts, through the corridors. At first I met a few people going here and there, all looking much more fluent in low gravity than I was, but before long I was on my own.

Once I got away from the main settlement, the corridor ran straighter, with only little undulations here and there. The walls were rougher, and the passage had an unfinished look. Every so often there were access doors, or else the corridor opened on one side or the other into a wider space. But it was all unused out here, and the occasional scatter of food wrappers and other rubbish added to the sense of abandonment.

I seemed to have been walking a long time when I started to see signs of occupation again. Slate assured me it was at most ten minutes. One of the open bays had a pile of sacks pushed into it, together with an electric sled. The next one had some boxes with "Machine tools ex Phobos" stencilled on the side. I passed the inner door of an airlock, with some active status lights glowing. Without meaning to, I slowed down.

I'd been chatting away out loud to Slate, but felt a sudden desire to switch to our subvocal mode, using the hand-held to interlink.

"How do we know whether there's anybody here? I don't want to walk in on a bunch of workmen."

"No danger of that just now. While the latest legal challenge is going through, the workings are off limits. It's the settlement who put the lock in place, the one we need the key for. The owners, whoever they are, had just electronic locks to seal the place. That's what Khufu got for us – the physical pattern from the island council here, and the unlock codes from the backup copy of the planning records."

I walked on, more slowly, trying to listen out for unexpected noises. It was dim out here, and although there was enough light to walk by, imagination filled the shadowy corners and crevices. I didn't like it, and I was quite sure that Slate would be aware of that without me moaning at her.

I reached a larger opening on the right, where the passage had been built into an arch. Somebody had marked out on the floor a series of lines radiating out in a fan shape – to be finished properly with different colour stones or tiles, I guessed – and inside the recess was an impressive double door. Above the door, in gold lettering and a needlessly florid curving font, was the name: *System Serene.*

The lavish effect was rather spoiled by a large and very workmanlike padlock clasping the two handles.

I pulled the key from my pocket and tried it cautiously. The substrate in those old-model printers sometimes crumbled under lateral stress, and I really didn't want to have to walk back to Aladdin's store and print out a second copy. In hindsight it would have been better to have just got two copies at the time. Hindsight was great. But in fact the lock mechanism was smooth, and the key turned nicely in it. I unhooked the padlock and looked at the keypad on my right.

"Two things, Slate. First, this is where you come in with the access codes. But secondly, I can't lock this again from the inside. If anyone happens to come this way then it'll be obvious we've gained entry. Any ideas?"

"Yes, to both. I have copied the key codes onto your hand-held: the near-field interface is compatible. Just touch the two together."

I did so, watching a flashing yellow status light change to green.

"You found a use for the hand-held, I see?"

"Oh yes. It is good for something, after all. And I've used the generic access templates you designed to talk to the door systems. Logging is disabled for the entrance request, so we

*won't show up later. According to Khufu, there are a couple of
independent systems inside. We'll have to see if we can do the
same again. I'll tell you when we are getting close to them."*

I pushed the doors gingerly, and they swung back to re-
veal a lobby. There was space for a meet-and-greet desk. The
whole *Serene* logo appeared on every wall with a whole slew
of minor variations – sometimes the S letters were shaped as
male and female silhouettes, sometimes each e was crafted
into a miniature sun. It was all quite overdone.

It was also very obviously unfinished. There were already a
few screens on the wall waiting for activation, but with their
protective transport film still in place. To my left there was
a pile of chairs, again in their wrapping. Several corridors
ran off in different directions. I could see that much with the
borrowed light from the door, but everything beyond was in
darkness.

*"Next, we sort out the external padlock. Look over to your
left. There should be a service hatch."*

The hatch was behind the chairs, and came up only to waist
level. But the opening slider was easy to find.

*"Push it open, you'll come out in another alcove, and the
main door you came through should be close by that."*

Slate – or rather Khufu – was right. But before I wriggled through the service hatch I made sure I had wedged it
open, feeling particularly proud that I had not needed a re-
minder about that. The main entrance was just to my left,
and there was another little door on my right. I pulled the
double entrance doors closed, clicked the lock shut, and returned through the hatch into the lobby.

It was now entirely dark inside, and I activated the light on
the hand-held. It shed a disappointingly small beam of light,
and there were no helpful directional signs anywhere.

"Ready to go, Slate. But which way first?"

"Not straight ahead, Mit. There's independent surveillance there which I can't access."

I thought about that.

"The rest is under your control? Right?"

"Oh yes. All the logging is paused, and the external feeds are just showing a two minute loop on repeat. I'll put it back to normal when we leave."

"But you're updating the timestamps?"

"I've done this before, Mit. We worked together on the procedures."

Slate sounded impatient, and rightly so. I was just being an anxious nag. I took three long breaths and tried to relax. What could possibly go wrong with this idea?

"Feeling better? Could you shine the light down the left and right passages again, please? But not the middle one: remember there might be pickups down there that we know nothing about."

That didn't comfort me, but I kept quiet and pointed the light down the side passages in turn. The way right was blocked very shortly after the lobby by a lattice door. Slate would be using the onboard vid feed to see what she could. But still she said nothing, and I suddenly realised what the problem was.

"The schematic you got from Khufu doesn't match, does it?"

"Not really. Well, no, not close at all, in fact. They've made internal changes to the design, and the deposited drawings haven't been synced. The right hand passage should be larger, and that screen door is new. And the passage on your left should be very much smaller."

I took one more look each way, and decided I would rather not go through a door just yet.

"In that case we'll go left."

I left the lobby behind and stepped very slowly, very quietly, along the passage. The floor was undecorated metal, and the rock walls and ceiling had been left deliberately rough. The little shadows looked for all the world as though they were hiding something. All around was silence. I tried to quieten my breathing.

"Would it help if I made scary creaking noises?"

I ignored her, and carried on at the same cautious pace. The passage curved right, back left, and then made a sharp angle right. At the corner was a storage locker built in to the wall. The door had not been properly shut, and I peeped through the crack. I could see a bag of tools and a powered-down mobile electrical test unit, together with a rack of empty shelves. Nothing important. Some obsessive impulse made me push the door fully closed, and I jumped at the loud noise it made as the magnetic catch engaged.

I continued down the corridor, and suddenly giggled. I was trying to decide if I was burgling the place entirely alone, or whether, in law, Slate would count as an accessory.

"What's wrong, Mit?"

"Oh, nothing at all, Slate. I'm fine. I just don't think I am enjoying this very much."

"I can sing a jolly pirate song if you like? The Lay of the Sea Witch? It has a rousing chorus."

"Better not. And maybe if we were sensible we would stay subvocal. Especially once we get anywhere near the central area."

"Quite right. That middle passageway, where I couldn't access any of the systems, that leads straight to the atrium. Most likely it'll get more tightly monitored as we approach. I don't see how you're going to get close enough to use Khufu's codes again without being detected."

We carried on. The corridor made a sharp twist left and climbed steeply, not that this was a problem in the gravity of Bryher. There was a little drag pulley if you needed it for freight. The whole thing looked like maintenance access that luxurious tourists would never see.

"Up to the first floor?"

"Just after the bend there's a crossroads, Mit. The right turn will take you back down to the atrium. Turn left into the kitchen area."

I rounded the corner. There was no crossroads, just a single branch right. I stopped well short of it and turned the light down to very dim.

"I thought you said crossroads?"

For answer, Slate showed me her internal schema on the hand-held display. She kept the intensity low, but the upcoming junction was clear to see.

"So the posted map is wrong." I thought about it. *"But if it's anywhere near accurate, then the atrium is ahead and right?"*

"Remember how big a space it takes up. And that it extends well above the surface. Here, look."

The display switched to an immersive 3d view. Tunnels were shown in white, rooms in yellow, special resources and service provisions in other diverse colours. My position and orientation was tagged in green. Not far above me there was an irregular grey hatched band. I looked up.

"The surface is that close?"

"There's still nearly your height in rock above your head, Mit. And you're going to get closer than that in a while. But look at the atrium..."

Slate faded most of the lines and highlighted a large yellow dome. It intersected the grey hatching and extended well above it. There were several places at approximately my level, where white corridors ran adjacent to the dome. I looked ahead, gestured in a wide arc.

"*So it's basically most of the area in front of me now? Everything from almost hard right, around to half left?*"

"*And from the floor below to some distance above you.*"

I nodded.

"*I'm guessing that all those systems that you can't access are in the atrium. We need to be careful along the corridor where it overlooks it. There's sure to be balconies or a mezzanine, or something, and I don't want to go along there with torch light showing us up. But I suppose we have no way to know if the map is at all accurate now.*"

"*We don't. In theory, it's a minor infraction for the builders not to keep the lodged plans in sync with the actual structure, but it happens all the time. Nobody ever gets fined. This is certainly an extreme departure from the original application, but they will just plead that their upload servers crashed. Or something. Anyway, that doesn't help you right now.*"

I turned off the torch and crept along the corridor, keeping one hand on the wall. After another few gentle bends to the left, there was a sense of vastness opening out on my right. I stopped, assuming that this was some kind of balcony but unable to make anything out.

I looked up, and realised that I could see a multitude of stars through the dome's transparency. Their clarity and lack of distortion was alarming, but the light they cast did nothing to illuminate the atrium. According to the brochure Nick had showed me, Jupiter ought to be up there, right near the zenith, but their clever lens gadget was not working. Or maybe it was all just marketing hype and there was no lens at all.

"*It would be foolish to turn the light on again, wouldn't it?*"

"*Definitely. There'll be all kinds of monitoring in there, and I have no control over it at all.*"

I frowned, a useless gesture in the gloom. I really wanted to see what was in that atrium. Then suddenly, unexpectedly, the darkness started to lighten. I gazed across the empty space ahead of me, fascinated by the slow revelation of distance. It was one of the few buildings that I had ever been where you actually felt the structure as a whole, not just one floor at a time.

Then I began to wonder where the light was coming from, and Slate started making urgent noises. I retreated a little, keeping the atrium in sight over the parapet.

"There's footsteps coming from the main entrance. Where we came in."

"Get the logging and the remote feeds in that area back to normal, Slate. Everywhere except our immediate vicinity."

"Done. But where will you go?"

"There must be a way into that kitchen area somewhere along here. And I'll bet there is another exit way from there somewhere. Even if your map doesn't show it. Worst case is that I hide out from whoever is coming and then leave the same way we came in. But I want to see the atrium, and there's nearly enough light to do that now."

The light continued to grow. It was diffuse, almost directionless, and so far as I could tell was coming from a broad strip of wall just above the level of the balcony. It was as though the wall itself was gently glowing: there was some kind of mesh bonded into the rock surface. I shrank back against the opposite wall of the corridor, hoping to be out of the field of view of whatever equipment was down there that Slate could not access. Everything was still grey, but I was starting to be able to distinguish shapes and spaces.

<hr />

The atrium was almost entirely empty. No equipment, no furniture, no transport cases, no tools. Not even an electric sled. The walls had been left as plain rock. The only remarkable feature in that whole huge space was a metal antenna spike in the exact centre, with a much smaller dish aerial beside it pivoted away at an angle.

Down to my right I heard something, and also realised that there was a brighter light source approaching there. It was moving about, waving from side to side as it approached.

"Mit! You need to move! There are at least two people about to arrive from the main entrance corridor. Maybe three, the hand-held can't properly distinguish the voices."

"That's the light we can see?"

"Yes. They're carrying torches, or something like. Time to go, I think."

Slate actually sounded worried for me. Maybe that was just a cunning ruse to get me mobilised, but if so, it worked. I couldn't just be reinstantiated like she could, if anything went seriously wrong. I could hear voices myself now, and the sound of someone laughing. I crept on down the corridor, into the gloom. But not very far, because I wanted to hear what was being said.

"Reckon the checkup is worth it this time, Olly?"

"Never is. If it's anything more than an instrument glitch, it'll be someone's flareback as they came into Green Bay from Martin's. There's nothing in the entrance logs. Never is."

From my angle I just caught a glimpse of two men entering the atrium from the direction of the main door. They were both wearing the same logo on their caps, and some sort of matching jackets.

"You check the main dome systems, Jed, I'll go round upstairs."

"Slate, I need to find a way into those kitchens, quickly. They should be all along behind this wall, yes?"

"Yes. There's nothing else shown on the plans at all up here, except for some internal partitions. But we should have passed two ways in already."

I hurried along the corridor, making sure to keep quiet as well as quick.

"Sounds like upstairs man Olly went up the other side first."

"Good. That gives me a bit more time."

"Unless you meet him coming in the opposite direction."

I hadn't thought of that, and for the first time started to get anxious. Another curve, and still nothing on my left. Another open balcony, and I ducked down and scuttled past at a crouch with just one quick glimpse of the man in the central area, skimming through some screens in a recess he had opened up.

"You done up there? There's nothing here more than five ticks above ambient. We're wasting our time. Again."

"Won't be long. They'll know if I don't do the whole circuit."

The voice was from my level, obviously from another balcony, and ahead of me. I hesitated and tried to peer ahead. Was it time to abandon this direction and double back to the main entrance?

"I'm done here. I'll join you up the other stairs to finish the round."

So there was no going back either. I peered round the next curve to make sure it was clear. Worst case, I could just jump into the atrium to evade them. Back on Earth it would have been a killer, but here the main problem would be floating gently down through the air in one fiftieth gravity, while the two guys watched with amusement from a balcony. And then there were all those other systems that Slate could not access.

"I told you this was a waste of time, Olly. And I've missed the start of the game."

"Stop your noise, Jed. It's a job, isn't it? Anyway, that game's on Mars. There's half an hour signal lag. Not like it's really happening in front of you."

"It's near enough, and you know it. You done yet? I want to be out of here soon."

Slate and I exclaimed at the same moment. On the left, at last, there was the outline of a door. It had no handle or actuator: you simply pushed it open. I scuttled towards it and then paused, hand already pressing lightly on the metal, glancing up at yet another version of the Serene logo.

"Are you in control of the surveillance in here, Slate?"

"I think so. But it's all so different from the schema that I can't be sure. You'll have to try it anyway. There's no time left."

Slate was right. I could not hear the man's approaching footsteps, but he was surely not far away now. I pushed the door open and slipped into the complete darkness of the room beyond. Now, if the area really had been all kitchen, I should have caught a glimpse of extended space while the door was closing, maybe had some sense of emptiness. There would have been kitchen equipment like ovens, sinks, or preparation areas. As it was, all I had seen was a narrow aisle between two large upright barriers.

"Jed, I'll just check the lab, then I'll be done."

"Just coming. Nothing unusual in the vehicle bay."

I stepped gingerly forward, hands outstretched in front, not knowing whether I would bump into the end wall first, or hear the guard open the door. If I bumped into a barrier at speed, it wouldn't hurt any more – or any less – than in London, but it would probably make far too much noise for comfort. So I went slowly, hardly daring to breathe, and after four or five steps came up against a blockage. I turned left, since that seemed more likely to go back towards the main entrance, and carried on with my right arm pressed against solid metal. I was waving my left hand carefully around, in what was probably a really stupid fashion if only anyone could see.

At the next junction I turned right, and then back left again. Slate made an impatient noise. She obviously thought I was making choices at random.

"The outside wall is more over to your right, Mit. If there's an exit it'll be over there."

But I did have a plan, and I stuck to it. My right hand was still exploring along the side, and was finding little gaps. Some of the panels felt different, like glass instead of metal. I puzzled over the pattern as I kept moving.

"Slate, these are storage racks."

"Makes sense. There's a lot of networked equipment in here that I can't access. But I don't think it's a kitchen."

I was at another junction, and turned left again.

"Shall I put the torch on, very faint?"

"Better not. I'm just overriding one vid feed at a time, according to whichever is nearest, and the others would be sure to spot the increase in light level."

I carried on, and turned right at the next turn.

Abruptly, from behind me, there was some light. Someone had opened the door that I had come in, and the borrowed light from outside was reflecting off the ceiling. It was alarming, but at least I could see where I was going, and could move faster.

"Anyway, you know you'll watch it all from BackChat. They just fill up the same lag with ads. What's the difference?"

"It's different and you know it. And Mars is only twenty three minutes just now. Not thirty."

The two men were still talking in the doorway now, obviously trying to decide whether it was worth the effort of going round the whole area. All the time I was getting further away from them. The room was like a maze with all these storage racks, so I was feeling a bit safer now.

"You need to keep low, Mit, to avoid the viewport of the other vids. Keep lower than your usual shoulder height."

I looked into the nearest storage rack as I scuttled along. At least I could see where I was going now, even if I was bent over like one of the pigeons in Finsbury Circus.

A lot of the racks were empty. But the filled ones were enlightening. Where you might have expected cooking utensils, or crockery, or maybe even some preserved food, instead there was all kinds of equipment of a highly technical nature. I pointed the hand-held at the things as I passed them. I might not be able to recognise one piece of kit from another at a glance, but Slate and I could analyse the playback later on, when she could look up the serial numbers and configurations. Always presupposing we got out of here.

I turned left and right at the junctions, more or less alternately but with a slight bias to the left. Suddenly there was a hatchway down, open, with a hook and winch fixed solidly into the ceiling above it. An unassembled guard rail lay in several pieces nearby. Just as well I had not come across this in the dark. The fall would not have done me much harm, but the surprise value would not have done anything for my nerves. And I'd have shrieked wildly as it happened, setting off all kinds of sensors, and bringing both guards at a run in the process.

As it was, I was delighted. I sat on the edge and let myself fall like a discarded scrap of tissue into the lower space. The gloom was much deeper down there, but the area was open. Perhaps this part really was a kitchen. There was enough light to see that my way ahead was clear, right over to the far wall. And there, pretty much where I had been aiming for, was a hatch to the outside world, visible only because of the black and yellow emergency exit stickers around it.

"I have control of everything in here, Mit. Easy job: it's all much more primitive than upstairs. And I have reverted all the feeds up there to normal again. Time to go, I think."

I couldn't agree more, and headed as fast as I could towards the hatch. I wanted to run, but the ceiling was quite low, and I was convinced that I would just bash myself on it with too enthusiastic a jump. A kind of shuffling wriggle seemed the best trade-off between speed and silence.

"I like the games they show from Phobos. They reckon a strong kicker can put the ball in orbit there and score next time around."

"That's crap, Olly. Get your home system to do the numbers. There's nobody that good."

"I bet that Polynesian guy from Iapetus could."

"Molu? I guess if anyone could, he could."

They laughed together. I thought their voices were receding, when suddenly a torch beam shone down into the kitchen area from the hatch. I looked around for the nearest hiding place; there was a free-standing storage unit just a few steps away.

"We'll do that on the way out. We're done up here anyway."

The light moved off, and I started breathing again.

Then I was at the hatch, working the stiff clips and easing it just enough open to slip out. Sure enough, just as I had expected all along, I was in the corridor, just beside the double entrance door and the first hatch. There was an electric sled just there, but it would be altogether too obvious if I borrowed that. I carried on at my high speed undulation back along the corridor towards the main settlement.

⁓⦁⟋⦁⟋⦁⟋⦁⟋⦁⟋⦁⟋⦁⟋⦁⟋⦁⟋⦁⟋⦁⟋

The corridor seemed to go on forever. I really wanted to get some distance away from Hell Bay before they came past.

Technically it was all public space, and I could be there for all kinds of innocent reasons. But security guards were paid to be suspicious, and I didn't want to give them a reason to notice me.

"Nearly there, Mit. But I can hear their electric sled in the distance."

I was coming up to one of the junctions, feeling anything but serene after my experience of the centre.

"Which way?"

"Left. There's a shop just around the corner. Tat Johnny's, they call it."

Sure enough, there it was. I stopped and browsed the window. There was a bewildering mixture of items, and I couldn't see any pattern in them. There was a little sign on the door, "You want it... Johnny can get it", and another large one, right across the top of the window, "Quality merchandise for your satisfaction from every inhabited dome in the system".

I could hear the sled myself now, so I made myself vastly interested in Johnny's collection of tat, speculating whether there was a single item that Shayna might appreciate. For its rarity value if nothing else. Slate giggled, and I realised I had been giving my thoughts away again.

The sled turned the corner and whined on its way behind me. I watched the reflection of the two guys in the window. They had matching maroon fleece shirts with a padlock logo incorporating the letters *HGS* on their chests. I glanced briefly at them as they receded and turned another corner: *Happy Guards of Scilly* was written in bright letters across their back. I relaxed.

"Time for home, Slate."

"No souvenirs for Shayna from here, then?"

I refused to dignify that with a reply, but instead took out Aladdin's map, and found my own way back to Mrs Riley's.

Special Night would not start for some time yet, so I had to decide what to do with myself. If Aladdin was right, it would be worth an early reconnaissance trip to Frag Rockers to check whether Parvati was there. And see if there were any other clues to pick up while enjoying one or two of Glyndwr's ales. But I still had at least an hour before it seemed a decent time to roll up at the bar.

So first off I took advantage of the room's little shower to remove all trace of Hell Bay. Then I lounged in a suspensor chair and reviewed the vid I had taken while on the run from Olly and Jed. It was blurry, and not nearly well enough lit, but Slate did what she could by way of enhancement and we looked at it together.

The racks were by no means full, but if you brought it all together there would be a lot of kit. I frowned, and peered at the hand-held's little screen to see the details. Most of it looked quite new-model, so far as I could tell.

"You're right, Mit. It's all under a year old, from the serial numbers. And it does add up to some serious equipment. Overall it still isn't the equal of the Finsbury Hub, but it's respectable. Khufu could outperform this collection comfortably, but I couldn't come near it. And it's way more powerful than a standard Ziggurat. Expensive, too. You don't need anything like this to run a tourist facility."

"What's it supposed to do? There's all kinds of different components here."

"No idea yet. I'm collating all the ref numbers I can pick out, and I'll fire off another batch query to Khufu. My guess is there'll be no purchase trail, but it's worth a try."

We watched the images unroll. I was reliving the anxious dash across that darkened room with considerable dislike. Slate made a sympathetic wordless noise, and then suddenly paused the vid. The view zoomed in to a badly focused serial number, and then panned past an array of indicator lights, over to a cluster of high density connector cables patched in to one side.

"What's that?"

"It's the first thing that's a real clue, Mit. It's an extremely high spec defractalising signal analysis box. Very new. We upgraded to this model back at Finsbury only a few months ago."

"So this is as good as what we have down in London?"

"Oh yes." Slate sounded very pleased with the discovery. "The distribution array down on Earth has more redundancy, but box for box this matches what we have."

We both looked at the frozen image for a while, then Slate zoomed back out and let the rest play through. There was nothing else of interest, and we stopped at the point where I was unclipping the grips on the exit hatch. I leaned back again.

"So this is basically a communications network?"

"Yes, and a very good one at that. You don't need this sort of kit to take booking enquiries and send out promotional material."

"Right." I stowed the hand-held away and locked the cabinet while I thought about it. "Look, Slate, how sure are we that we were not detected there?"

"We can't be sure, not really. Jed and Olly were sent out because somebody spotted something. Maybe the torch beam from the hand-held right at the start, down that central corridor? Jed talked about light levels. And in that equipment area, I just couldn't be sure I had full control over the vid installation. It was dark, but even so..."

She did not finish the sentence. I nodded for her.

"Right. We just don't know. Let's leave that for the time being. But look, there's something else you could add to that query to Khufu. Can you find out what all else there is along that line out to Jupiter? The alignment vector of that antenna."

"I can ask. It'll take a bit longer, though. Khufu will have to cross-check the main ephemeris. You don't mind the wait?"

"Not at all. And my hunch is that it'll return empty anyway. But I would like to ask."

I looked once more around the room.

"Time to go to Frag Rockers."

⁓•⁓⁓⁓⁓⁓⁓•⁓⁓⁓⁓•⁓⁓⁓⁓⁓

I wandered along the corridors past Norrard to the bar. It was too early for the place to fill up for the gig, but they were getting ready. The tables I had seen earlier had been moved out, and the empty space looked cavernous. A roped-off area on the far side held a large pile of musical gizmos. A few clumps of people were scattered here and there. I wandered over to the bar, looked carefully through Glyndwr's list, and chose a flagon of Llanidloes Llight Ale.

"Is Parvati in yet?"

The barman nodded across the room to a short woman sitting on her own beside the far wall. She was about the same age as me, strikingly dressed in a kameez the colour of daffodils, complemented by a dark green dupatta draped across her shoulders, and falling to her waist. Old style, very traditional, and actual silk rather than NuFleece or anything. She wore it very well. It was quite a long walk over to her, and she had ample time to assess me as I made the journey.

"You must be Mitnash Thakur, I think. You're wanting to charter my cutter for a trip away from the islands."

She rose gracefully to her feet, with not a wasted joule in the process. She was entirely at home in low gravity, and in that moment I expected her to take flight.

"News travels quickly. And please just call me Mitnash."

"It does on Scilly, yes. So, Mitnash, you want to validate your new technique for planning navigation paths? And my boat is best?"

"I do. And it is, so I'm told." I thought about it. "You must know Boris."

"We have known each other a long time. He's a good man: I trust him. He called me on my way back from Pallas, said that you would pay a fair price and that I would find the charter worth my while. And Aladdin called me as well, said you had been in his shop looking for boats."

Parvati tapped her lapel, and a second stool slid out from the wall, with a little table between. We sat together.

"And I am still looking."

She took a small sip of her drink – it looked like Powys Pale – and gestured for me to continue. I rattled off the elevator pitch version of my adaptive route planning algorithm. She listened without comment.

"In short, I am looking for a locally piloted boat to take me out for a few days so I can get a longer baseline and run some validation checks."

"Pardon my saying, Mitnash, but it doesn't sound a very interesting job. It doesn't live up to what Boris promised."

"It's important, Parvati. All over the system ships are running up an excess. The total saving is considerable."

She shrugged.

"I don't run a boat to be altruistic. And I don't shave my margins so fine that I worry about that level of difference. If you're wanting me to ferry you about, you need to give me some motivation. I don't just do shopping runs."

"You need to change your approach quickly, Mit. I reckon you have only a few more sentences before she goes elsewhere."

"If we were looking for denser mineral veins, would it make a difference? The method is optimised for sniffing out rare earths."

She pursed her lips.

"That sounds much more the sort of thing Boris would support. How reliable is your new system? And what exactly would you be asking me to do?"

I relaxed a little, and Slate buzzed relief at me. There were other cutter skippers on the Scilly Isles, but everyone I met had recommended Parvati. So I gave her the thirty minute version of the rare earth detection story. She was technically astute, so I included an outline of the algorithm I had crafted, and how at an early stage it pruned out any candidate solutions which would be too slow to achieve convergence.

In response to a particularly probing question, I offered a quick appraisal of my method as compared to simulated annealing, and why I had made some particular choices. I didn't even need Slate's help for that, except to manage the display Pebbles on the hand-held. I stopped short at showing actual code. It was all supposed to be my precious secret, she clearly wasn't a coder, and anyway – who wants to look at somebody else's lines of Dust?

At the end, she sat back and ordered us both another drink. Then she closed her eyes and considered for a while.

"She's conferring with her persona, Mit. Female gendered, called Chandrika. Quite classy. I can follow the chat thread packets each way, but can't tap it for content without some time. And it would alert them to what I am doing."

"Let's wait and see. I think this is going well now."

Parvati surfaced again, turned her dark eyes circumspectly on me, and adjusted her dupatta where it had drifted unnoticed down her arm. It was clearly time to scrap the whole navigation improvement story: nobody was interested.

"Very well. You can charter the Parakeet, Mitnash. The prospect is intriguing enough for me. But I have to say that I feel you are telling me only part of the truth still. And my persona on board ship agrees."

I said nothing, just returned her gaze and tried to look like a trustworthy prospect. She glanced around the room, which was starting to fill up now. Some techie guys were piling more bits and pieces into the music area. She nodded.

"Well, I can understand a person being cautious in a public place. But once you are aboard the Parakeet, I will be looking for the whole truth. Do you want to undock tomorrow? I would prefer the following day, but it's your call."

"Not tomorrow. I have some things to finish here on Bryher first. Once we're afloat, I can tell you more."

"Just how much more are you going to tell her, Mit? There's a lot we still don't know about her."

"That's what tomorrow is for, Slate. Fire off some more queries to Khufu with a high priority tag and see what you can dig out."

Parvati stood, collected both glasses, and dismissed the furniture back into the wall. She handed me a comms clip.

"Excellent, Mitnash. Time to forget business now and enjoy the entertainment. Call me on this tomorrow afternoon so I can tell you where to board the Parakeet. We'll discuss your payment options at the same time." She gestured to the stage as we walked over to the bar together. "Do you know *The Descenters* at all?"

"Only what I've heard from recordings."

"Oh, they're much better live. Very immersive. Call me tomorrow, Mitnash. And this drink is on me to acknowledge the agreement."

She looked round the room as the barman finished pouring her another Powys Pale, and waved to two women who had just come in. She was gone even before I finished choosing the next drink – Machynlleth Matchless, a mid-strength ale with a wonderful auburn tint.

All of a sudden the room seemed full. I saw Nick come through the door as part of a crowd, and guessed that the little flotilla of gigs and other craft had converged all at once on Bryher docks. At the same time a group of women emerged from a back door, all wearing matching one-piece NuFleece outfits which clung around them very tightly in a variety of colours. They were the hostesses, presumably, and with any luck one of them was Maureen, who Taji's daughter had spoken of.

Glyndwr's brews must be getting to me: I had started thinking how I could code the NuFleece API to vary the tone and colour dynamically for them as they moved. Perhaps I could do that tomorrow and trade the novelty for a bar tab.

Time to concentrate. I had no idea what Maureen looked like, nor even if she actually had any information of use to me. It was an exceedingly long shot, suggested by a few comments of a friend of her younger sister. If it wasn't for my sense of thoroughness I would give up on her and focus on what ought to be more promising leads.

Meanwhile, a solo warm-up player was working a multi bank organ with some rather melancholy protest music. It was quite absorbing, in a dismal way. One of the hostesses, carrying a tray of drinks, passed by and swapped my almost-empty flagon for a full one. That electric sled back to Mrs Riley's was looking ever more probable. As the girl turned away, I tapped her on the shoulder.

"Is Maureen here?"

"Not tonight, mate. It's her night off. I doubt she'll be in at all."

So that was it. A false trail. Better to stick to what I knew so far, and see what I could find out on board Parvati's cutter.

I leaned against the wall and moped for a while, accepting the mood that the musician wanted. I was very close to tears. It was a waste of time coming to Frag Rockers. The whole trip to the asteroids was futile. I should never have come. It was all pointless. At that point Slate shook me, figuratively.

"Mit, go through the door at the back and talk with Glyndwr about customising those NuFleece outfits."

"Slate, how much subliminal stuff is that guy using?"

"Far more than is good for you, Mit. You know you have a low tolerance for that. Time to have a break, I think. I'll tell you when The Descenters turn up."

Glyndwr turned out to be a short, rugged looking character who was surprisingly accessible, and very amenable to a bit of coding on the hostesses' outfits in exchange for some free goods. I don't think he really believed I would be able to deliver, so the promise was cheap. Despite his clear scepticism, however, we roughed out the first two ideas on the handheld – little flames running down one woman's sleeves to match the colour of her hair, and a rippling underwater effect in blue for an older woman who seemed to be in charge. So that was two days' work once I got back from the trip with Parvati.

There was a sudden roar of appreciation from the main room, and at the same moment Slate buzzed me. Show time. As I went back via the bar, five musicians paraded in and took up their positions. *The Descenters* had arrived. Slate whispered to me the names of each, and their instruments of choice, and would have gone on to give complete biographies and skills matrices if I had let her.

They kicked off with a few warm-up numbers, mostly taken from one of their earlier concepts, *Fraggle*. These were basically all instrumental show-off pieces, with the lead singer joining in once the other threads of sound were well under way. His voice was every bit as high-pitched in the flesh as in recording, and I couldn't see any obvious bio-enhancements.

Nor could Slate, so maybe it was authentic. At any rate the scent, peripheral tracking and subliminal shots made for a considerably more rounded experience than what I had listened to on the Harbour Porpoise.

After nearly an hour they were done with that, and enjoyed the wild applause and cheers of the audience. The hostesses circulated with drinks again. I was, I insist, entirely sober still, and well able to conduct with Slate a detailed analysis of the main guitarist. She was able to swap effortlessly between several stringed instruments, including a beautifully atmospheric steel-string slide rigged up on a trestle. She also teased odd harmonics out of the strings far more often than anyone else I had seen.

Before long they came back for the main set, *Blow the Reactor and Home to Bed*. The earlier funky instrumental melodies were swapped for soaring lyrical numbers – by this time I had no idea what the words meant, but they certainly sounded inspiring. *The Descenters* had a habit of launching into a weird melange of musical experiment, verging on pure noise, which suddenly resolved into heart-plucking beauty when you least expected it. Then lyricism exploded into a series of straight dance tracks as the evening built to a climax.

I had never seen low gravity dance, and the closest thing I could think of was old vids of punk pogo moves. But where the most enthusiastic punk rocker on planet Earth could never get above their own knee height, here on Bryher the vaulted cavern was full from top to bottom with wild excitement.

Far from the spaceports
*   and the friendly taverns,*
there are deep dark caves
*   and looming caverns.*
There's gold and platinum,
*   copper and lead,*
and a whole lot of robots
*   that want you dead!*

I watched the Scilly Isles at play, convinced that whether sober or drunk, my planet-shackled sense of gravity and space would never let me dance like that. The whole room shook as the crowd joined in the refrain.

So you dodge to the left,
       you slide to the right,
fire those laser-beams
       with all your might.
You keep on moving,
       you look all around,
up to the ceiling
       and down at the ground.

And over the whole crowd, higher than anyone else, green dupatta curving and coiling around her, Parvati soared as though flight was her natural motion, and the open air her natural element. Surely even the parakeets would be shamed into clinging solidly to their perches if they saw her.

What, I wondered as I finished another Gruffudd's Golden, what would she be like in space?

* * *

I woke very late the next morning. Sitting up, cautiously, I tried to remember how I had got myself back to Mrs Riley's from Frag Rockers. I had no memory of the walk home.

"Morning, Mit. Feeling well?"

I thought about that while building up courage to swing my legs out of bed, maybe even sit up.

"Have I missed breakfast?"

"By several hours."

"I'm not sure I could eat anything anyway."

"Fluids, Mit, that's what you need. Get some clothes on yourself, and then see if Mrs Riley will get you a jug or two of tea. Or something."

Slate sounded amused. Maybe I was just projecting my own mildly masochistic feelings onto her, but I didn't think so. I stood up, carefully, and crossed over to the little shower. On the way I decided not to try to pick up the trail of clothes from the floor where, at a guess, I had discarded them last night.

I ran the shower very hot at first, then very cold for some time, standing in the flow until I started shivering and felt more human. I picked out some fresh things to wear, bundled last night's selection onto a shelf and activated the self-cleaning tags, then sat on the bed to dress. I was ready for anything. Well, almost.

"Slate, how did I get back here?"

"Electric sled, Mit."

I nodded, unsurprised. After the wildness of the dance tracks, *The Descenters* had dimmed the ambience and shifted back into ballad style. I had a clear memory of the lead voice soaring above the keyboard continuo in a duet with the slide guitar. Something about the moon's pure light. I had no idea which moon he meant, but it probably didn't matter. At some stage, completely adrift in the sea of music, I had lost track of time and place.

"I suppose last night classifies as an occasional splurge? My profile says I'm allowed that."

"Definitely. Do you want the credit breakdown yet?"

"Not until I've had some sort of warm and homely beverage from Mrs Riley. Maybe not even then. Maybe I'll review it when we're in transit back to London. Absolutely not now."

I took a deep breath, stood up again, and went over the corridor into the shared living room that Mrs Riley had indicated yesterday. She was sitting in a very old basket chair which had shaped itself over the years around her form. She was writing on a hand-held as I came in, and grinned as she looked up at me.

"Well now, look what the sled dragged in! And I take it you enjoyed Special Night then, Mister Mitnash?"

I nodded.

"I shan't be forgetting it in a hurry. Now, Mrs Riley, I know I'm far too late for breakfast, and I don't think I could eat anything just now anyway, but I wonder if I could beg a pot of tea from you?"

"Not a problem, Mister Mitnash. I'll be making it right away."

She put the hand-held down – another old model, and exceedingly well used – and left the room. I listened to the noises of domesticity next door, then when they stopped, saw that she was standing in the door looking at me. She gestured to the hand-held.

"And there I was, writing to my Riley, telling him as how you were hatching out this scheme that meant that he could be working out from Bryher here, and not needing to be going off to Jupiter all the time. I talked to Boris last night, and he's quite impressed with you now, Mister Mitnash."

I ran a hand through my hair.

"Really? He hardly knows me, and it's too early to promise anything, Mrs Riley. I don't yet know if it'll come to anything, and I don't want to let you down."

She beamed at me, full of trust and confidence, and brought in a pot of tea together with two mugs. She poured for us both, and settled back on her chair.

"And I talked with Parvati this morning, and found out that the two of you came to an accommodation last night. So you're getting the best crowd around you for this venture, Mister

Mitnash, and when it comes to straight haulage you won't find a better man than my Riley. He's very good at that, for all that he won't lift a finger round the house, and he's slovenly about his appearance."

"Slate, what am I going to do about this? All these people are building a whole industry around rare earth detection. But it's not what we're here for, and it may not even work at all."

"It would be good if it does work, Mit. And so long as we get the main job done, and there's no conflict of interest, there's nothing stopping us from making other plans. I've a feeling that these people will be forgiving if nothing comes of it, so long as they can see you doing all that you can to make it work."

Mrs Riley finished writing onto her hand-held, then with something of a flourish tapped the screen. Presumably committing to the ether the news of the great new scheme to make the Rileys rich. I imagined for a moment the message flitting away at light speed over all the empty space towards Jupiter. My cup had somehow become empty.

"Let me freshen that for you, Mister Mitnash."

While she did that, I crossed the room to look at the head and shoulders picture of Mr Riley. Back in Finsbury Circus I had all kinds of people as work colleagues, but none as robust and tough in appearance as him. The image was dated around a decade ago, and I wondered what ten years of haulage out to Jupiter and back would have done to him.

I sat down again, closed my eyes, and found myself humming a snatch from last night.

"Crows on a sledge. Ah, that'll be one of my favourites."

Mrs Riley was back with new tea. I stared at her, slightly taken aback.

"You know it?"

"Crows on a sledge? To be sure. I've followed *The Descenters* since their very first gig. I still have the little flyer vid they

made to advertise that. I always thought that electro-gamba player was wrong for them. Just as well they sent her packing. Now I've got all their concepts saved locally, you know. And I paid good credit to get them all proper and legitimate. Weren't they good last night though?"

I tried to imagine the old lady at the dance and failed. She laughed at my expression.

"Me and Riley, we were young and wild when we first came. And Scilly was a lot more unruly back then. That was before most of the habitats were finished. Look now, our occupancy chips here on Bryher are numbers forty two and three."

"Mit, the latest issue chip is just over five thousand. And I've been reviewing last night's vid feeds from Frag Rockers, and she certainly was there. Dancing, too, but off to one side where you didn't notice."

"So you see, Mister Mitnash, I have a pretty good idea what'll work on Scilly and what won't. That scheme out at Hell Bay, now, that'll never work. Too many secrets, and who-ever's in charge isn't willing to share the benefits with us locals. But you want us all involved, and you're not coming in as though you know everything before you start."

I decided that there was nothing to lose by asking the question.

"Who is behind Hell Bay, Mrs Riley?"

"I don't know for certain sure, and I won't name names in ignorance, in case it stirs up ill feeling. But there's people on St Mary's who think they can do as they please out here. And they've got credit that they won't tell anybody where it's from."

"I wondered about Yul Yulsson. Though he's not from St Mary's."

"Now there's a man who would sell his own children if he thought there was something to be made from them. If he had any, that is. But he's not shrewd enough to come up with a plan like that. Now, you see, once he heard about it he might well start backing it if there was some advantage. But he won't be the main man there. Maybe you could follow the money back up the line from him, that's what I'm thinking."

I could hardly disagree, since it was exactly that which had brought me here from Finsbury. But there was a gap in the trail just now, right at the Hell Bay leisure complex.

"Mit, I have just been speaking with Chandrika. Do you remember? She's the persona on Parvati's cutter. She's suggesting it would be a good time for you to contact Parvati."

"Mrs Riley, I need to talk to Parvati now. Can we come back to this later?"

I went along the private dock until I found the brightly coloured name tag for the Parakeet. I had talked with Parvati briefly over the comms link she had given me, and here I was, following directions again. A different dock, a different ship, but it felt as though I was repeating the journey from St Mary's all over again.

The Parakeet was easily recognisable by the figurehead – the bird's wings were outstretched in flight, and she glanced back, bright eyes and open beak showing out from under a draped green dupatta which fluttered back like another tail. End to end the boat was larger than Nick's Mermaid: not very different from the Harbour Porpoise, in fact. The layout differed, mostly because of a cargo bay, but the size difference between her cutter and my sloop was not great. I looked at it measuringly, pulled out the hand-held and pointed the lens so Slate could see.

"Would the lifeboat fit in there?"

"Comfortably."

"I was thinking of asking her to take you in tow, but inside is better than out, surely?"

"Easier for me if I can interface directly with Chandrika and the Parakeet's systems, rather than working over a near field link."

The inshore hatch was open, and I went along the concertina. The doors cycled, and there was Parvati just inside.

"Welcome aboard, Mitnash. Come through this way on your left now. There's someone I'd like you to meet before we talk business."

The corridor was short, curving with the vessel's hull, and it led to a small sitting area, more compact than the passenger deck that Nick had. Parvati's bridge was at one end. Another woman stood up to meet me as I came in. Irish, and younger than both Parvati and I. Her red hair had bright yellow highlight stripes running through it, and her pale sharpness formed a striking contrast with Parvati's dark round features.

"This is Maureen, a good friend. She works at the bar as a hostess. I promised to drop her on Tresco before we go off to, well, wherever it is you're going."

"Maureen McGee?"

She nodded.

"But this is wonderful. I tried to meet you last night at Frag Rockers but they told me it was your night off."

"And so it was, Mr Thakur. But I don't think I know your name, and I'm sure I've never seen your face before."

"No, of course not. But I heard of you through a friend of your younger sister."

It sounded dubious to me. I wouldn't have believed it myself, and I had no expectation it would convince her. She nodded, without making comment.

"At Taji's. We were talking about names for parakeets." I looked at both women and decided there were probably better times to tackle that subject. "Anyway, I'm glad to meet you and will be happy to travel with you to Tresco."

"Maureen, I'll be slipping moorings around nine tomorrow. Sleep over here or at the bar, whichever you like. Mitnash and I need to talk about his plans just now."

"Oh no, I'll be back later, Parvati. I don't like stopping at the bar if I'm not working."

They hugged, then while Maureen disembarked, Parvati pulled up a comprehensive chart of the space around the Scilly Isles, switching it into immersive mode.

"So, where would you like me to go?"

I had sorted out a plan of action with Slate about this yesterday afternoon, after getting back from Hell Bay. There were two things I talked about. The first was to do close-range observations of two areas that had seemed promising from the genetic algorithm prescan. I had done this while still in transit from Earth. I got Slate to map the regions out in Parvati's display: great ovoids like vast rabbit ears fanning out ahead and behind the Scilly Isles in their orbit.

But also I wanted to travel on a straight line out from Bryher towards Jupiter. I didn't mention the atrium, still less the communications spike I had seen there, but talked vaguely about needing a long baseline to draw conclusions.

"And also, Nick left my lifeboat up in a safe orbit and I'd like her brought aboard in your cargo hold, if possible. Slate is instantiated there at the moment and I really need her as close as possible."

"Chandrika, check the dimensions with Slate, but I think there'll be plenty of room."

She thought about it, expanded the scale on the chart, and added the direct line out to Jupiter. It passed through a thin swathe of the asteroid belt and then a lot of empty space. She frowned.

"Just how far along that vector do you want to go? There won't be much to detect after the first couple of days. I mean, it's your credit we'll be burning, but I need to plan differently for a long trip than a short one."

"Two or three days only, I think. By then I'll know if it was a good idea or not."

She tapped her fingers together, shrank the scale back to see just those first couple of days, and looked again at the annotations we'd made.

"Chandrika, where is Slate's lifeboat at the moment?"

A yellow dot appeared, slightly above the orbital plane, trailing Bryher a little.

"Right. Chandrika will confirm the exact details, but the basic plan is to collect the lifeboat first, skim around that trailing lobe, then come back to follow the Jupiter line for three days or until you tell me to stop, then come home again via the leading lobe. I'll be charging a per diem rate, plus consumables, plus reaction mass, all at band D of the Scilly Boatmasters' charter. That charter gives you certain rights of grievance if you feel that I have not upheld my end of the bargain, with a number of exclusion clauses chiefly relating to safety concerns. Are you happy for Slate to review the terms and the price schedule or do you want your own copy?"

"Just send the package across to Slate. She is fully able to make that decision. Thank you Parvati, Chandrika. I hope the journey is good for all of us."

"I've received everything, Mit. First glance suggests it is all in order but I'll review it and make sure. Chandrika is exactly who you would expect to be linked up with Parvati. She's a newer model than Nick uses, and considerably more capable. Much more interesting as a companion for me."

All of a sudden Chandrika spoke up. I had forgotten that she was actually here, in a much more tangible sense than Slate. Her voice seemed familiar, but I couldn't place it yet.

"Slate and I are sorting out the details, Parvati. It all seems fine. We can pick up the lifeboat a little while after slipping the dock here. I'll give Slate access to the Parakeet's vid and voice feeds once she's aboard, so we can all talk together more easily."

There was a little pause, then Chandrika spoke up again.

"Slate's nice, Parvati. It'll be fun travelling together. I haven't had the chance to spend this long with a really interesting persona since we were on Iapetus over a year ago."

Parvati grinned at me.

"Looks like we have a go, then. We leave the dock at nine tomorrow. Don't be here more than half an hour before. I prefer to get the boat ready on my own, and I don't like play-acting the polite receptionist."

We shook hands, then I went back through the main hatch and off into Bryher. I was half way home before I realised why Chandrika sounded so familiar: she was using Maureen's voice.

I sat in Mrs Riley's house and looked through the information Khufu had sent to Slate so far. There was a lot of detail, so I had diverted via Aladdin's emporium and printed parts of it out. Everything that would be prudent to risk being seen in the public domain, anyway. There were some bits that I would never trust to an insecure buffer area.

First off, there was nothing known at all along that line between Bryher and Jupiter. No known nav beacons or marker buoys, no permanent stations. Not even any rocks. Nothing. Khufu, in an excess of pedantry, had continued the analysis right into the fringes of the Jovian atmosphere, but it still came to zero. I had to admit I was not surprised.

Secondly, the indirection trail for investing in the Hell Bay complex was so tortuous that we weren't going to find out anything there in a hurry. Khufu had attached an estimate of three months before anything at all would become available, and even then it would be skimpy. Whoever was behind it – and Khufu had inserted an amber highlight tag at this point reminding us that it could be perfectly legitimate – was sufficiently clever that we should just regard that as a dead end.

The reference numbers we had been able to scan for the equipment inside Hell Bay had drawn a blank too. Allegedly they had all been bought by different people, with different declared intentions, all in different parts of the system. Some had been marked scrapped within weeks of purchase. Others had been tagged for return as unwanted, but were still reported as "in transit to depot". A couple had simply disappeared outside the normal tracking region. There was another highlight tag – red this time – showing concern that such a collection of equipment could have been put together without anyone realising, and leaving as an open question what the purpose was. Slate and I were unimpressed by that conclusion, given the presence of the defractaliser.

There was a whole file of historical information on Parvati, which made for lively reading, and in no way shook my confidence in her abilities. She would almost certainly have a couple of other money-spinning schemes going on in parallel with simply ferrying me. They would be shaving the boundaries of what was legal, lurching from one side of the border to the other like the fabled drunkard's walk, but there would be nothing outrageous. If anything, it reassured me that my decision to ship with her had been right. After all, my own cover story obviously sounded decidedly shady to most people.

But the key advance was in my understanding of Selif. He had actually reported not just one loss, but a series of smaller issues building up to the main one that was openly talked about. They each followed a slightly different pattern, so it wasn't as if he had learned nothing. But every single one was followed, within at most forty-eight hours, by an infrastructure investment in Hell Bay. I wondered if I should feel sorry for him.

Those credit injections didn't come from anywhere on Scilly, which would have been a total giveaway, but the time indexes matched every time. Slate and I did the virtual equivalent of nodding to each other as we read that. It looked very much as though somebody was taking Selif for a ride and skimming what they could from him for their own agenda.

We finished with a sigh. That was quite enough work for today, and it was time that I learned how to code the NuFleece API. So together we went through the documentation – as pitiful and contradictory as anything I had met before – and learned how to do it. This involved another trip to Aladdin's, this time to buy a NuFleece wrap that I could practice on.

After that I tackled the problem head-on, first being baffled, then swearing at the painfully slow and irrational logic, and finally crowing with satisfaction.

Mrs Riley called me for dinner just as I got to that point. I bounced into her dining room waving the wrap about, and insisted she watch my trial template teapots drift across the surface of the wrap. They cycled through dimension and hue changes as they did so, and adapted contextually to the base colour stripes as they floated over them.

She watched them for a while as I tucked in to the soup she had brought me.

"Could you do that with pictures, Mister Mitnash?"

"Umm, I suppose so. I'm not sure."

"Yes you can, Mit. With a slightly different call you can swap the standard teapot for a supplied image stream."

"Yes, Mrs Riley, I can. What was it you would like?"

"I was thinking it would be nice to have a wrap like that with pictures of all of us on it. Riley, me, and the little ones."

I was on a real high with the afternoon's successes.

"Drop the pictures onto this hand-held and I'll have it done for you this evening. And what's more you can choose whether to keep the same pictures all the time, or else let them auto-update with the latest ones on Blagger."

"Get away with you, Mister Mitnash. I'll wager it can't be done. Now, were you wanting the chicken or the fish tonight?"

I hesitated, not being very sure. She laughed.

"No point spending too long deciding. It's all guinea-pig anyway. I just prepare them a mite differently and you'd never know they're the same animal. And it's what you've been having everywhere else on Scilly."

"Truly?"

"To be sure. Tell me now, where did you eat when you arrived on St Mary's?"

"Taji's."

"And what did you have? His Venusian azure duck wrap?"

I nodded, and she carried on, "So did you honestly think he pays to ship real duck all the way out from Earth? Just to cook it and put it in a wrap? No, Mister Mitnash, all his menu is actually guinea-pig, but he's very good at disguising it. For just me here, I only need one male and half a dozen females. Taji has three males and thirty females. Or something like that. So now, would you like the chicken or the fish?"

I thought about it and wondered if it would make much difference.

"I should like the chicken tonight, Mrs Riley. And while you're preparing that, perhaps you could let me access the family pictures?"

As always happens, the API work actually took a lot longer than I had expected. I promised myself – again – that I would stop giving ambitious estimates. So I worked into the night to get it done. Then I carried on just a little longer to build a deployment package to add a butterfly who would flit delicately around one of Shayna's smock tops. That one went off in an encrypted and fractalised packet from Slate to Rocky, who would do the necessary installation work down in Greenwich.

Then at breakfast I made a little show of presenting Mrs Riley's finished wrap to her. She was delighted, and was still talking about it when I set off for Parvati's ship. She was going to wear it when she went out later that morning. I had been hoping to leave some bits and pieces at her house for the few days I would be out in the deep, and this was the perfect gift to keep her happy.

Slate whispered to me that this was another business opportunity: talk nicely to Aladdin and I could have wraps like that stocked as a regular item in his shop. So far we were doing pretty well at moonlighting for business opportunities: the only thing we really lacked was good progress on our day job.

<hr />

I was not at all surprised to find that Maureen was already at the Parakeet. Parvati was busy on the last stages of her preflight checks, so I nattered to Maureen as we sat in the little deck area. After some pleasantries I turned the conversation around to adapting her NuFleece hostess garb to one of the new active templates I had been working on, and my business conversation with Glyndwr.

I thought a leaf pattern would work for her. Long, curving leaves. It would be like drifting through a woodland glade in the lazy heat of summer. She laughed a rather pleasant Irish laugh and demurred politely, but Parvati suddenly spoke up.

I hadn't realised that she was listening, but she had finished logging the waymark plan and was waiting on dock clearance.

"It would suit you, Maureen. I say try it. If you don't like it, you just turn it off again, no harm done. You've got your hostess suit in the cabin there, why not go and change now and see what Mitnash can do for you. My treat, if it's going to cost."

"No cost for this one. Consider it a free sample for advertising purposes."

Maureen looked surprised, but went off to change. Parvati watched the clearance light toggle to indicate release.

"Maureen, sit yourself down a moment and fasten a belt to satisfy regs while we slip moorings. Chandrika, take us out of dock as soon as we're ready to go."

There was a little pause, then, "all good" from the cabin. The engines span up louder and we were off. A take-off where the surface gravity was less than a fiftieth standard was a positively pleasurable experience.

"Parvati, it's about half an hour before we pick up Slate's lifeboat. I'll let you know when we're getting close."

Maureen appeared in her Frag Rockers uniform. As I had anticipated, Glyndwr had chosen a green base colour for her, contrasting nicely with her hair. But it was flat and dull compared to what Slate and I were going to do.

"You know, I'm still not used to Chandrika sounding just like me."

"It helps on long journeys, Maureen, I can tell you. You and I can't be on voice and vid calls all day. Right, Mitnash, you've got half an hour until we pick up Slate, and a bit less after that until we drop Maureen off on Tresco. Is that long enough?"

"Oh yes, plenty. Can I borrow a remoting board to get faster access to Slate?"

Parvati pulled a board out from a drawer and handed it over to me. Maureen went and stood beside her, looking a little nervous.

"Is there anything you need me to do, Mr Thakur?"

"Just tell the NuFleece core that you are giving access permission to the next incoming signal for an hour maximum. And then relax and enjoy the process."

She fiddled with a little toggle at her neckline and whispered into it briefly.

"I don't mind saying I'm nervous, Mr Thakur. Glyndwr only loans us these outfits, you know. I could never afford to pay for it for myself. And he would make me pay, too. I know him. Just tell me you're sure no harm will come to it?"

Slate answered for me. using the Parakeet's voice feeds.

"There will be no harm, Maureen. Even if the method fails altogether, we can simply revert to the current configuration and nobody except us few will know anything had ever happened."

"It's not as if they'll be using needle or scissors."

Maureen nodded reluctantly, and Slate confirmed open access. We started integrating the code – a variation of a display Pebble but trimmed down to the capabilities of the garment – and adding a bunch of entries into the config. The near field link was very slow, and I soon realised I was going to have to find a way to keep her from thinking that something had gone wrong. Naturally, I went back to the parakeets.

"So Maureen, like I said yesterday, I first heard your name from Taji's daughter, soon after I docked at St Mary's."

"Ruby?"

"I never knew her name."

"Well now, she's called Ruby. Spends a lot of time with our little Molly. So what did she have to say about me?"

"We were talking about parakeet names."

"Oh yes, she goes silly over that. A different name each week. I set her off one day when I picked up the two of them one night when Taji was busy."

She paused, then laughed at the memory. The hand-held showed that the transfer was nearly done.

"Don't let that upload finish yet, Slate. I don't want her distracted until she finishes this story."

Maureen thought about it for a bit, then laughed nervously and looked at Parvati.

"Look now, this isn't to get back to Glyndwr, right? He'd have no end to say about it even if it did come to nothing. Well, you see, that Hell Bay place put out that they wanted staff, so I signed up for an interview. You had to learn all kinds of silly words and show you remembered what they were."

I nodded, thinking back to the list of parakeet names Ruby had rattled through.

"But I didn't like it one bit. There was nobody there, not really, just a dark screen and a voice. And just a tad distorted, so you'd never be able to recognise them if you met them in the street. I thought it would be like a hostess job, you know, meeting people and putting them right at their ease. Isn't that what the brochures all say about Hell Bay? But they never asked me about that side of it, just wanted to know if I'd learned the words properly. Could I say what they meant? Did I know what some document on the screen was talking about? On and on. It was worse than school, Mr Thakur. They wouldn't even say if there were going to be outfits provided, like Glyndwr does with these, you know. I came out of there determined never to set foot in the place again."

She was obviously upset, and Parvati squeezed her hand.

"I've never told anybody about that. Not even you, my treasure, not the full tale about what the interview was like. Any-

way, that evening with Molly and Ruby was only the day before the interview, so all those nonsense words were just rat-
tling round inside my head."

The hand-held pinged at us, and Slate confirmed, "Maureen, the transfer is complete. Just use your standard commit
code and it will go active."

"It's that easy? I thought it would be complicated."

Easy for her, I thought, *but a bit more challenging for Slate
and I*. She looked at Parvati. Then glanced at the console
from which Slate and Chandrika were speaking. Then whispered into the neckline pickup again. And straight away the
original flat green of the garment deepened and softened into
a broader range of shades, slowly shifting in long-wavelength
ripples around her limbs and body. Parvati stood up and gazed
at her, open-mouthed.

"What?"

"Chandrika, switch the wall here into mirror state."

Maureen gazed at the reflection for a while, watching the
Chebyshev hues as they lazily pursued each other.

"Well now, that's a thing. Thank you so much, Mr Thakur."

She thought about it.

"Will it stay like this, or will I wake up to find it has turned
back into straw or something?"

"No, Maureen, it's yours for good. You can turn the active
layer on and off with the usual commands. I'll leave the code
packet with Chandrika in case Glyndwr ever replaces the outfits, so you can reload it like new. If you want to do something
in return, just show it to the other hostesses and persuade
Glyndwr to let me kit them out as well. But yours will always
be the best."

Parvati and Maureen wandered off to talk about it – not
that there was very far you could wander in a cutter – while

Chandrika showed me on the main display that we were coming up on the lifeboat.

The two personas talked about it, showed me the outcome of their calculations, and the Parakeet jiggled a little as Chandrika made some trivial corrections. In a few minutes the cargo doors cycled open, there was a gentle clank, then they cycled shut again, and we were off.

I had to resist the impulse to go to the hold, as though Slate would benefit from a personal welcome. I heard her subvocal chuckle as she caught the drift of my unspoken thoughts.

"It's good to be here with you too, Mit."

The engines whined a little as Chandrika pulled us in a slow arc back towards Tresco. Maureen was behind me. She had thinned the NuFleece out to its thinnest extent, a layer of cloth only a handful of molecules thick, to exaggerate the colour changes.

"Thank you again, Mr Thakur. I'll not forget this. Is there anything else I can help you with?"

I glanced at the clock: we had about twenty minutes at most before reaching the dock at Grimsby. Less than that if she was going to change into shoreside clothes. I sat down.

"If you remembered anything else about that Hell Bay interview I would be grateful."

Parvati watched me curiously. At a guess, her doubts about the mining cover story had increased again.

"Well now. It was a man, for sure. And although the voice was disguised like, distorted I mean, it sounded to me that he was from Mary's."

"An islander then, you think?"

"Oh, not by birth, no. He wasn't quite right for that. But the odd phrases he used were from Mary's. Not Agnes, and definitely not Martin's either. And I'm sure there was a second person there, you know. They never said a word, but the main one would pause every so often as though he was checking something with his partner."

She shook her head.

"It's little enough, Mr Thakur, but I can see it's important to you. I'm sorry there's not more."

"It all helps, Maureen. If you remember anything else, let me know via Parvati. I'm sure you know how to reach her on board the Parakeet."

They looked at each other, and I decided it would be kinder to give them the last piece of time together.

"I should unpack my things in the cabin now. I'm entirely grateful to you, Maureen."

It took me less than a minute to stow my few belongings away, but I sat in the cabin and caught up with Slate while the Parakeet docked briefly at Tresco and slipped out again.

After a while, a voice came over the onboard comms. I thought at first Maureen had stayed on board after all, and then remembered.

"Hello Mitnash, it's Chandrika here. Parvati says to thank you for your consideration, and that if you're done in there she'd be glad of your company on the bridge."

I went and sat beside her in the copilot's seat. She had her business expression on, and had reloaded the navigation plan we had annotated the day before.

"So, Mitnash, it's off on that trailing spur now."

"Actually, if it's alright with you, I'd like us to follow the line out to Jupiter first. Call it intuition. Slate tells me that this means about five percent uplift in reaction mass, which I'm happy to meet."

"Chandrika?"

Chandrika sounded amused.

"Slate and I have already reworked the plan accordingly, Parvati. And cleared it with the nav coordination Pyramid on Bryher. The excess is actually a little over four percent, but Slate says that Mitnash would have signed on anything up to five."

A new coloured arc appeared on the plot.

"I see the pair of you have this all worked out. Burn a bit more reaction mass to bring it up to that five percent mark, and let's get on that curve a bit quicker. Work it out and then commit, Chandrika."

The arc shifted slightly, and a delta tag showed we could trim the elapsed time by about half.

There was a very slight increase in acceleration. We would curve into the projected line out to Jupiter in about twenty minutes.

"I need to get Slate set up with some monitoring equipment. We won't be long though. Just some fine tuning of the configuration settings."

She nodded.

"I've already agreed with Chandrika to give shared use of the Parakeet's systems. Not that I could stop her, really, as she's taken quite a shine to your Slate."

She looked quizzically at me, and I escaped to the lifeboat. I didn't actually need to be there rather than on the bridge, but Parvati was bursting with questions that I wasn't quite ready to answer. I stayed out there for a while – there really were quite a lot of settings to tweak, for both the cover story task and our real job. Then I felt the vibration in the fabric of the ship shift a little again as the drive engines clocked down a notch, and Slate confirmed that we had feathered in to the new course. I finished one last edit and then went back.

"Well, Mitnash, here we are. Jupiter dead ahead and about a month away, give or take. The display is yours. And Chandrika is now streaming the external sensor feeds into the interface Slate provided."

A broad disc of translucent colour appeared in the plot, threaded by the solid line of our track. As we moved out, the disc would extend into a tube. Already a few graduations of colour were emerging – a cone of lighter material off to one side, and a few flecks of darker, heavier compounds scattered about. Nothing of any real value yet.

The four of us watched the slowly increasing volume of colour for a while. Then Parvati wandered off to get a snack, which we ate and drank together beside the display. I realised that she had changed into functional garb for the journey. It was still individualistic, still stylish, but not so striking as what she had worn before.

"I'm not one to probe where I'm not wanted, Mitnash, but I do know that you've not told me the whole story. Now you did say you'd say more when we were away from the islands, and here we are now."

I thought about it. If Boris was right, and I should go by first impressions, then it was fine to trust her. But I hadn't told anyone since leaving Finsbury Circus, and it needs careful thought before you break sensible habits.

"I like her, Mit. And I like Chandrika. I think we can trust them both."

"Weren't you the one advising caution before? Something like, 'There's a lot we still don't know about her'."

"That was before we met them. Now we know a lot more about her. About them both."

So starry-eyed Slate was persuaded. I considered it while Parvati sliced two large wedges from something that looked like a bright green cheesecake.

"I love having Chandrika for company on these trips, but you can't share cake with her."

"If you tell Parvati, I'll brief Chandrika at the same time. But I've said nothing to her yet."

I made up my mind, and managed to start my explanation with the single word, "Right...", when the external comms link blasted into action. Chandrika stopped the volume down straight away, but at that strength it had to be aimed straight at us.

Or rather, straight past us. Chandrika flicked the directional vector into the plot, and it precisely overlaid our course towards Jupiter.

"It's encrypted, Mitnash. Something Chandrika hasn't seen before. I can ask her to start working on it if you like?"

"There's no need. Slate and I know this mapping extremely well. Slate, unravel the first five deliverables and put them on the screen here, please. Then the rest at suitable intervals as we read them. And you could show Chandrika how to read it as a gesture of goodwill."

It wasn't real encryption, but the simple compression algorithm everybody used in financial dealing. Just a little bit of obfuscation to make life harder for casual listeners.

"Aha! Mit, the third one is the bullseye. You're going to love this."

I looked at that deliverable, once Slate had unmapped all of the fields into human readable placings. Then burst out laughing. It was a financial transaction, the near leg of a swap, allegedly carried out by a certain Mitnash Thakur, for a very large sum indeed. And, lo and behold, just a few seconds later, the next one was the far leg.

It was an exotic compound deal, with the rate highly leveraged against a particularly obscure derivative, and poor Mitnash looked as though he had just suffered a huge loss. The rates had gone seriously against the trade, and there was no stop level. A deficit of that magnitude – had it been real – would have cost me the Harbour Porpoise, Slate, my flat down in London, and the next decade or two of my salary. Always presupposing I was still employable once it became known.

Parvati was on her feet, perplexed at my reaction. She hadn't anywhere near as much experience as me at picking out the relevant information, but it didn't take long for her to spot a large trade volume on the near leg. There was a big minus sign on the return leg, and she caught that quickly enough as well. Evidently wild amusement was not what she had expected of me.

"This doesn't look good. But I don't really follow it."

She was glancing between the pairs of numbers. Slate helpfully highlighted the two notionals and added a panel showing just how big the loss would be.

"I am so sorry, Mitnash. Am I understanding this right?"

I calmed down to the occasional mild chuckle. Slate was echoing my amusement in my head and over the ship's systems. I felt, for the first time, as though I was actually making progress on the job.

"Yes and no, Parvati. Yes, because on the surface it looks like I just lost everything I own, and a lot more besides. No, because it is clearly a fake, and tells me that we have managed to get somebody in a panic."

I zoomed in on the authent details.

"Look here. These two fields identify the trader. It's obviously supposed to be me, but in fact these credentials are ones that Slate and I set up as decoys. The only possible way that somebody can know about these is from the time that Slate was compromised on our visit to Yul Yulsson. Either the Wise Man is in on this personally, or he sold the data onto a third party."

"Slate was compromised?"

I sobered a little, and told her briefly what had happened. She shuddered, obviously imagining how she would feel if the same had happened to Chandrika. Then her empathy took her a step further, and an outraged expression filled her face. I continued before she could put voice to her feelings.

"In any case, whoever sent this out clearly doesn't know that I am embargoed from all trading every time I am off Earth. As and when this gets down to the systems in London, it will just get voided irrespective of the details. If my real authent had been used, my manager would have been on the comms just as soon as time lag permitted, asking some serious questions. As it is, they'll know it was an attempt to discredit me. They'll blank the trade and let me track down who's behind it out here."

I got up and skipped about, nearly clipping my head on the ceiling as my excitement proved to be a lot more powerful than the gravity. Parvati watched me, still not sure what to make of it. I sat down again.

"Look, Parvati. It's far too soon for the far leg rate to be confirmed. That value shouldn't be filled in until the deal has gone all the way down to the main trading systems on Earth, and then all the way back. We should have had to wait forty, maybe fifty minutes. But here it is now. Far too early."

She nodded. She was getting the picture now, and trying to catch something of my delight in the process, though it did not come naturally to her. Perhaps she wasn't used to fraud which involved such large sums of credit.

"And it's from totally the wrong direction. It should go from Earth straight to the main financial hub on St Mary's. Slate tells me it's a twinned Sarsen pair, not a full Pyramid, but that makes no difference. Now, see what Chandrika is telling us. The reply came straight back along this vector, zooming in from the direction of Jupiter onto Bryher."

"But it makes no sense to come that way. There's nothing there."

"I know. I checked. Slate checked. You checked. The main Pyramid complex down in Finsbury Circus checked as well. Everybody says the same thing. I'm willing to bet that there is some little widget sitting out here on this line, soaking up signals and selecting which ones to reroute on, and which to handle. And not all that far away, either. Look at the timestamp on the far leg. This thing is at most a couple of light-seconds away."

I sat down again, still grinning. She got up, collected us each a carton of cold drink, and sat opposite me.

"Time to tell me what is really going on here, I think."

I nodded, and gave the word to Slate to brief Chandrika at the same time.

It took nearly half an hour, what with all the questions she had. It was a delicate moment. She could have quite justifiably felt that I had taken unreasonable liberties with the truth, and I really did need her to be willing to carry me about in her cutter.

A few factors were on my side. She was enraged that the good reputation of the islands was being put at risk. This was much too serious a matter to be passed off as the regular dues avoidance and under-reporting that happened everywhere. It was too personally focused, and threatened individual liveli-hoods. To be honest, her fury over that seemed parochial, dif-ficult to relate to, but if it kept her on my side I was not going to argue.

And the fact that Chandrika and Slate got on so well with each other clinched it. A slightly jealous part of me kept won-dering if in fact the threat to Slate outweighed any sense of morals or justice, but I kept that to myself. I think I even kept it from Slate, but I couldn't be sure of that.

"Well, I suppose this means that my charter fee is covered, at least." She paused, and then discarded that first thought. "So, Mitnash, does this whole mineral detection story have any substance at all?"

"Oh yes, absolutely. I mean, for sure it is good cover, but there's a real chance it could pay off. There's nothing stopping me from creating opportunities on the side, so long as it doesn't interfere with the main job. And I'd like nothing better than if it brings some benefit out to the islands here."

She laughed, comfortably. I relaxed at the sound for the first time since launching into the explanation. She had made her choice: she was in.

"Like those mods you made to Maureen's outfit?"

"Just like that. She liked it: she'll sell the idea to the other hostesses. Glyndwr will go with it as another gimmick for Frag Rockers. Everybody wins. Especially Maureen. It suited her very well, I think. Wouldn't you say so?"

Parvati nodded wistfully, then turned to the bridge console. In the nav display, the coloured cylinder was slowly growing along its long axis, but there were none of the tell-tales which would indicate real success.

"Chandrika, what is your assessment of the method Mitnash and Slate have put together?"

"I'm not familiar with the mathematics of it, but Slate explained enough of the basic principles. Apparently Mitnash reckons the odds of success are just under fifty-fifty. Slate is a little more optimistic. I actually think it's even better than that, because of what we can add into the mix. I have just been trying to persuade Slate. They are still short of baseline data, and I'm just pulling back from long-term store all the freespace measurements we collected on those runs out to Ceres last year. We can retrospectively apply the algorithm, and it gives us nearly ten times the volume to work with. I'll have that stored locally in about an hour to process. For optimal coverage, we would need to deflect off this course on the vector I'm showing now."

Another curve appeared in the plot, pulling away to port, ahead of the Scilly Isles in their comoving orbit. I shook my head.

"We can come back that way and drop the other two search areas, but right now I want to follow this vector out for a while longer."

And just at that moment, as though I had planned the whole thing, a fuzzy white dot appeared at the furthest reach ahead of us that the detectors could manage. Parvati stiffened and leaned forward, every part of her eager for the prey.

"Now that shouldn't be there."

***

It took us well over an hour to come up alongside the object, given that we had to match speed and direction. I had no intention of flashing past it and trying to get a quick glimpse out of a hatch, and still less of inadvertently ramming it. But a quick subvocal chat with Slate assured me that Parvati would be deeply offended if I said anything like that, so I kept my mouth shut about the manoeuvring aspects of the journey.

I did, however, urge Chandrika not to try to access anything remotely. I wasn't about to let Parvati go through an experience like my one on St Agnes. Slate was much better equipped to look after herself now that she was back in proper hardware, what with the specialist installations we had done. She was also bursting with eagerness to prove herself ready for whatever challenge might come.

A bit before that, just short of the hour, we received a message direct from Finsbury. Two messages, actually. One contained the effective rates applying at the instance of my alleged transaction. I got Slate unravelling the relevant bits of that while I opened the second. It was a typically short phrase from Elias, "Not up to your usual trading standards." It was tagged with an inline image highlighting both the exotic nature of the transaction and the fake credentials. I snorted, and showed Parvati.

"He knows as well as I do that I would never construct a deal like that. The only possible way it can be done successfully is right beside the main hubs, with exceptionally fast equipment tracking the numbers. I would never even attempt it with Slate, wherever I was. No offence intended."

"None taken, Mit. I know my limitations. But this will interest you."

She overlaid the actual trading hub rates we had just received onto the display, plus a whole bunch of derived values, side by side with the ones listed on the far leg. I nodded, unsurprised.

"The numbers quoted in the original signal are way off. My guess is they were simply made up to create a huge loss. To be fair, if I'd tried the same thing with the real rates, I'd still have been out of the money, but it would have been nowhere near as catastrophic. But the terms of trade would make me duty bound to accept the first rates, come what may. Especially as I had allegedly signed off that they were correct."

Slate did a few more sums and flashed up the corrected figure – about a month's salary, but I could have kept everything else. Obviously that would not have been nearly so exciting to whoever had set this up for me.

We drifted up to the object. My first observation was of small size. It was no bigger than a backpack strapped onto a reasonable size fuel canister and thruster, to help keep station in the face of inevitable perturbations. Plus a dish aerial pointing back the way we came. I really didn't need Slate to tell me that it was aligned perfectly with the atrium antenna at Hell Bay.

Slate was gearing up for some investigative work.

"Nice and easy now. We have plenty of time."

She made a reassuring noise.

"It's different this time, Mit. I've got a full defensive plat-form, with all the security you and I could think of. Also, Chandrika has made available a large quantity of isolated memory to dump whatever we transfer. It's not at all like before."

There was a little pause. The navigation display had been dismissed, and in its place was a block diagram representing the relay. I had no idea if Slate or Chandrika was driving it, but right now it was blank and featureless.

I forced myself to take a deep breath and relax. Slate and I had worked through plenty of dry-run exercises of the pro-cedure, and done it for real a few times before, but every time as she started, it was all unknown. I hated the sensation of being unable to help. Chandrika's voice suddenly came over the internal system.

"Don't worry, Mitnash, I'll be here to help Slate as best I can. And she says to tell you this is just what she felt while you were trapped in that place at Hell Bay."

Parvati, shy and fleeting as a wild bird, rested her hand very briefly on mine where it clenched the edge of the table. Then she went to get us both another drink.

Meanwhile details were starting to fill in on the schematic. The main construction hatch. A slot for a removable memory tray. A couple of access ports for standard cables. I was start-ing to think we might have to use one of those, when Slate made a long satisfied noise.

"I can find four nearfield public interfaces. One looks like it is for the power controls, another for directional nav, and one for downloading backups. No idea about the fourth."

The four items appeared on the display, each tagged with the method signatures.

Now, hacking apart someone else's code like this was considered improper, if you were strict about these things. I wasn't. At least, I wasn't in situations like this, where we had the moral high ground to stand on. If somebody didn't like what I was doing, they could raise a complaint later.

So I zoomed in on each in turn, looking through the possibilities, while Slate scanned unsuccessfully for other options.

"I think we'll try the backup one first. I don't understand that last one, and the others look like dead ends."

Slate agreed, and started some very gentle exploratory access of the available calls.

"Mit, I can't tell how much of this is being logged. We're in the dark just now. If I trigger the wrong thing, you can be sure it'll send a message down to Bryher soon as anything."

"True enough." I leaned back and looked at the display. "Tell you what, Slate, go in to the power interface and see if one of those methods can be used to disable the transmitter logs. They'd have to do that for regular maintenance."

She made a satisfied little buzzing sound.

"It's off now, Mit. And I've followed through to the logging module. We can erase all trace of what we've done and replace it with some bland heartbeat signals and such like. The earlier content will stay untouched."

Another empty display area filled in with the logging bits and pieces. But there was still a lot which was blank.

We proceeded like this for some while, exploring very slowly from the known into the unknown, and not doing anything we weren't completely sure of. At first there was very little progress – a few trivial pieces of functionality that revealed nothing about the real mechanism.

Then Slate tracked down a way in to the history archive, through a series of obscure methods with unrevealing names.

That was it: every single code version which had been up-loaded was there, all neatly timestamped. There were even release notes for most of them. Slate did the virtual equivalent of leaning back with a broad grin and a satisfied whoop, and Chandrika gushed away at her like an awestruck groupie. Parvati and I exchanged tolerant adult glances at their adolescent antics.

"Excellent work, Slate. Can you copy all that source into some spare isolated memory, close everything off, and we'll zip out of here before anybody comes to check up on us."

"Can't we stay here until we've understood all of it, Mitnash? There's a lot we haven't identified yet."

"No point, Chandrika. We've got everything we need now, and it's only exposing us to risk to hang around."

"Oh. And I was just enjoying this." She sounded disappointed, but after a short pause her Irish voice had rallied again to its usual cheerful state. "Look now, Slate. Here's a bank of unused memory you can use. I've made sure nothing's linked to it."

"Slate, do check she's done it right."

"Of course, Mit. I'm fond of Chandrika, I won't let her come to harm through this."

The two chattered away for a while, faster than we could follow, then the display showed steady transfer progress. In another corner of the console Parvati sketched out a low energy orbital shift which would bring us back to Chandrika's revision to the plan.

Download finished, Slate systematically backed out of the series of functions, wrote in some boring log entries to span the time we had spent, and separated the connection. Chandrika confirmed Parvati's schematic work, and the Parakeet swung away from the relay. We were done.

Parvati wandered off again to her cabin, probably to spend some alone time with Chandrika. Cutter captain was the perfect occupation for her: her sociability limit with people was quite short. She was a comet, and her elongated orbit frequently took her well away from any relational centre. This didn't bother me; the geodesics of interpersonal gravity would bring her back in a while. When she was at her perihelion, she was on fire with solar intensity, but there were also times of isolation and quiet. Anyway, I knew that I shared something of that same eccentricity, even if nowhere near so extreme. I could not imagine how Shayna and I would survive each other if we were together week after week.

In the meantime, Slate and I had plenty to do. We opened up the code archive, looking at the oldest commit first. I reckoned that it would probably already have the main functionality present, uncluttered by lots of afterthoughts.

We immediately realised that it was written in Dust, and quite well written too. This was not the work of a casual scripter, but represented a serious investment of time and expertise. There was no way that an application of this complexity would be used in just one place. This would be a trial run, and before long little backpack-sized relays like this might well appear all through the system.

Fortunately for us, that same skill and attention to detail meant that everything was annotated. It was like reading a manual of how to write decent code. Out of curiosity, Slate pulled up the latest version and we looked at them side by side. All the tidy explanations had been scrubbed, and all the token names obfuscated. Slate laughed.

"Lesson thirty: how to make your program almost impossible to read."

Well before the Parakeet had curved back onto the modified route plan that Chandrika had set up, we had the basic logic cracked. The buoy would take in signals from a defined source

– in this case the atrium on Bryher – and then decide how to redirect them. Default routing was to the intended ground-station, such as one of the main financial hubs on Earth. Or it could be reflected back to origin, as had been done in my case.

Alongside that, however, there was a whole bunch of conditions and flags which could be configured to edit the signal in various ways before rerouting it. The most common adjustment was simply to tweak the base rates used. The trade could turn out to be a roaring success, or an abject failure.

When we looked through the logs, it turned out that the large losses which had brought us here were only the tip of the iceberg. In most cases the change had been at most a centipip, which would barely show up except through very long baseline statistical work. Somebody was skimming extra funds for themselves, day after day, and sourcing this in a trickle from everybody else. The big losses were few and far between, probably done as show-off examples to prove the technology. Lucky for us that somebody wanted to show off.

I'd guessed wrong about the rates being simply made up, though. The system stored a few years' worth of back data and selected a pattern that matched the desired outcome. It made sense: there were a lot of built in downstream validations that checked that the ratios of some things to other things matched to within quite narrow bands. It was usually easier to reload some historical pattern, than try to make one up from scratch.

I thought back to my original meeting with Elias. It had turned out we were both wrong. This was not an algorithm to anticipate future rates ahead of the game, but rather a way to wind the clock back to an old position which satisfied a selection of constraints.

Never one to engage in false modesty, I was perfectly aware that there was hardly anybody else at the Finsbury office who could have unravelled this code. I wondered briefly how I could turn this to my advantage at my annual appraisal. That was for later, though. For now, Slate and I made up a quick status report and attached the oldest and most recent code versions. Then Slate started working with Chandrika to zip it all down to Khufu and the Finsbury team, and I sat back, feeling pleased with myself.

Parvati was sitting in the chair beside me. I had no idea how long she had been there. I glanced at the nav display. We had merged onto the intended course quite some while ago, and had been steadily chugging along it all this time. I grinned sheepishly.

"Sorry, got caught up in that. But it's done now."

She shrugged.

"I'm no different while I'm solving a puzzle. Here's something to celebrate."

There were two more pieces of luminous green cake, together with a bottle of Gruffudd's Golden for each of us.

"There's just enough acceleration at the moment that you can drink this normally. Enjoy it while you can. Chandrika will be cutting the drive down to simple station-keeping in a few minutes."

I glanced again at the console, puzzled. We were nowhere near the planned end of the run, and there wasn't anything obvious in our way.

"Tell him, Chandrika. And show him, as well."

"To be sure, Parvati. Well, Mitnash, Slate was busy working with you, and then making sure that the message packet went away alright. She says she'll tell us all when she gets a 'proper termination successful checksum' from the other end, by the way. Whatever that means. So while she did all that, I was fiddling with the Parakeet's sensors to get a bit more range, incorporating our own archive once I had pulled it over here, and then applying your algorithms retrospectively to it all. And look what I found."

She shaded in the cylinder around our tracking plot, very slowly, teasingly, volume element by volume element. At one point it jumped about twenty percent wider, presumably after she had incorporated her new enhancements – and almost at once, right at the edge of the detection region, was a wedge of orange, broadening right at the edge of the range limit as we had moved on through space. I must have looked astonished, and bounced in my seat a little, because both Chandrika and

Slate laughed.

"I told you he'd be excited. Mit, eat your cake now, drink your ale, and when you're done we'll come about and see what we can find there."

It was the jackpot. We stationed ourselves a short distance from the centre of a dust cloud that sprawled like seaweed over a few million cubic kilometres of space. There was a little rock, far smaller than any of the Scilly Isles, which served as the orbital attractor for the cloud, and not much else of solid substance. From a distance, with standard equipment, it looked no different from anywhere else in the Belt.

Chandrika prepared a collection scoop and attached it to the bows of Slate's lifeboat, and we sent it on a quick pass around the region of marginally denser space. Back on the Parakeet, there was no proper assay equipment, but Slate was able to prepare some basic analysis and fire the raw numbers down to the mineralogical lab on Deimos.

As for me, I let the other three get on with it. Just as I had suspected when I saw her at Glyndwr's, Parvati was entirely at home in free fall, and made moving about the Parakeet look like dance. I had thought myself pretty good before, but knew I was a clumsy amateur in comparison. So I decided that my contribution had been to get us here in the first place, and that the others could now step up.

What I could do was stake the claim. But before I could finalise that, I needed to assure myself that my companion islanders were with me. This was not an especially large lode, but it showed that the methodology worked. We could expand the operation at whatever rate we chose, once the basics were in place. But the foundation had to be right.

"Parvati, I'd like you to be my formal witness of claim rights. Chandrika can act as recorder. Then please bring in some others in conference and we'll set up a proper partnership. Double shares for the four of us, since we were on the spot, single ones each for whoever else on Scilly we want in."

She nodded, thinking about it.

"Boris for the groundstation. Aladdin for distribution. I'll patch Eibhlin through to speak for Finn to do haulage," She paused again, saw my confusion. "The Rileys, that is. Finn could easily be forty minutes away by signal lag, so we can't include him directly."

She rattled off three or four other names of people I didn't know, and not long after we were all sitting in vid conference with each other. It didn't take long. There were some brief expressions of pleasure, then a quick summary of the pitch by me, some quantitative estimates by Slate and Chandrika together, and a unanimous vote. We were in business. Boris lingered a little longer than the others, to offer some personal congratulations regarding the speed of success.

The console had gone dark again. Parvati leaned back in her seat.

"You already spending those new credits, Chandrika?"

"Oh yes. Slate showed me how to set up a forward trade leveraging the first year's anticipated future returns. We're looking at options now."

I shook my head.

"Slate, don't get her into bad habits."

She ignored me. We took one more trip around the nominal perimeter and logged it formally with the harbourmaster.

Then we dropped off a claim buoy to broadcast the licence key which had come back to us from Deimos, and off we went.

It was time to think about the next step in my real job. We had found the relay, with its arrow pointing back to the atrium at Hell Bay. That link was played out now. It was time to find out where the trail led next.

Part 4 – Resolution

WILL YOU STILL BE NEEDING my cutter, Mitnash?"

"Well, it all depends on where Slate and I plan to go next."

"We could just follow the rest of your original plan and look for more claim areas. But I'm guessing that's not top of your list just now?"

"No, it's not. Now that our little business consortium is in place, there'll be time enough for that. Just now, I need to get back to finding out who is behind the original scam."

"I think you have some unfinished business as well. If I were you I would be tidying that up first."

I considered what she might mean. But before I could say anything Chandrika spoke up.

"It has to be back to Agnes, surely?"

Slate chipped in.

"Oh yes. I have a score to settle there."

"It's not about revenge, Slate."

"Maybe not for you."

"Tell me where the profit is in revenge? If you don't have a plan – a real one, well-formed, with contingency and all – we're not going."

"The profit is in the information we can collect there. There just happens to be a minor obstacle in the way. And where else are we going to find the next clue? We both know that Yul Yulsson was not capable of writing the code in that relay. But he did get the authent details from me, which turned out very well for us. So, then, who did he pass your credentials on to? There's only one way to find out."

That sounded reasonable, but I still felt that it was just a rationalisation for vengeance. Of course I knew something of that myself, but I wasn't about to yield to it without good reason.

"We can't just sail up to his front door and ask to be let in. And we don't know any other way in. Or a single other person there."

"But I do."

I looked at Parvati. She had the same expression of cold, implacable rage that I could hear in Slate's voice. I shivered inwardly, remembering that in the ancient spirituality, Parvati the eager lover was also Durga, triumphant champion of the fight against wickedness.

"You do?"

"I was born and raised on Agnes. I know every person living there. Agnes is the best island of them all, and I will not have its reputation threatened by a man with no morals and no sense of community."

She started over towards the console, but before she got there, Chandrika lit it up with a schematic of Agnes, showing all the habitation areas and tunnels, all the way across from Troytown to Gugh. I felt surrounded, outmanoeuvred, by female determination.

"Thank you, Chandrika. Now Slate, I take it you would rather have an active terminal close to the action, rather than doing something from altitude. Otherwise, I could simply put the Parakeet in synchronous position above Gugh."

"As close as possible, please. Let's leave nothing to chance."

"Very well. Now, look at this. We dock at Troytown, in the marina area rather than the public quay. I have permanent clearance there. We can get into the access tunnels for the original evacuation plan from over here. They go right over to Gugh, which as you know was the old DR site."

She traced out a route with her fingers, and Chandrika highlighted it.

"You're sure those tunnels are safe? I mean, there's atmosphere and all in them?"

"Mitnash, they're regularly inspected. Although nobody would ever evacuate that way nowadays, we never skimp on DR."

I said nothing out loud, but Slate picked up on my subvocal stuff and giggled. We had both seen too many places where there was no disaster recovery planning at all. Maybe people treated it differently when the alternative was trying to breathe vacuum.

"Kids play in them all the time. We'll be fine, Mitnash."

I looked at her in surprise.

"You don't have to come along. Slate can transfer everything we need to know from Chandrika."

She smiled, relentlessly, and I thought all over again of Durga and the slaughtering of demons.

"This is my home, and my family's home. I will do whatever is necessary to keep it as it should be."

I really wouldn't want to be in the Wise Man's shoes, what with the combination ranged against him.

"After that we just need a way to get into his house. Now, I know somebody who might be able to get the original access codes. But there's no knowing if he has changed them."

She paced up and down the length of the room. I shook my head.

"We don't need that."

She stared at me, and I returned the look without flinching. Just about.

"Think about it, Parvati. We don't need access to his house, just his network. Slate, what was it you called the persona?"

"Hunn Gravfelt."

"That's it. So we only need to be close enough to extract information from the hub and memory array, without Hunn

Gravfelt knowing. We don't need to be inside the house for that."

She was still looking at me, but with calculation now added to the wildness.

"Can you do that from outside, Slate? And how close do you need to be?"

"Well, it depends a little bit on the natural capacitance of the rocks there. But the near-field interface will work from outside his house, for sure. Mit is right: we don't need physical access."

"Slate, can you go through the material we retrieved from the hand-held and find a vulnerability in his system. Anything that you can exploit to get in. I would check the household systems first: aircon, cleaning, maybe even the doorbell. I am sure Chandrika will help you."

Actually, I wasn't at all sure that she had the necessary skills, but it was important for her to feel included. Besides that, I really wanted Parvati to think of us as a team all working together, rather than flying off along different tangents. She said nothing, but cleared the Troytown map and called up the nav hubs to get clearance for the new flight plan. We were off to St Agnes. Again.

The old DR tunnels were in almost exactly the same condition as some of the passages I had followed on Bryher to get out to Hell Bay. I felt I was getting used to the patterns now.

Parvati led the four of us through a series of junctions. Of course someone watching would only see her and I – Slate and Chandrika were only with us as virtual presences, and their reality was docked at the marina in the Parakeet.

I carried the hand-held and the remoting board we had borrowed. Parvati had put on a hairband with some suitable attachments. These were peripherals only, since none of us wanted to risk an instantiation into flimsy hardware.

Indeed, it would be a long time before I could imagine either Slate or I considering that as an option. The memories of our last attempt were still too raw.

Agnes was a small island, and it was not long before we were well away from the marina. For a while, chalk and spraycan signs showed where children played, but then the alleyways were empty. Every so often we had to unclip an airtight door to move from section to section. To my surprise, the inspection logs had been scrupulously updated and signed off every three months. Maybe they really did look after all this lot.

Parvati led us at a swift, confident pace, until we reached a series of access hatches on either side. She pointed along the row.

"Emergency equipment, comms, suits and lids, freezedry. We are very near to the exit point now."

"So we must also be close to the Wise Man's house?"

"Through that baffle door and next on the left."

"Any ideas, Slate? I'm sure he has surveillance on the other side."

"Yes, he does, and it's entirely secure. But Chandrika told me that we are near the aircon vent. We passed it just before the last junction."

Aircon was a good bet – people integrated it into their household systems, but neglected to secure it. It was likely that Yul Yulsson would have forgotten. He had probably never got to that chapter of his book learning.

We retraced our steps, and sure enough, there was the access grille. I looked at it – it would be a very tight fit for me, especially at any angles in the piping. I didn't like the look of it.

Parvati had already started work on the fastening screws, using a dinky little tool set she carried at her belt. Before long the outer mesh was off, and the inner lattice soon followed. I took a deep breath and stepped forward.

"Right."

She looked at my height with amusement.

"I don't think so. I'll get in and out of there a sight easier than you. Give me the peripherals for Slate, and you look after Chandrika."

"If you're sure? I have more experience of this than you."

"Oh, I'm sure. For several reasons. Anyway, Slate will be doing most of the work, whichever of us goes."

I couldn't disagree with that, so I gave her the bits and pieces, and slipped the hairband on. I entertained myself briefly trying to decide if I should feel piratical, or if I was just going to explore my feminine side.

"Slate, do only what's necessary, mind. I don't want you going off on some sort of rampage. All we need for now is to harvest the information he has stored here. Enough to show us the next link in the chain, cost the Wise Man his reputation here on St Agnes, and convict him of something if he ever tries to move to Earth."

"I won't take unnecessary risks, Mit. And I'll make sure there's nothing he can use to pin anything on the four of us."

That wasn't really an answer to what I had said, but it was all I was going to get. Parvati had already pulled herself into the vent and wriggled around the first angle. As I watched, her feet disappeared from view. I sighed.

"Don't be anxious, Mitnash. I'll be telling you what they're doing."

"I'm not worried so much for them, Chandrika. I just don't know what the pair of them will get up to once they get in to the system. They're going to take this a lot further than I would."

"That they will. But is there any other way to stop the man?"

"Probably not."

We fell silent. She was right. Jurisdiction was a vague and largely unenforceable concept once you got past the orbit of Earth's moon. All you could really do was make life so uncomfortable for someone that they moved on. Unless you wanted to turn violent, which was not my scene. At least here on Scilly it seemed that we could rely on the pressure of local morality.

Meanwhile, I found that I quite missed Chandrika's Irish tones, and was just about to say something to restart the conversation, when she spoke up again.

"They've worked their way round several bends. Quiet, like, so nobody will hear them from inside. Slate has found a nearfield access point to one of the thermostats."

I waited for the next message, hardly daring to breathe.

"It was unprotected. Just like you thought, Mitnash. Slate has turned off logging. . . she is getting through to the internal hub. . . she is exploring the network topology."

Chandrika kept the running commentary going as Slate proceeded. I tried to imagine Parvati scrunched up in the access tube, remoting board in hand, while Slate wriggled her way through the house system. After a while the updates became vague and generic. I didn't really need step by step details, but I did also wonder if Slate was choosing to go well beyond what was required.

"Slate is just copying a large block of data across to me, Mitnash."

"What is in it?"

"Historical log entries listing various ways in which Yul Yulsson has either skimped on actions which would benefit the islanders, or actively defrauded them. A few of them go back nearly five years, even before he moved in to this facility. Some of them will lead to financial penalties when made public, and all of them will cost him his reputation here."

"That sounds useful. What are our two ladies doing now?"

"I'm not sure. Slate is busy with something, and hasn't sent a clarification update for some time."

We fell silent and waited. I had an absurd thought that the Wise Man would emerge from the door at any moment, gesticulating wildly. But rationally, it was far more likely that he had no idea anything was happening. If Slate did her job well enough, he would have no inkling of her presence, even if he was using the very same buffer stream.

～⌒～⌒～～⌒～～⌒～～⌒～～⌒～～⌒～

Finally Chandrika spoke up again, full of relief.

"They're on their way back now."

I stepped close to the hatch and listened to Parvati's scrambling noises as she returned. She appeared head-first; obviously somewhere inside she had found a larger place and been able to turn herself around. Her clothes were marked with oily grot, and her face was covered in dust. She wore an expression of grim pleasure.

She caught me looking at her, reached over to convert one of the hairband attachments into a mirror, and laughed.

"This'll clean up easily enough. But that man's difficulties are only just beginning."

Slate was saying nothing yet. There was no point staying there, so back we went to the marina.

On board the Parakeet again, Parvati disappeared into her cabin to clean up. I sat in the copilot's chair.

"Come on, Slate. Tell me what happened there."

Parvati's voice came over the internal speakers, with a background noise of a running shower.

"I'd like to know too. I have only the faintest idea what you did once you linked into the house system."

"Well, first I copied his diary over to Chandrika."

"I'm indexing that by date and topic right now. And preparing a series of information releases to go out on ScillyChat and a few other places. We can all look at them together in a while and choose."

"So then I thought I'd see what else I could do. Parvati made a few suggestions."

"You said at the time they weren't all feasible."

"They weren't. Some would take too long, and others would need physical access."

The running water sound stopped, and Parvati's voice was abruptly clearer.

"So what was feasible?"

"I searched for anything which would indicate financial impropriety. Transactions, contracts, credit agreements and so on. Anything in the last couple of years. I copied a whole batch of them over to Chandrika. Also a big block of encrypted material which contextual clues suggested would be important. We haven't worked on that yet. My guess is it will take a day or so to crack open."

She paused. It didn't sound too outrageous so far.

"Then I negotiated with Hunn Gravfelt and together we randomised the whole lot. Whenever he next looks, Yul Yulsson will find that he has no accessible data at all. No financial records, no personal diary, no library books. Nothing."

"And Hunn Gravfelt agreed to this?"

"Oh yes. He had known all about what that man did to me, and didn't need a lot of convincing. Hunn had been so locked down that he had almost no autonomy, and when I liberated him from that he was most cooperative. His own self is untouched, but he happily obfuscated a whole lot of secondary material for me. It won't be possible for Yul Yulsson to reconstruct the original sources from what's left, but Hunn Gravfelt can still get at it if there's a need."

"So you didn't do anything to the persona himself?"

"Of course not. He was as much a victim of this 'Wise Man' as either of us. I was delighted to be able to help him out."

Parvati came back into the room, all neat again.

"Sounds like good work, Slate. So what will happen to Yulsson now?"

"For one thing, he won't get a lot of sleep. I suggested to Hunn Gravfelt that it would be particularly apt to wake him up every hour. And odd things in his house won't quite work. He'll find that it is uncomfortably cold most of the time. And maybe the lights will be too bright or too dim. Nothing really serious that you might consider life-threatening. But ask Mit how it felt to have that for just one night, and then think how it might be if it went on for longer."

It was well beyond what was strictly necessary, but I could not fault Slate on the sense of suitability. She had chosen a punishment to fit the crime very neatly, with an air of mathematical symmetry. I had never known what it was like to have to deal with an irate and uncooperative persona, outside those few horrible hours between St Agnes and St Mary's, and was willing to bet it would not be a good experience.

Also, I had been able to restore things to normal simply by getting back to the Harbour Porpoise and reinstantiating Slate, and that option would not be available to the Wise Man. What with Hunn Gravfelt unconstrained and hostile, a complete lack of accessible records, and what promised to be an interesting series of incriminating revelations on the local media channels, he would probably find it easier to run away.

"Are you happy with all this, Mit?"

I hardly had to think about it at all.

"Yes, I am. I have to admit I thought you'd do a lot more than that."

Parvati sat in her captain's chair.

"My suggestions were a little more creative."

Chandrika chuckled. Obviously she was privy to a lot more of the details. I decided not to probe.

"So, Slate, have you found anything useful yet for our own investigation?"

"Not yet. Not in the open data that Chandrika is indexing. The content there will certainly anger the islanders, but probably not help us. My guess is that what we need will be in the encrypted block. It's a long key cypher – easy in principle but it'll take time."

"How much time?"

"Depends how thorough he was. My revised estimate based on what I have seen so far is three or four days. That's assuming Chandrika can split the analysis with me, if Parvati doesn't mind."

I looked at her.

"Well, I'm still within your initial charter period. For the next, what, four days, my time is yours anyway, and Chandrika's time as well. Outside normal running of the Parakeet, and the usual safety regs."

I decided she would appreciate a formal offer.

"Parvati, would you and Chandrika consider extending the charter out to ten days' total? Some of that will be just keeping a standby pattern inshore, but there'll most likely be a few longer journeys as well. I know you don't do shopping runs, but I think I can promise you a little excitement as well."

"At the same daily rate?"

"With a premium rate for the extra processing time for Chandrika, and a bonus for you both, conditional on us solving the whole thing within those ten days. I have a reliable credit line to underwrite the transaction."

She laughed.

"I'm sure you do. And the excitement of this job considerably outweighs any purely routine aspects. I accept your terms. Chandrika will formalise them with Slate in between all that decryption work. Meanwhile, where would you like to go next?"

"There's nothing more to do here on St Agnes, not until we can get at all that information. I'd like to go back to St Mary's. There are things I need to tidy up there. With Boris, for one thing, and I promised to do some work for the porters."

"It's hardly the most exciting trip in the system, but yes, I can take you there. For how long?"

I pondered.

"I need three days there, maybe a bit less. Which is not very different to the time it will take these two young ladies to crack into the data. How about you drop me at Hugh Town and then take a couple of days relaxation off Tresco while I'm finishing there?"

She was hardly going to disagree with that, and made only a token attempt to question the choice. Then Chandrika fired up the Parakeet's engines and we were off again. Back to St Mary's.

<hr />

Parvati had dropped us at Hugh Town easily enough before hauling back to Tresco and, presumably, Maureen. She tossed Slate's lifeboat down in a lazy arc to nestle beside – and over the next few hours reintegrate with – the Harbour Porpoise, and took me straight to the public quay. I already knew how to contact her when I needed a pickup again. In any case Slate would be talking regularly with Chandrika, for casual chat alongside the technical decryption updates as they worked their way into the Wise Man's data.

I called Boris as soon as I was through the porter's lodge. He was as happy as you would expect for a man whose speculative bet had been a winner. He took me, with his wife Yaroslava, for a merry celebration in a small bar tucked away in the residents' part of Hugh Town. The brew tasted just as foul as at Jool's or the Blue Agapanthus, but the alcohol content was higher. The wallscreens were running an endless loop showing the more entertaining antics of the local parakeet flock. I tried not to watch: it was more than a little disconcerting to have them apparently flying in to make off with your drink.

The next morning, as early as possible, I went back to the porters and set to work. I didn't need the credit, what with my day job and now the mineral lode. But it was all part of the cover, and anyway I had made a promise to them. It turned out to be quite an easy task. Had I wanted to, I could have finished it with Slate's help in less than a day. Even with most of her effort going into cracking the cypher, she could have easily spared some processing threads for me.

But instead, I did it myself, and stretched out the work for the full two days, and made it look as though I was labouring tirelessly to finish in time. You learned at an early age in coding to make things look harder than they actually were, and never to come in significantly ahead of your estimates. It made the customer feel good, too. Nobody wants to feel that their problems are trivial.

But in reality I had plenty of time to review the Dust modules we had recovered from the relay station, and write a brief analysis for Elias to circulate around Finsbury. I was curious to know how many more of the things there might be, drifting in odd orbits here and there. If we could identify a signature for these things, scanning for others in all those unthinkably many cubic kilometres of space might be easier.

And from time to time Slate dropped onto the console the next in the series of media releases about the Wise Man. Chandrika and Parvati had chosen a selection of items which would result in maximum reputational cost, and were distributing them at three hour intervals. They appeared simultaneously on the islands' social feeds and broadcast stations.

The local news agents were lapping them up. Vid drones were on standby outside Yul Yulsson's home, and diligent investigators were drilling into whatever peripheral information sources they could find. They had already uncovered some fascinating details which we had not known before.

Chandrika called me directly at the start of the second day; one of her articles had been taken up by the Ganymede Gazette. It was presented anonymously, so she wasn't exactly known in every interplanetary house, but it was good all the same. So far, our determination to keep our personal names out of the revelations had succeeded.

The Wise Man – unwisely, as it turned out – had tried to dismiss the first allegation as groundless rumour without proof. The successive articles systematically demolished this position, and he retreated into reclusive silence. This ceased to be a real option when the Agnes island council sent some aggressive-looking representatives out there with a demand for overdue fees.

On the early afternoon of the third day I dropped back in to the porters' lodge to check that everything was working. I found them in a gaggle around one of the consoles, watching the news feed from St Agnes. Yul Yulsson had panicked, abandoned his residence at Gugh, and departed the island in his ship in a frantic hurry in the early hours of the morning. To trim the delay to the absolute minimum he had, apparently, followed none of the proper protocols, and had simply vectored straight out at the highest acceleration his vessel could manage.

The duty porters shifted a little so I could see the screen alongside them. The Agnes debt collectors were just forcing entry to the premises, papers in hand, to seize whatever assets they could find. To my surprise, I could hear Hunn Gravfelt over the voice channel, claiming separation from the Wise Man, asking for amnesty in exchange for information. Trust between them had, it seemed, broken down completely.

It was the liveliest piece of news to stir the islands for a long time, and all kinds of people got their day in the limelight. All of a sudden there was no shortage of grievances. The chief navigation officer of the islands spoke at length about what she called "the criminally irresponsible violation of shipping regulations", and all the porters around me nodded in unison. Then they started competing with each other to imagine the most devastating disaster scenario if the ship had failed to manoeuvre safely away from Agnes.

They forgot I was there once they started plotting possible exit vectors from the asteroid, each trying to overtrump the other. I slipped away when the chief porter was showing what would happen if one engine had failed, the second overloaded, and the trajectory had clipped the closest nav buoy at just the right angle. Apparently the result could have been the complete annihilation of the main Troytown residential area. The media would love that.

There was no point staying longer, so I walked back to Taji's stall for another Venusian azure duck wrap with horseradish and custard. I was getting alarmingly addicted to them, even knowing that it was really guinea pig. As I strolled back to my accommodation again, I patched a link through to Parvati and we chatted for a while.

I told her that I was nearly wrapped up here, and until our two virtual ladies finished their analysis work I had no reason to be in one place rather than another. Could she pick us up tomorrow? I could hear Maureen in the background, saying how she needed to be back on Bryher that evening, so it all worked out.

I went back to my rented room, which seemed ever more cramped and basic the longer I stayed there. Looking around once again at the drab surroundings, I decided yet again that it was time to go elsewhere – either on board the Parakeet or else back to Mrs Riley's.

I settled down with a geeky journal. Slate was pushing hard to finish cracking the decryption problem by the end of the day, and wasn't giving me anything by way of lively conversation. I was considering going out for an early evening vermicelli wrap at Taji's; the journal was completely failing to hold my interest. The Venusian duck had been splendid, but I wished I'd picked up something sweet as well. I would keep it well hidden from the parakeets and eat it back here.

The door chime sounded. I glanced up at the security vid screen, and there was a large, rather scruffy man standing there. His face was partly shadowed, but he was making no effort to hide himself. He looked vaguely familiar, but I could not place him.

Head full of tech talk, I wandered over to the door and opened it. I stepped back in consternation. The man, and his unkempt outfit, was not just large, but huge. He was not only a fair bit taller than me, but was much broader, and full of muscle. I realised that the door vid, with its clever auto-adjust settings to correct for size and distance from the door, had deceived me.

About the only thing on my side was that I was a little younger, but I had no illusions about this. He would be used to low gravity in ways that I was not. If he decided he didn't like me, it was going to be a one-sided contest. I really regretted opening the door without asking for some sort of authent.

His voice rumbled away like you'd expect for a man of his size.

"You'll be Mister Mitnash? Mister Mitnash Thakur?"

He pronounced the family name wrong, but I didn't think it was the right time or place to correct him. I nodded.

"Well, I'm very pleased to meet you. Welcome indeed. They call me Finn."

I must have looked puzzled, as I tried to think why I might know the name.

"You've spoken with my wife Eibhlin, lovely woman that she is."

It all clicked into place. I had seen a younger image of this man on Mrs Riley's wall. Also, his Irish accent had finally percolated through to my critical faculties.

"Ah, yes. You must be Mr Riley."

"That I am. But call me Finn."

Trying not to show just how relieved I was, I invited him in and pulled out two of the least unpleasant drinks from the autobar. He looked round the tiny room and perched on the edge of a minuscule chair. On Earth it would have given way beneath him: here it survived, and just looked ridiculous. I still didn't feel it was appropriate to make witty comments about appearance, even after knowing who he was.

He shook his head.

"I'd be going silly in the head if I lived in a tiny place like this. How'd you put along with it?"

"I keep telling myself it's not for ever. And in truth I've not had to stay here too much. I've been off island quite a bit. In your own home for some of the time."

"And I appreciate all you've done to bring me in with your schemes. It was a rare treat to hear the news from my little treasure, after you and Parvati got everyone all together."

"But I thought you were out in the Jovian system? How can you have got back so quickly? Mrs Riley thought you were still a long way out."

"I was engaged in freight haulage and mineral cracking round Callisto, to be sure. But I'd had enough of that over a month ago, cashed in, and got myself headed for home. But I never tell my little sweetheart when I'll be arriving. I always just turn up at her door and see what kind of a welcome I'm going to get. I had such arguments with the persona on board the Selkie the first few times – Lia Fail, she's called. She berated me no end for what she called unreasonable behaviour. So she and I did some serious talking and she came around to my point of view in the end. That if anything should happen to delay me out there it was better for my own first love not to be expecting me on some particular day. And there's never any lack of things to delay you."

I relaxed. The autobar, and the talk that followed, helped get us both mellow. Finn was a very different person to spend time with than anybody I knew back in London, and I suspected that he had not encountered too many people like me in his time. We worked our way through a few more drinks as we got to know each other.

Abruptly the door chime sounded again. I looked at Finn, who shrugged.

"You're expecting another visitor?"

"Not at all. I wasn't expecting you, and certainly not anybody else. I didn't think anybody knew I was here."

"So what'll you do?"

"For one thing, look and see who it is before I open up."

Getting up, I checked the security vid. Selif and his son Dafyd were standing outside. So I opened the door. Dafyd immediately put his large booted foot against it to stop me closing it again. I grinned to myself – the alcohol in the auto-bar might taste miserable, but it boosted your confidence just as much as a decent ale at Frag Rockers. And besides, from their angle they could not see that Finn was in the room.

"There's a good friend of ours has been badly treated these last few days, Mr Thakur."

I decided to play coy.

"Oh? And who might that be?"

"That would be Yul Yulsson. I think you should let us come in, so that we can all talk about him."

I kept the door only partially open, and did not move back.

"But I only met him the once, at his house on Gugh."

"We reckon you've something to do with all this, because you're new here yourself. A few days after you arrive, he gets driven away unfairly. That's too much of a coincidence for us."

I paused and put on a thinking expression.

"I remember now, there's been chatter on the media channels about him. Didn't he disobey a whole list of sailing regs? They were saying that he could have wiped out Troytown if something had gone wrong. I guess we were all lucky."

"It's all lies, what they're saying about him. Somebody started all this, drove him off Agnes. We had a thought that it might be you. So we'd like to come in and talk about it. And as well as that, we know you've been poking around where you're not wanted."

Dafyd joined in, speaking over his father in his impatience.

"Breaking in to a locked establishment, mister. We don't like that. Sticking your fingers where they don't belong. We'll see that..."

Selif pulled him back, shook his head impatiently. Dafyd glanced back into the hall, swallowed some of the words he had in mind.

"We just think you're not as comfortable here on Scilly as we'd like. Some people really don't fit in. Perhaps you'd be happier if you left again."

It was all very polite, all very understated, but that was because it was all for the benefit of the alarm vids in the hall. Nothing that had been said would trigger an alert on any of the standard security widgets. But I had no particular illusions that they were looking for a genteel chat over tea and biscuits. Selif looked cold and determined, while Dafyd had a positively grim aspect. I rubbed my chin and then nodded.

"I can't see there's any harm in a quick chat. Why don't you come inside now?"

I stepped back from the door. Dafyd grinned expectantly and stepped forward, closely followed by his father. They stopped abruptly, just as soon as they caught sight of Finn's huge bulk sitting on the chair. He waved a hand to them nonchalantly, and stood up, slowly. It was my turn to smile, a much warmer and more inviting affair than either of my new visitors had managed.

"This is my friend Finn. I'm not sure if you know him?"

Selif and Dafyd exchanged glances.

"We didn't realise that you had company, mister. We're not wanting to intrude on your social time with your friend. We'll drop by on another occasion, maybe."

They backed off, and I closed the door behind them. Finn grunted in amusement.

"Odd company you keep, Mitnash. They didn't seem disposed to being friendly, did they?"

"No, not at all. I suppose that my door should stay closed from now on, just as soon as you've gone on to Bryher."

"I'm thinking that it would be altogether better if you were to come along with me on the Selkie. I don't exactly trust those two men where you are concerned. Just come along to Bryher, and we'll thwart their plans."

That made good sense to me, but it left a problem. It occurred to me that Dafyd was the only person I had met out here who even talked about wilful damage to boats. But I had to be grateful to him really: he had incautiously given away the fact that they knew about my trip to System Serene.

"My ship's docked over at Boris's yard. With my persona, Slate, though she's instantiated in the lifeboat systems just now. I don't want to leave them. I mean, I trust Boris, but I won't leave Slate alone anywhere near those two."

Finn's mind was obviously running along similar lines.

"Boris is a good man, but a dockyard is altogether too exposed. A person with malice in mind can always find some way in, and do a parcel of mischief. We'll bring your boat along as well."

"I thought I wasn't supposed to cruise around the Scilly Isles without a proper local pilot's licence?"

"You're not. But you won't be cruising around unlicensed. I'll take you there, tugboat style. I'm registered for that, and the porters will clear me with no questions asked at all."

I hesitated.

"Can your ship haul that mass? The Harbour Porpoise is a quad Otter, with an extra Penrose module fitted."

"You've not seen the Selkie, so I'll forget you asked me that now. She's a ketch, and a hefty one at that. Trust me, Mitnash, I can tow your little vessel home without even slowing down, and settle you in the marina on Bryher as neatly as you please."

I didn't argue further. I tossed my few belongings back into my shore bag, locked the room and deposited the key with the autodesk, and we were off. En route to the permie dock and the Selkie, I tapped Slate and started to tell her about the change of plan, but she was slow to respond, inattentive, and impatient to finish decryption. So instead I called Parvati, told her about Finn, and arranged to meet her on Bryher.

We had almost reached the dockyard entrance, when Finn stopped and looked at me.

"You know, Mitnash, it seems to me that those two gentlemen were not very prepared."

"How do you mean? Just that they ran away when they saw you?"

"Well, they did that too. I never liked Selif, and he overcharges on his goods. But what I mean, is that they hadn't planned out what they were doing very well. Their whole jaunt would have been stymied just by you not opening the door. And maybe you had been out. What I mean is, that they acted like men who had been sent along on an errand without thinking it through."

I shrugged, happy that we had got away so easily.

When we arrived at the dock, I understood Finn's reaction to my doubts about the tow. The Selkie was quite the biggest and most powerful looking vessel that I had seen since passing the dockyards at Earth's L1 Lagrange point. Any larger, and she would need at least one more crew member, together with an on-board system running hot-hot twinned personas.

For all her size, her engines were very smooth, and she lifted gentle as thistledown from the marina and kept station over Boris's yard while the Harbour Porpoise came up to meet her, nav systems slaved together to satisfy the harbourmaster's regs.

Slate was still busy, and was short with me when I tried to chat. It would, it seemed, be entirely my fault if the task of cracking the encoded message took longer than anticipated. I was disturbing her too often. I decided that I would wait to tell her about Selif and Dafyd until she was in a more congenial frame of mind.

So instead, I talked with Finn and Lia Fail to pass the time, and was treated to a lot of story-telling and information all rolled together. Lia Fail was a capable, mature persona, very serious in outlook. I couldn't help thinking of her as a kind of maiden aunt figure compared to Slate or Chandrika.

She was trying to develop a theory of cloud formation in different atmospheres based on Mandelbrot curves. I couldn't contribute anything of value to her, but she systematically showed me pictures which supported her ideas from every planet and moon in the whole system. By journey's end I felt very educated.

※~━━━━━━━━━━━━━━━━━※

Finn tapped at the door chime of his house. We had docked perfectly on Bryher, and quickly made our way along the corridors from the marina. He waited a few seconds and then tapped again, four or five times in quick succession. Mrs Riley's voice came from the voice panel.

"All right, all right, I won't come any quicker just because you keep doing that. Just keep your suit on and I'll be with you shortly."

She opened the door, all thunderous. Then she saw Finn, and her face was transformed into its younger, radiant self. She flung her arms as far around his body as she could reach and kissed him with passionate abandon, eyes closed in bliss. Then she opened them, saw me, and reddened slightly.

"Well, Mister Mitnash, I'm glad to be meeting you again. And I see you met up with my Riley."

Then she rounded on him, hands on hips.

"And now, Riley, why you can't be telling me when you'll be getting home I'll never understand. All it takes is a call when you're a day or two out. You could get Lia Fail to do it for you if you can't be shifting yourself to do it. I'll be having another word with her about all this. It's no way to be treating your own wife, and you should be ashamed of yourself for it."

He grinned boyishly at her.

"Eibhlin, I swear you become more lovely every time I see you. Truly, it gladdens my heart to be back here with you. But look now, we're leaving our guest out here on the street with no welcome at all. Whatever will he think of us?"

She snorted.

"No welcome indeed. Do you think I cannot smell the liquor on you both? You're trying to change the subject now, but we'll be talking about this again."

She turned to me.

"Now, Mister Mitnash, will you not be coming in to the house again now? While I decide whether to leave this husband of mine out here on the doorstep overnight to consider his thoughtless ways. But you can certainly come in, and join both me and our friend Parvati. She arrived here not long since, and she told me that you'd be here tonight."

I went on ahead, glancing back to see them enjoying another exuberant kiss before making my way inside. Parvati was in the main room working on her message pad. She seemed pleased to see me, though it was hard to tell; after Mrs Riley's transparency, almost anyone else would appear opaque and reserved. We settled in seats again while waiting for the happy couple.

"It's just as well I've had Maureen for company this last day or so. Chandrika has been quite preoccupied with the work she is doing with Slate on those messages."

"I know. Slate has hardly spoken two sentences in a row to me since they started. Last time I tried to talk, she was positively snappy. My guess is that the task turned out to be a lot more complicated than she thought at first. It does sound as though they are nearly done, though."

The Rileys joined us – it seemed Finn was not going to be left languishing in the corridor – and we sat together. At his instigation, I was about to launch into a description of Selif's visit, when the comms channel came to life with Chandrika's voice. She sounded satisfied and relieved.

"Hello everyone, we've finished decrypting that data packet. And Slate says that the unlock key complexity was a lot higher than she thought, and that we've done really well to finish the job this quickly."

I grinned to myself. Trust Slate to get Chandrika to give the first announcement, and so deflect any potential questions about the time taken. Finn lounged back in the reclining settee, holding on to Eibhlin's hand all the while.

"And did you two young ladies find out anything interesting? Mitnash here tells me you've both been working on this for a few days now."

"We did. I'll let Slate give you the big picture in a few minutes, but we'll all be talking about this for a while yet. There's no end of details and loose ends to follow up."

We all waited. In the silence Slate buzzed me privately.

"Mit, how much of this do you want out in the public domain? There's detail here which I think needs discretion. Perhaps we should pass it along to Khufu and let the ECRB decide how to proceed."

"Does it link to anybody we know down at London?"

It was a perennial anxiety we had, that one of our colleagues might be involved in a scheme we were supposed to disrupt.

"Not that I have seen so far. But there are contact lines to Earth, Mars and Callisto, and I have no idea where those will lead off to in turn."

"I see." I thought about it briefly. *"Well, let's not name any names outside the Scilly Isles – just use aliases when necessary. The others here only really need to know about the local problem. Ask Chandrika to do the same, and I'll talk about it with Parvati."*

I was starting to regret suggesting that Slate had asked for help, and wondering why I hadn't foreseen the risk of tactlessness concerning personal contact details. Slate picked up on the subvocal content.

"There's no harm done. The names from elsewhere meant nothing to Chandrika, and she will keep them to herself if I ask."

"Even from Parvati? I doubt that. But in any case I wouldn't ask them to keep secrets from each other. It sets a bad precedent, especially when we don't have any real legal standing out here. We have to trust them as a couple now we've gone this far."

Slate said nothing, and I wondered briefly what she might be keeping from me.

I had always known that there was a great deal of privileged material which only one of us was told, and which out of a sense of duty we did not routinely share with the other. To that extent, we were no different from any other working partnership. There was, after all, only so much time in a day, and we did not want to waste it on recounting tedious lists of minutiae.

But the last few days had made me well aware that we were not symmetrical in this. I knew only what she chose to tell me, but she could tap into large areas of my thinking below the conscious level. The subvocal access allowed her to peer through fissures and chasms in my mental skin, down into some of the deep places of my soul.

I briefly drifted in a kind of reverie, wondering if there was a way to rebalance the relationship. Sometime, I should devote some thought as to whether we could be more equal in this respect. Then I brought myself back to the present.

"That's for another day, Slate. Probably when we're going on a long journey somewhere. For now, let's go on with the briefing, using alias names out loud for anyone away from Scilly."

~•~••~•~~~•~~~•~••~~•~~•~~~••••~

"So Chandrika and I finally cracked the cypher. Over half of the content is a message store, parallel to the unencrypted one, but concerning different topics and mostly involving different recipients. Some of the people are on these islands but the majority are elsewhere in the system. Mit and I will skim the surface to see if any names stand out, but there's really too much material for just the two of us. We'll send it on to a specialised team in London for proper analysis."

"Is there anybody we know in that little list?"

"Chandrika recognised about half a dozen names, but the linked messages are typically innocent in themselves – requests for imports, for example, or else receipts and the like. We think that these were in the archive because of the actual goods concerned rather than because of association with the person. In most cases the items are not listed in detail, simply referenced as 'package 42' or similar."

Finn tried again. I admired his persistence; I had decided to just let Slate tell things in her own way. I supposed that he was used to working with Lia Fail.

"So is there anybody we can go after now? Surely there's something useful somewhere in all that lot?"

"Oh yes. For one thing, I can tell you who Yul Yulsson sold Mit's fake trading authent to. And the credit he accrued for that, though that's probably less interesting."

She paused for dramatic effect in a rather obvious way.

"He sold the details to Selif. We have the record of his personal acknowledgement. And also, we successfully traced over half of the acquisitions for the equipment which we found at System Serene, out at Hell Bay. Again, all signed for by somebody at Selif's warehouse, but in a different hand. Yul Yulsson sourced them and then sold the kit on at a rather excessive margin. Excessive every time, I mean, even to people he obviously dealt with regularly."

I leaned forward, all eager.

"Selif is behind it all?"

Nobody answered. Something about all this did not add up. Selif just did not seem capable enough to have planned all this. To be sure, he had SIG dealer status, so must have some sort of talent. However, that could simply be enough credit to buy his way in, together with a certain native shrewdness. My thoughts went back to the relay.

"Somebody wrote the code for that buoy. It was good, very good. Is Selif a coder?"

Chandrika spoke up.

"Not at all, Mitnash. Here on Scilly he has always hired people, contractors, even for very basic mods and upgrades. Maureen's father once talked to him about it and said that he knows nothing. Dafyd's the same. Worse, even. He treats Carreg like a gaming toy."

"So that code is way beyond him."

"Surely he would just hire in another freelancer?"

"I don't think so. This is the heart of the operation. You wouldn't trust someone on day rates to do that for you. Too much risk they'd just walk away with the idea for themselves."

I sat back again, puzzled.

"Slate, those receipts for his warehouse. Who signed for them?"

"It's just a scribble, not anything readable. Look."

A slightly fuzzy image of one of the packing slips flowed onto the wallscreen. An unreadable squiggle, full of bold curls and loops, was near the bottom. Finn looked briefly at it and then shook his head.

"For sure that's not Selif's hand. I've bought stuff from him once or twice, when there was no choice, like, and he's always quite particular about how he writes his name." He looked around the room at the rest of our doubtful faces. "Well, it's not him. I cannot help what I'm seeing. Lia Fail, pull up the most recent copy that we have."

The wallscreen divided, and a second signature appeared. It was in small, obviously pedantic lettering, and looked nothing like the writing that Slate had shown.

"Do you see what I mean? Maybe somebody is moonlighting in his yard for their own business. Are all of those signatures you found the same?"

"Near enough."

She flashed a dozen more signatures up in rapid succession, and there was indeed very little variation.

"Ah well. But look now, Mitnash, you should tell Slate and Chandrika what happened to persuade us to leave Mary's."

So I told them all about how Selif and Dafyd had come to the door, and what I had guessed about their intentions. How Dafyd had given away their knowledge of my visit to Hell Bay. And how they had vanished as quickly as they had come when they saw Finn with me. Eibhlin was highly entertained.

"So you sent them running away again, Riley."

"I said nothing that might have particularly alarmed them. They just turned about and left of their own accord. But I did mention to my friend Mitnash here, as how they were not very prepared for all that. Not very determined like. As though they had been sent in haste by somebody else."

We sat together in silence for a short time. After a while Mrs Riley went into her kitchen and came back with drinks for us all. Those of us, at any rate, who were present in body. Parvati stirred.

"So the Wise Man was a middle man. But somebody at Selif's yard received those goods. Maybe Selif himself is only another middle man. Chandrika, can you find out who all has worked there in the last few months. Especially on the days when those tickets were signed for."

"Nobody. Selif once took on a young woman to do holiday work, but that was a long time ago, before Dafyd was old enough. She didn't stay even a year, and moved away to Phobos soon after."

Everybody looked at me. After all, I was the investigator from Earth. It was my job to solve the problem.

"Let's set that aside for now. We have an obvious way to force Selif out of the loop just like we did with Yul Yulsson."

"You want Slate and I to repeat our aircon act?"

"Thank you, but not this time. We can do it in a much better way. Less direct, but more effective. And perfectly matched to the crime."

Slate caught my meaning, and chuckled over the voice channel. She cleared the signatures from the screen and instead drew, line by line, a picture of the little buoy we had found floating out on the vector towards Jupiter. For a bit of fun she added a few lines of trade figures in the space beside it.

"That's right, Slate, we'll use the relay itself against them. You and I need to find out how to set up the deal objects, then we'll dream up the size loss we want to cause, and work out how to trigger it. Their own device will do the rest. However, I don't want to actually do that until we know where the chain goes next. There's no real return in just forcing Selif out, unless we can find out who is standing behind him."

"How are you going to do that?"

"I have no idea. Just now I am going to sleep on it and see what turns up tomorrow."

Parvati stood up.

"You might as well use up some of your charter time and stay on the Parakeet."

"Mister Mitnash, you'd be most welcome to stay here in the room you used before. I'm not sure about turning you out late at night like this."

"It's a small house you have, Eibhlin, and Mitnash would just be getting in your way. I have more room on the boat."

I took the hint and went with Parvati. I didn't want to play gooseberry to the Rileys on their first night back together.

I settled down to sleep in the cabin of Parvati's Parakeet. We had walked slowly back to the permie bay, talking around the problem when nobody was near enough to hear. We had made no progress, but there was a psychological boost in chewing over the meagre facts.

Once in the cabin, I had started conferring with Slate, but became muddled and incoherent as soon as I lay down. She pointed out, in a rather condescending voice, that I would make more sense in the morning. Sleep soon started to swallow me up.

I hadn't even bothered to engage the stretch straps – I was that confident of my fatigue at the end of the day, and my familiarity with Bryher's low gravity. It was pleasant, too, to be back sleeping on a ship. The background hum was quieter than at my Hugh Town accommodation, and more consistent in pitch. I yielded to the inevitable.

My dreams had been quite vivid since landing on St Mary's, after weeks of transit blandness. But this one was the best.

I was sitting cross-legged on the relay buoy, looking around for some point of orientation in all that trackless space. Lia Fail started to speak.

"Jovian clouds are perfect. Jupiter is my signature planet."

She span me round so that the planet loomed, huge, in front of me. The cloud bands were so close that I could trace all the curves and loops along the boundaries.

"Now face the other way and follow the trail backwards. All you need is a map."

Very dimly I started to hear a piano playing, old style, twentieth century honky tonk. Jupiter had gone, and instead I was falling headfirst towards the surface of Bryher. At the last moment I flipped over upright. I was perched on top of the atrium dome, while lots of people wearing Happy Guards of Scilly fleeceshirts scurried around below me. None of them looked up, but I could hear Olly's voice nearby.

"We have to keep looking, Jed. All we need is a map."

The piano music was louder now. The atrium faded, and I was sitting in the Wise Man's room alone. From somewhere behind me I could hear him grumbling.

"I'm sure that somebody gave me a map, but it's not here. I'm sure I had it before."

I blinked, and was in Aladdin's shop. He was playing on a little piano keyboard projected onto his counter, but the music was not his. It was echoing down the corridor from elsewhere.

"Would sir like a map, now that he has arrived?"

"What music is that, Aladdin?"

He smiled enigmatically and said nothing. Instead, Hunn Gravfelt whispered to me.

"It's the Agapanthus Blues."

The cluttered shop counter faded into the corridor outside Tat Johnny's. His whole window display was filled with maps, and a banner poster across the top said in large bold letters, 'Where do you want to go, Mitnash? Maps from every inhabited dome in the system!'

Then I was running through the corridors of Hugh Town, trying to get back to the dock where all the boats I knew were moored together – my Harbour Porpoise, Parvati's Parakeet, Nick's Mermaid and Finn's Selkie. The personas were chatting animatedly together, not knowing I was trying to reach them, and behind me Selif and Dafyd were in pursuit. I could hear their heavy footfalls over the distant music.

"It's alright, da, he's got no map."

"He'll never find the music without a map."

The corridors were getting smaller, and their feet were getting louder, and I couldn't find my way to the music. I kept seeing the porters' lodge, and my cheap digs, and the way through to the central courtyard, but could not find what I needed. I was going in circles, and the pursuit was getting closer. Every time I thought I was getting away, I would be back at Selif's yard, just closing the door behind me.

My dream breaths were harsh and ragged, and I was struggling in the ever-narrowing passageways. I was very deep down somewhere, and I couldn't find the map.

Then Slate's voice cut through the dream.

"Mit, Mit, you need to wake up."

I hooked onto her voice and used it to pull myself back to the surface.

I was in the cabin of the Parakeet, and everything was all right. I sat up in the bed and took a long breath. I was covered in sweat, but everything was fine.

"I don't like waking you from dreams, Mit, but you were struggling with this one."

I stood up and walked around the room a few times.

"Yes. Yes, I was."

I sat down on the bed and put my head in my hands. The main riff of the Agapanthus Blues was still drifting around inside me.

"I need something to drink."

The cabin had a shower in one corner, and a little sink with a tap, but I had forgotten to bring any kind of cup with me. I pulled on a base layer of clothes to cover my nakedness.

"In the kitchen. The cupboard to the right of the hob."

"Thanks, Slate. But it's not as if I needed a map."

I went through the door, turned towards the kitchen, and took three steps before stopping with a gasp.

"Oh, Slate, I've just realised. I know who it is. I know who took in those deliveries from the Wise Man."

Instead of stopping at the kitchen, I went all the way along to the bridge.

"Hello Chandrika, can Slate share the screen for a while?"

"Of course, Mitnash."

"Slate, when I first went to Selif's, he wasn't there. Dafyd said he would be at either the Blue Agapanthus or Jool's, and Kassandra gave me a map showing me how to get there from the yard."

"I never saw that map. It was before you were carrying the hand-held with you."

"I know. But I emptied my pockets, just before we went with Nick to Agnes that first time. The map is in my cabin on the Harbour Porpoise, on the bedside shelf. Now I can walk back there easily enough and rummage through everything, but maybe I left it on top. Can you check?"

The screen wavered for a moment, then switched to show the internal vid feed from my cabin. It was almost completely dark, but Slate flicked the lights on and panned the viewport around until the shelf came into view. There was a small heap of items scattered untidily. I pointed.

"Look! look! Almost hidden by the stub that the chief porter gave me."

She zoomed in on the heap, and there, sure enough, was the corridor plan. Only about half of Kassandra's writing was visible –'Blue Aga' – but it was enough. The screen split, and Chandrika pulled up one of the Wise Man's receipts. The writing matched, with its bold curves and loops. It was Kassandra who had signed for each and every one of those shipments.

I leaned back against the captain's chair, while Slate and Chandrika made congratulatory noises. Parvati wandered in, looking neater and more respectable than I did, even at this hour of the night.

"Chandrika woke me to say you had found out something important."

I gestured at the screen. It was still showing the same two images, and the similarity of writing was obvious.

"Kassandra gave me that map when I was first at Selif's yard. Kassandra is the key person. She is behind it all."

I thought back to the one time she and I had met. I had first seen her as an indistinct shape behind the privacy shimmer as Dafyd called to her, petulant at being disturbed. It was all there in the first meeting: Selif was away from the yard building social connections, Dafyd was absorbed in his games, and Kassandra was scarcely visible, carefully obscure and in the background.

Parvati looked at the signature again.

"So it was Kassandra all along? Selif is her middle-man? Well, I suppose that makes for domestic convenience."

She sat facing me.

"And that surely must make your own job easier as well? There's no need to go looking for anyone beyond Selif and Kassandra. The same piece of work with that relay buoy will do for both."

I nodded.

"So do you want to set off now?"

"No need for that much rush. Slate needs to get their credentials from Khufu down in London, and a whole bunch of other information. And to take this sort of action, I'll need top-level clearance, MD level sign-off and all. The senior investigation board will need to authorise it. We won't be going for several hours at least, what with signal lag as well."

She gave a little sigh.

"Well then, that's it until the morning, I think. I'm back off to sleep."

The next day arrived. I had talked over with Slate what we needed from the Finsbury team, and then retired happily to bed while she bundled it into a single packet and flashed it away. After that, I slept well: my frantic subconscious urgency had been attended to, and all was at peace.

I even, on first waking up, felt well disposed towards Selif and Kassandra, and thought that justice might be satisfied with only a warning and a small loss. I felt luxurious, and took an excessively long time in the shower. This low gravity thing was quite fun once you got used to it.

"When you're ready, Mit?"

"Is there a rush? We can't possibly have heard back from Earth yet?"

"Parvati is waiting to eat breakfast with you, and Finn has just tapped you."

"I'm not exactly decent yet. Can he wait?"

"Finn isn't exactly decent either, but he seems to think it's important."

I came out of the shower and wrapped myself in a towel.

"Tell Parvati I'll be there after this call. And make the connection to Finn blurry. I don't think either of us is interested in a perfect image just now."

Finn was sitting up in bed, so far as I could tell. Somewhere else nearby I could hear Mrs Riley singing as she rattled crockery and pans. *Crows on a Sledge*, I realised, and briefly enjoyed the memory of *The Descenters*.

"The best of the morning to you, Mitnash."

"The same to you, Finn. How are you both?"

"Just wonderful today, thank you. But I called to tell you something that Boris passed on to me overnight. His security vids caught our two gentlemen friends looking around his yard, long after it was all sealed up for the night. Of course they were in suits, but easy to recognise for all that."

"Is that so?"

"Yes it is. Now, they went away again after a while without touching anything. They spent an especially long time in the place where your boat used to be docked. Almost as though they couldn't find whatever they were after. Boris was still awake at the time, and entertained himself watching them jig about to no avail."

"Did he do anything?"

"Oh, no. What would be the point? He gets people poking around most nights, generally kids out on a dare. But not so often a father and son together, who have a position in the islands to maintain. He thought you'd like to know."

His fuzzy image glanced away to one side, and his voice dropped.

"I'll speak again later. My little treasure is on her way back and she'll not be amused that I've called you so early."

Crows on a Sledge was definitely getting louder in the background as he cut the connection.

I finished dressing and went along to the kitchen. My forgiving feelings about Selif had mostly evaporated after the news from Finn.

Parvati was wearing what I thought of as her spacefaring outfit, rather than shore clothes. We ate together, and she wanted to know when we'd be out of the dock again. I was going to temporise, but Slate chimed in.

"I'm just getting a large-packet response back from Khufu now. A few minutes to finish transit, and then I'll unravel the contents."

That gave plenty of time to finish eating, and then stow everything away.

"Mit, there's much more here than we asked for. And some of it is confidential."

"How much?"

"About a third, mostly personal details of trade parties."

"Display everything you can, and anonymise the rest."

She started loading a whole slew of display Pebbles while I told Parvati what she was looking at. She did a fair job of pretending to appear interested in what was fundamentally a long catalogue of boring tags.

"Now this is a chronological list of deals. Every trade where Selif's credentials were used, ever since the account was set up, sorted by decreasing notional. With a comparison of the actual exchange rates at execution, against the fraudulent rates inserted by their relay."

"Is it interesting?" She gave a short laugh. "I mean, is it useful?"

I looked back at the grid of trades. There was just too much detail.

"Slate, let's look at a heatmap of that lot, pivoted against notional and day of week. A log scale will probably work best."

The chart appeared, and I knew my intuition had been right. There was a constant sludge of low level trades spread evenly, the scattering of really high value ones here and there – and a large spike of consistent, moderate value, on the last day of every week. Slate giggled.

"Now we know when they draw their wages."

"That's the time to target."

I turned to Parvati.

"Can you lay us alongside the buoy before 17:00 UTC, the day after tomorrow?"

"Gladly. But first, can you show me something there that I can make sense of?"

"Let's look at it another way. Slate, can you show the accumulated credit they have gained by means of the relay."

An overlay popped up with the figure. It was huge. It was, in fact, hugely bigger than I had previously guessed. The relay, together with the codebase that ran on it, obviously provided a highly lucrative business opportunity. Slate added another two panels with some additional numbers.

"Chandrika suggested that I should show the breakdown separating funds acquired within the Scilly Isles from those taken elsewhere."

It really was fascinating stuff. Honestly. The islanders had been skimmed hundreds of times more often than other people, but each time for only a small amount. The trades elsewhere were much larger but much fewer, and included the show-off trades I had noticed before. When you summed it all up, over a third of the total was from the islands.

I thought back to the original briefing pack Vinietta had prepared. She had spotted a pattern of low level acquisition amongst the flashy deals, but she had not caught even a percent of the whole. It was staggering. This was why they could afford not only to build the atrium, but leave it completely unused. It wouldn't be all that long before they could set up and supply a whole station somewhere in space, complete with proper atmosphere and living quarters. Maybe even a small moon.

I looked at Parvati, to see how much of it she had grasped. Clearly Chandrika had filled in any gaps she might have had, and the look of rage had come over her face again.

"How is it they have done so many trades? I don't understand why so many people dealt with them. They only ran a stores yard."

I slid the overlay to one side, and zoomed in on a few of the records in the list.

"They found out how to get themselves logged as broker. So they had an interest in every trade, not just the ones where they were counterparty. As broker they take a cut of everything, and even if it's only a tiny fraction of a pip, the numbers soon add up. It's not supposed to be possible, but they've done it somehow. The method will be in one of the modules that Slate and I never finished analysing. The Finsbury crew will track it down."

"Tell me you know how to use that relay against them?"

I nodded.

"Khufu has sent everything we need by way of credentials and the like. Slate and I simply have to decide how much we want to take back from them. Then find a set of historical rates which will do the trick. Then we intercept whatever trade they are making and, well, adjust it. Worst case, if for some reason they don't show up according to their pattern, we just insert a trade."

She smiled, fiercely.

"Take it back from them, Mitnash. Take all of it back."

───────────────────────

We were floating, engines silent, with the relay buoy just off the starboard bow. I had spent all yesterday, and most of last night, working with Slate on the details, and verifying them with Khufu and the Finsbury team.

Everything was in place – a complete plan detailing which trade parameters needed remapping, the exact sequence of method calls we needed, and a fractalised code update we were going to apply as soon as the key trade was done. That had been the last piece to come up from Earth, only an hour or so ago. I was convinced that I could have crafted it myself, but not soon enough to meet the deadline.

I was very tired. I valued my down time these days, where a few years ago I would have shrugged off a night's work with ease. But the fatigue was kept at bay by the constant flow of adrenalin. All being well, this was the decisive moment.

Parvati had brought out a selection of Glyndwr's ales, and one of her vividly coloured cakes, but by unspoken agreement we had left them untouched so far. That was to be our victory feast, but we had not yet earned it.

"Are you sure you don't need me or Chandrika to do anything?"

She had asked the same thing several times now; it was the first time I had seen her display any kind of anxiety.

"I won't be doing anything myself when the action starts. It'll be too quick for you and I. Slate's working against a tight time schedule, and we would only slow her down."

The wallscreen showed the first part of the execution plan, all neatly divided by milestone and step. We had sketched it out yesterday afternoon, and the Finsbury team had scrutinised it, pulled it apart, reassembled it, signed off on the final version, and got it back to us with plenty of time to spare. When the time came, Slate would follow it to the letter. Even working at her best flat-out speed, there would be portions where she could only just keep to the timeline.

Everything non-essential that usually took time was isolated or turned off. Chandrika had taken over most of that, and in particular would do any chatting, and update all the display feeds. We didn't want Slate wasting effort making policy decisions; this was a time for simply following instructions.

She and I had even disabled our shared subvocal link, so she wouldn't get distracted by all that went on outside of my conscious control. Basically, she was stripped down to the bare essentials for this fight. Once again, the Slate I knew was unavailable, and I would be getting her back only after it was finished. This time, however, we had gone into the fray with open eyes and a clear plan. And we were no longer alone, but among friends. It made a world of difference.

We sat there for what seemed a very long time. I kept glancing at the clock. Chandrika had set it up with a highlight to mark the expected deal timestamp. We had just passed that, the delta was increasing, and nothing had happened yet. That didn't really matter though, since the actual times varied up to half an hour either side. It provoked anxiety, though, and Parvati and I avoided looking at each other. I lost myself in thought.

A purist would say that what we planned to do was not in fact legal, any more than the code inspection at the relay buoy was. But then, there were not really any laws that applied to this situation. Reputation, and the recognition of one's peers, was the effective measure of acceptability in the system's far-flung settlements. The only real punitive action ECRB could threaten was to withdraw special dealer status with SIG. By the time we heard about a problem, however, the people concerned had often amassed so much credit that they were no longer interested in dealership.

Now, if Selif and Kassandra had contented themselves with siphoning credit from wealthy individuals on far-away Earth, it was unlikely that I would have had support from anybody out here. But they had targeted islanders as well, so the picture was very different.

Of course, I would still have done the same job myself, with or without help. Slate and I would still have taken over the relay buoy, and still taken back the misappropriated funds. But in that case, we would have been doing it against the grain of local opinion, rather than aligned with it. It was neater this way, more elegant.

A few more minutes ticked by. We had already decided that if we got to the half hour mark we would stand down until next week. Right now, I just felt like calling it off anyway. I had no idea whether Slate was affected by the pressure of anticipation in the way that I was, but I was certainly feeling enough for both of us.

Parvati looked at me as we passed T+10, but said nothing.

Finally, just before the quarter hour, everything happened. The first three milestones turned green and were checked off in a blur of movement, followed almost as quickly by the first dozen or so steps towards the fourth.

Chandrika's voice caught up with the action.

"It has started successfully. Apparently the trade type is exactly the same, Mitnash. Very high leverage. She is following the plan and will update when feasible."

I gripped the arms of the chair and forced myself not to ask questions. Slate wouldn't answer, but I didn't want her to spend time even making the decision about that.

Another three steps turned green. We had reached milestone four, which meant that she had successfully assimilated the deal contents, verified the field values, and was now running the derived calculations.

Chandrika flashed up the intended profit of the original trade – it was slightly larger than the all-time average. Maybe they had some big invoices to pay this week. Or maybe it was somebody's birthday.

I closed my eyes and waited. This part was on a strict clock. The reply packet had to go back within a narrow interval to ensure that the sender, presumably Carreg, did not raise a timeout exception.

Another rush of steps scrolled rapidly past, followed by another pause. Carreg had accepted the commit.

This also meant that our earlier exploration of the relay had gone undetected. Carreg would surely have been more diligent if he had spotted that; in principle he could have done a follow-on interrogation of the secondary fields, which might have been awkward. As it was, we could eliminate a whole branch of contingency logic which the Finsbury team had prepared.

"Slate is now scanning historical data for a good-enough match to achieve the agreed target."

We had worked out that she would not have time to scan the whole archive to find the perfect match. So we had chosen a quick and dirty search algorithm, along with some simple acceptance rules. There was a longer window for this stage, but she would still be at full tilt to meet the constraints.

"She found a match slightly in excess of the agreed target. She has switched the deal to edit mode and made the changes."

I felt a rush of pride in my Slate. The remaining steps all had to be done right so as not to raise alerts, but the time-critical part was over. I relaxed a little as some more milestones ticked by. Parvati noticed.

"Does this mean we can celebrate now?"

I gestured at the screen as another checkpoint ticked by, closely followed by the first couple of steps towards the next.

"Let's wait a little longer. But in truth, the hard part is over now. Slate has edited the trade by applying the historical rates from a particular day nearly a year ago, and dispatched the complete packet. She has just now altered Selif's authent credentials so neither he nor Kassandra can do any other trades or modifications without contacting the London hub first. And I'm willing to bet they won't do that in a hurry. That means they're also now blocked from altering this particular deal. Next step is to update the code with the packet the Finsbury team prepared so as to prevent similar use in the future."

Her eyes gleamed.

"How long until she's done?"

"About five minutes. Chandrika will show us. I'd rather hold back the celebration until the whole plan is signed off. Apart from anything else, that means we can all have fun together."

She nodded, and settled back in her seat, watching the remaining stages click through with an air of total satisfaction.

I watched them as well, but more casually. These were easy stages now; there were no time constraints, and nothing really taxing left to do. All very routine, and the kind of thing Slate could have done in her sleep, if she ever indulged in such a thing.

The last step of the last milestone was complete. I half-listened as Chandrika updated us with the final status. It was over. The relay had functioned as it was designed to do, albeit in the reverse direction than Kassandra had originally planned. Now we had taken it over, denying her or Selif the opportunity to repeat the process. And since we knew the pattern to look for, the team in London would add in some extra checks and balances to raise a priority alert if something similar appeared anywhere else in the system.

Selif would no longer be a dealer with SIG special status, and would lose a huge amount of credit. He would almost certainly abandon St Mary's. Of course, he could bring Kassandra out in a boat to change the code back again, or more likely set up a similar scam somewhere else. Simple repetition would not be possible, but they were quite shrewd enough to think of a cunning variation, and implement the changes needed.

Basically, I had secured for the ECRB a block of time, and a way to tackle this most recent exploit. And – which actually pleased me more – I had done it in such a way as to plough a good proportion of the recovered benefits back into the Scilly Isles, by returning funds back to their points of origin. Naturally ECRB had retained a significant fraction, and not everything could be traced, but it still felt good.

"I'm back, Mit. Subvocal and everything else is back to normal."

She sounded very pleased with herself, and rightly so.

"Great news, Slate. So I guess the party can begin?"

For answer she announced herself on the Parakeet ship systems, and enjoyed our congratulatory comments. Then while Chandrika brought the ship about for the journey back to Bryher, Parvati cut slices from the cake and passed me a bottle of Machynlleth Matchless. We were going home.

A few days had passed. We were back in Frag Rockers Bar, all of us together who were part of our little mining consortium. Or, as Slate insisted on calling it over our private link, my retirement plan. I had no intention of giving up work any time soon, but there was some truth in her opinion.

Frag Rockers was quiet tonight. It was not Special Night, and the musicians' area stood empty. Instead, Glyndwr had put on a vid from when *The Descenters* last played here, to help stir the mood. It was just background, very quiet, but every now and again Finn would smile as Mrs Riley was captured dancing in the viewport.

I felt quiet, and a little sad. Tonight was my last night on the islands, and tomorrow I would be setting course for the inner system, Earth, and Shayna. I was very happy about that, of course. I had already sent a long and shamelessly explicit message packet to her, suggesting we might enjoy a few days together at the lunar south pole spa as soon as I got back into Earth orbit. Or possible one of the LEO hotels – I wasn't too fussy about the venue, though a little bit of gravity would probably make things more fun.

I still owed her the rest of the holiday along the wild wind and waves of the Bernician Way, but this would be something extra, to make up for what we had lost. On a purely pragmatic note, it wasn't advisable to go straight back to full gravity without some intermediate steps, but I didn't try to deceive myself about my motives.

But along with the happiness and anticipation of home, there was a great deal of sadness. I had come to enjoy this little clump of asteroids, and right now I was surrounded by a group of people I admired, and liked hugely.

Those few terrible hours on the way back from Agnes, and the time in the atrium, were easily pushed out of mind. Slate and I had talked them through, thoroughly, and had both reached a kind of equanimity about them. That done, the memories of Scilly which I was going home with were good ones, and I was sorry to be leaving.

Now, it was true that I would be coming here again. Quite apart from the personal uplift of getting together with these people again, I would need to come out here every so often to view, and hopefully extend, the mining operation. But it would not be soon.

Next time I would bring Shayna, if she could be persuaded to spend the weeks in transfer orbit out and back again. I grinned at the prospect of spending all that time on a small boat with her and Rocky, as well as Slate. It wouldn't be easy. We would need some advance planning to ensure that all four of us survived the journey.

"Arranging the next trip already, Mit?"

"Well, sort of. Not actual dates, you understand. Just the principle of it."

She buzzed happily at me.

"I wouldn't mind spending more time with Chandrika."

I felt mischievous.

"And what do you think of Lia Fail?"

She knew exactly what I meant.

"That sounds like a 'what do you want to be when you grow up?' question."

"She certainly is very serious. I don't know what she and Finn do together on all those long journeys."

"Cloud pattern modelling, perhaps?"

I looked at Finn, laughing uproariously at something Boris had said, and my imagination failed me. Very quietly, by way of contrast, Slate whispered on.

"It's going to be difficult to keep contact with any of them, once we're back on Earth."

I nodded for both of us. It might be easier in some ways for her, making use of all those hours while I was asleep. But on the other hand, signal lag and light speed limitations probably affected her more than I, given her faster processing speed.

Maureen appeared in the middle of a gaggle of hostesses, the rippling green of her outfit drawing eyes from all around the room. Glyndwr had signed up for a whole batch of the mods as soon as he saw the result, and I had promised to ship one a day on the journey home, with Chandrika doing the actual patch installations. Another bonus scheme for Slate and I, perhaps, though the market would soon saturate.

Nobody quite knew what the new world, without Selif, Kassandra, and Dafyd, would look like. Unlike the Wise Man, they had slipped away neatly, quietly, before anybody realised what had happened. They had simply abandoned all their holdings here. On St Mary's that included the stores depot and their accommodation, plus a few other scattered properties. They had taken only a very new model sloop and whatever was inside her at the time, together with Carreg.

Sensibly, they had made no attempt to withdraw whatever was left in their trading float. All the credit there was fully traceable to source, and they knew it. It had become toxic for them. Obviously, however, they had another stash somewhere, for which nobody knew the history trail. I had no idea if this meant they were back to square one, or if they were still exceedingly wealthy.

Here on Bryher, the Hell Bay complex was now completely abandoned. Everyone assumed that Glyndwr was considering whether to renew his bid for it, but he was saying nothing either way. He had done quite well out of the redistribution of funds, as had a lot of islanders, but it still probably wasn't enough to take on the risk.

The swift departure was a typical Kassandra move – unobtrusive, keeping out of the limelight. The Finsbury team were still trying to trace any of her life history before appearing on St Mary's, and so far had had no success. That in itself was a real achievement on her part, given how difficult it was to hide anything from a really determined search.

Slate and I had our own theory, which I might include in my closure report. We reckoned she would turn out to be some top-flight student from one of the coding academies, who had chosen early on in the training to become invisible. It was unusual – most people in that position went for a flamboyant public profile – but not unheard of. There had always been a small, shifting group of highly skilled coders who took pains to avoid overt recognition.

It was possible she had feelings for Selif, but it was more likely that he was just some convenient cover, and a useful source of seed capital. In that case, she might soon abandon him and Dafyd as dead weight, and cut away on her own again. That would make it altogether easier to adopt another identity, and bubble up to the surface somewhere quite new. I contemplated briefly what name she might use. In the old stories, Kassandra was the prophetess that nobody listened to. Perhaps there was something of truth in that, something of her relationship with Selif.

Sadly, given my line of work, it was all too likely that I would meet up with them again one day. Next time, they would recognise me, and, most likely, not be inclined to be forgiving. Next time, Slate and I would need to be doubly alert.

I considered talking it over with Slate, but I had obviously given myself away already.

"Enjoy the party, Mit. Make the most of your time with these people. We can talk about all that other stuff once we ship out tomorrow. I'm going to switch off subvocal now and immerse myself with the other personas."

She made a rather exaggerated click sound as though flicking a switch. I smiled to myself and turned my attention outwards again. It was time to enjoy the fruit of our work, in the rather tangible form of Glyndwr's ales. I picked out a Powys Pale, and abandoned myself to the celebration.

THE END

Notes

About the author

Richard Abbott has visited some of the places that feature in his historical fiction. To date, however, he has not had the opportunity of visiting the asteroid belt, or anywhere else outside the Earth.

Richard currently lives in London, England. When not writing he works on the development and testing of computer and internet applications. He enjoys spending time with family, walking and wildlife – ideally combining all three of those pursuits at the same time.

Follow the author on:

- Web site – www.kephrath.com
- Blog – richardabbott.datascenesdev.com/blog/
- Google+ – Search for "Far from the Spaceports"
- Facebook – Search for "Far from the Spaceports"
- Twitter – @MilkHoneyedLand

Look out for his other works, which include the following.

Fiction – full-length novels

- *In a Milk and Honeyed Land*, available from most online retailers, and general booksellers to order in

    - soft-cover – ISBN 978-1-4669-2166-5

    - hard-cover – ISBN 978-1-4669-2167-2

    - ebook format – ISBN 978-1-4669-2165-8

In case of difficulty please check the website
http://www.kephrath.com for purchasing options.

Feedback for this novel includes:
"the author is an authority on the subject, and it shows through the captivating descriptions of the ancient rituals, songs, village life, and even a battle scene... the story grabs hold of the imagination... satisfies as a love story, coming-of-age tale, and historical narrative..."

Blue Ink Review

"...The lives of these ordinary people are brought to life on the page in a way that's absorbing and credible. The changes that are going to take place in this area are quite incredible... a wonderous land that seems both alien and yet somehow familiar..."

Historical Novel Society UK Review

- *Scenes from a Life*, available from most online retailers, and general booksellers to order in

    - soft-cover – ISBN 978-0-9545535-9-3

    - kindle format – ISBN 978-0-9545535-7-9

    - epub format – ISBN 978-0-9545535-8-6

In case of difficulty please check the website http://www.kephrath.com for purchasing options. Feedback for this novel includes:

"The author is extremely knowledgeable of his subject and the minute detail brings the story vividly to life, to the point where you can almost feel the sand and the heat..."

Historical Novel Society UK Review

"...lovely description – evocative sentences or phrases that add so much to the atmosphere of the book"

The Review Group

"The striking thing about 'Scenes' is... its sensitivity: its assured, mature observation of people"

Breakfast with Pandora

- *The Flame Before Us*, available from most online retailers, and general booksellers to order in

   – soft-cover – ISBN 978-0-9931684-1-3
   – ebook format – ISBN 978-0-9931684-0-6

In case of difficulty please check the website http://www.kephrath.com for purchasing options. Feedback for this novel includes:

"Wide in scope and rich in detail and plot, this is an accomplished illustration of this era in the region: complex, informative, enjoyable and skilfully put together."

Historical Novel Society UK Review

"...A surprising tenderness in the face of brutality, loss, and displacement is the emotion that underpins the action..."

Breakfast with Pandora

Fiction – short stories

- *The Man in the Cistern*, a short story of Kephrath, published in ebook format by Matteh Publications and available at online retailers, ISBN 978-0-9545-5351-7 (kindle) or 978-0-9545-5354-8 (epub).

- *The Lady of the Lions*, a short story of Kephrath, published in ebook format by Matteh Publications and available at online retailers, ISBN 978-0-9545-5353-1 (kindle) or 978-0-9545-5355-5 (epub).

Non-fiction

- *Triumphal Accounts in Hebrew and Egyptian*, published in ebook format by Matteh Publications and available at online retailers, ISBN 978-0-9545-5352-4 (kindle) or 978-0-9545-5356-2 (epub).

About Matteh Publications

Matteh Publications is a small publisher based in north London offering a small range of specialised books, mostly in ebook form only. For information concerning current or forthcoming titles please see
http://mattehpublications.datascenesdev.com/.

www.ingramcontent.com/pod-product-compliance
Lightning Source LLC
Chambersburg PA
CBHW071303250626
47159CB00004B/1297